PENGUIN CLASSICS

THE MAN WHO WAS THURSDAY

G. K. CHESTERTON was born in 1874, and educated at St Paul's School, where, despite his efforts to achieve honourable oblivion at the bottom of his class, he was singled out as a boy with distinct literary promise. He decided to follow art as a career, and studied at the Slade School of Art, where he appears to have suffered a nervous breakdown, before turning his hand to journalism, at the suggestion of his friend, Ernest Hodder-Williams. A prolific writer throughout his life, his best-known books include *The Napoleon of Notting Hill* (1904), *The Man Who Knew Too Much* (1922) and the 'Father Brown' stories. Chesterton converted to Roman Catholicism in 1922 and died in 1936.

MATTHEW BEAUMONT is Senior Lecturer in English at University College, London. He is the author of *Utopia Ltd.: Ideologies of Social Dreaming in England, 1870-1900*, which appeared in paperback in 2009.

G. K. CHESTERTON

The Man Who Was Thursday

A Nightmare

Edited with an Introduction by
MATTHEW BEAUMONT

PENGUIN BOOKS

PENGUIN CLASSICS

UK | USA | Canada | Ireland | Australia
India | New Zealand | South Africa

Penguin Books is part of the Penguin Random House group of companies
whose addresses can be found at global.penguinrandomhouse.com.

Penguin
Random House
UK

First published 1908
Published in Penguin Books 1937
This edition first published in Penguin Classics 2011

019

Introduction, chronology and notes copyright © Matthew Beaumont 2011
All rights reserved

The moral right of the editor has been asserted

Set in Postscript Adobe Sabon 10.25/12.25pt
Typeset by Ellipsis Books Limited, Glasgow
Printed and bound in Great Britain by Clays Ltd, Elcograf S.p.A.

ISBN: 978-0-141-19146-1

www.greenpenguin.co.uk

MIX
Paper from
responsible sources
FSC® C018179

Penguin Random House is committed to a
sustainable future for our business, our readers
and our planet. This book is made from Forest
Stewardship Council® certified paper.

Contents

THE MAN WHO WAS THURSDAY

Chronology

1874 G.K.C is born on 29 May in Campden Hill, London, to Edward Chesterton, head of a company of house agents and surveyors, and Marie Chesterton.

1879 Birth of Cecil Chesterton, G.K.C's brother.

1885 Publication of *More New Arabian Nights: The Dynamiter* by Robert Louis Stevenson and Fanny van de Grift Stevenson; and *The Science of Revolutionary Warfare: A Little Handbook of Instruction in the Use and Preparation of Nitroglycerine, Dynamite, Gun-Cotton, Fulminating Mercury, Bombs, Fuses, Poisons, Etc, Etc.* by Johann Most.

1886 Publication of *The Princess Casamassima* by Henry James; Haymarket Affair, Chicago.

1887 Attends St Paul's School, London.

1891 Co-founds the Junior Debating Club at St Paul's.

1892 Publishes 'The Song of Labour' in *The Speaker*; attends University College London.

1893 Attends the Slade School of Art; publication of *The Angel of the Revolution* by George Griffith.

1896 Publishes 'A Picture of Tuesday' in *The Quarto*.

1900 Publishes *Greybeards at Play* and *The Wild Knight and Other Poems*; meets Hilaire Belloc.

1901 Publishes *The Defendant* and, in *The Speaker*, 'A Defence of Patriotism'; contributes for the first time to the *Daily News*; marries Frances Blogg; moves to Battersea; publication of *The Eternal City* by Hall Caine.

1902 Publishes *Twelve Types*, and, with W. Robertson Nicholl, *Robert Louis Stevenson*; publication of *The Wonderful Story of Dunder van Haedan* by Edward Chesterton.

1903 Publishes *Robert Browning* and *Varied Types*; commences exchange of articles about socialism and Christianity with Robert Blatchford; publication of *The Riddle of the Sands* by Erskine Childers, *The League of Twelve* by Guy Boothby, and *A Girl Among the Anarchists* by 'Isabel Meredith' (Olivia and Helen Rossetti).

1904 Publishes *G. F. Watts* and *The Napoleon of Notting Hill*; publication of *England: A Nation*, edited by Lucian Oldershaw and containing an essay on 'The Patriotic Idea' by Chesterton.

1905 Publishes *The Club of Queer Trades* and *Heretics*; the British Parliament passes the Aliens Act.

1906 Publishes *Charles Dickens*; prints 'The Folly of Anarchists' in the *Illustrated London News*.

1907 Publishes 'The Diabolist' in the *Daily News*; appearance of a pilot edition of *The Man Who Was Thursday: A Nightmare*; publication of *The Secret Agent* by Joseph Conrad.

1908 Publishes *The Man Who Was Thursday: A Nightmare*, *Orthodoxy* and *All Things Considered*; anonymous publication of *G. K. Chesterton: A Criticism* by Cecil Chesterton; publication of 'About Chesterton and Belloc' by H. G. Wells, and 'Belloc and Chesterton' by George Bernard Shaw, in the *New Age*; publication of *The Bomb* by Frank Harris.

1909 Publishes *Tremendous Trifles* and *George Bernard Shaw*; moves to Beaconsfield.

1910 Publishes *The Ball and the Cross*, *William Blake*, *Alarms and Discussions* and *What's Wrong with the World*.

1911 Publishes *The Innocence of Father Brown*, *The Future of Religion*, *The Ballad of the White Horse* and *Appreciations and Criticisms of the Works of Dickens*; Belloc launches the *Eye-Witness* (later renamed the *New Witness*).

1912 Publishes *Manalive* and *A Miscellany of Men*.

1913 Publishes *The Victorian Age in Literature* and *Magic*; the *New Witness*, edited by Cecil Chesterton and abetted by G.K.C, is instrumental in exposing the so-called Marconi scandal, centred on allegations that the Liberal government had engaged in insider trading ('It is the fashion to divide recent history into Pre-War and Post-War conditions,' G.K.C wrote in his *Autobiography*; 'I believe it is almost as essential to divide them into the Pre-Marconi and Post-Marconi days').

1914 Publishes *The Flying Inn*, *The Wisdom of Father Brown*, *The Barbarism of Berlin*, and the privately printed *London*; suffers physical collapse at Christmas and lapses into a coma from which he recovers at Easter in 1915.

1915 Publishes *The Appetite of Tyranny, Including Letters to an Old Garibaldian, Poems* and *The Crimes of England*.

1916 Publishes *The Book of Job* and *A Shilling for My Thoughts*; replaces Cecil Chesterton as editor of the *New Witness* and edits it until 1923.

1917 Publishes *A Short History of England, Utopia of Usurers and Other Essays* and *Lord Kitchener*.

1918 Travels to Ireland; death of Cecil Chesterton in France.

1919 Publishes *Irish Impressions*; prints 'The Conversion of an Anarchist' in *The Touchstone and The American Art Student Magazine*; travels to Palestine.

1920 Publishes *The Superstition of Divorce*, *The Uses of Diversity* and *The New Jerusalem*; travels to the United States to give a lecture tour.

1922 Publishes *Eugenics and Other Evils*, *What I Saw in America* and *The Man Who Knew Too Much*; converts to Roman Catholicism.

1923 Publishes *Fancies versus Fads* and *St Francis of Assisi*.

1925 Publishes *The Superstitions of the Sceptic*, *Tales of the Long Bow*, *The Everlasting Man* and *William Cobbett*; founds *G. K.'s Weekly* (piloted in 1924).

1926 Publishes *The Incredulity of Father Brown*, *The Outline of Sanity* and *The Queen of Seven Swords*; foundation of the Distributist League.

1927 Publishes *The Catholic Church and Conversion*, *The Return of Don Quixote*, *Collected Poems*, *The Secret of Father Brown*, *The Judgement of Dr Johnson* and *Robert Louis Stevenson*; travels to Poland.

1928 Publishes *Generally Speaking*, *The Sword of Wood* and *Do We Agree?* (based on a debate with Shaw, chaired by Belloc).

1929 Publishes *The Poet and the Lunatics*, *The Thing: Why I am a Catholic* and *New and Collected Poems*; travels to Rome.

1930 Publishes *Four Faultless Felons, The Resurrection of Rome, The Grave of Arthur* and *Come to Think of It*; travels to the United States to give a second lecture tour.

1931 Publishes *All is Grist.*

1932 Publishes *Chaucer, New Poems, Sidelights on New London and Newer York* and *Christendom in Dublin.*

1933 Publishes *All I Survey* and *St Thomas Aquinas: The Dumb Ox.*

1934 Publishes *Avowals and Denials*; travels to Italy and Sicily.

1935 Publishes *The Scandal of Father Brown, The Well and the Shadows* and *The Way of the Cross.*

1936 Publishes *As I Was Saying* and *Autobiography*; dies 14 June at Beaconsfield.

1937 Publication of *The Paradoxes of Mr Pond*, by G.K.C.

1938 Publication of *The Coloured Lands*, by G.K.C.

Matthew Beaumont 2011

Introduction

Publisher's Note: First-time readers should be aware that details of the plot are revealed in this Introduction

The book's title – comic, no doubt, but at the same time faintly disconcerting – transmits the opening shock. At first, it looks like a typographic mistake. On its publication, in 1908, as Chesterton drily commented in his *Autobiography* (1936), some reviewers 'affected to mistake it for "The Man Who Was Thirsty".'[1] If the title initially causes confusion, though, it also inspires a sense of incipient excitement. *The Man Who Was ... Thursday*. The Man isn't simply called 'Thursday', Chesterton implies; he *is* Thursday. Why? Perhaps he is a remote relation of Thurse, the ancient heathen giant ... Perhaps he is the Man Friday of industrial modernity, the archetypal native of the imperial metropolis ... Perhaps ... The reader's adventure has already commenced. In the concluding sentence of his Introduction to the old Penguin edition of the book, Kingsley Amis claimed, in characteristically bombastic terms, that anybody who catches sight of its title and 'does not feel a faint tingle of excitement and a breath of wonder is not really a fit person to be reading the book.'[2] It is difficult not to agree. For, in carefully coupling these distinctly prosaic concepts – an anonymous man and an ordinary day of the week – the novel's title creates a peculiarly poetic effect. In its self-consciously unsettling use of the English language, it touches that sensitive spot which, in *Orthodoxy*, a spiritual autobiography that also appeared in 1908, Chesterton identified as 'the nerve of the ancient instinct of astonishment'. It inspires 'an almost prenatal leap of interest and amazement'.[3]

Orthodoxy, a book that, characteristically, adopts an attitude both combative and meditative, celebrates what Chesterton describes as 'a sort of secret treason in the universe'. 'It is this silent swerving from accuracy by an inch,' he avers, 'that is the uncanny element in everything.'⁴ The title of *The Man Who Was Thursday* itself swerves from accuracy by an inch. It is thus a potent example of Chesterton's aspiration, apparent in almost every article or book produced in his exceptionally prolific life, to inspire amazement at that which, perhaps because of some secret treason in the universe, simply happens to be. For Chesterton, whose philosophic outlook in the 1900s was informed by an increasingly profound Christian faith, everyday life was a fabulous, sometimes sinister fairy tale. In this respect, the novel's title anticipates no other title so much as *The Man Who Mistook His Wife for a Hat* (1986), the collection of case histories published to critical and popular acclaim by the psychologist Oliver Sacks. In the chapter that lent Sacks's book its baffling but strangely beautiful title, he describes a patient of his who 'saw faces where there were no faces to see': in the street, this genial man 'might pat the heads of water-hydrants and parking meters, taking these to be the heads of children; he would amiably address carved knobs on the furniture, and be astounded when they did not reply.'⁵ Chesterton, whose self-appointed spiritual vocation throughout his life was to irradiate the ordinary, to render it subtly fantastical, might have seen Sacks's patient as a saint.

If the book's title recalls a typographical error, then, or a phrase taken from an enigmatic poem, or even a fragment of some singular psychological case history, it also resembles the punchline of a nonsensical joke. 'The title of Mr G. K. Chesterton's new story,' observed the correspondent of the *Daily Telegraph*, 'reminds us of the anecdote of an intoxicated man who stopped a policeman in the West-end and asked, "Can you tell me if this is Regent-street – or Wednesday?"'⁶ Chesterton himself had some respect, as he admitted, for those reviewers who 'treated it as a mere title out of topsy-turvydom; as if it had been "The Woman Who Was Half Past Eight", or "The Cow Who Was Tomorrow Evening".'⁷ After all, the first book he published, *Greybeards at Play* (1900), had been a collection of nonsense poems; and in his 'Defence of Nonsense' (*The Defendent*, 1901), he had contended that nonsense is a type of literature absolutely replete with spiritual importance, because it so effectively communicates a sense of amazement at the 'huge and undecipherable unreason' of life itself:

> Everything has in fact another side to it, like the moon, the patroness of nonsense. Viewed from that other side, a bird is a blossom broken loose from its chain of stalk, a man a quadruped begging on its hind legs, a house a gigantesque hat to cover a man from the sun, a chair an apparatus of four wooden legs for a cripple with only two.[8]

The title of *The Man Who Was Thursday* is intended to reveal the other side of the detective novel, the other side of the adventure novel. It defamiliarizes popular forms from the start. Chesterton takes a code that is common to such fiction – Kipling's 'The Man Who Would Be King' (1888) might be one example, Chesterton's 'The Man Who Knew Too Much' (1922) another – and deftly deranges its logic. He deploys the *non sequitur*, a device the Surrealists subsequently used to such provocative effect, so as to deepen the sense of some almost inscrutable mystery that titles of this kind are intended to evoke. The title is a riddle redoubled.

'It is no use attempting to say what it is all about,' wrote Austin Harrison in a review of Chesterton's novel in the *Observer*, 'it is about everything, and that in curiously thrilling detective form.'[9] Ostensibly at least, the book is about a battle to the death between anarchists and anti-terrorist detectives in London at the end of the nineteenth century (the 'boom of bomb throwing', as Orson Welles so deliciously put it in the comments with which he prefaced his radio adaptation of the novel in 1938).[10] It begins in Saffron Park, a bohemian suburb of London, where the protagonist, the respectable young poet Gabriel Syme, encounters another poet, the aesthete and self-professed anarchist Lucien Gregory. After a heated argument about the relationship between politics and aesthetics, one that Gregory hopes to clinch by offering Syme irrefutable proof that he is committed to anarchism, in practice as well as in theory, the former takes the latter to a conspiratorial meeting of dynamitards, located in a subterranean chamber close to the Thames, at which he expects to be elected to one of the seven posts on the Central Anarchist Council. Moments before they enter the chamber, though, after making a pact with Gregory that requires both of them to maintain strict secrecy, Syme reveals that he is actually a police detective:

> 'Don't you see we've checkmated each other?' cried Syme. 'I can't tell the police you are an anarchist. You can't tell the anarchists I'm a policeman. I can only watch you, knowing what you are; you can only watch me, knowing what I am. In short, it's a lonely, intellectual duel, my head against yours.' (19)

Then, to Gregory's deepening horror, in the course of the more and more passionate meeting, the assembled anarchists appoint Syme rather than him to the Council, convinced by this secret agent's eloquent imitation of an extremist. It is therefore Syme, not Gregory, who subsequently goes to meet the other members of the Council, at a bizarre breakfast party in Leicester Square, where a plan to assassinate both the Russian Czar and the French President is being finalized. These exotic terrorists are all code-named after days of the week; so Syme, who takes up the vacant seat on the Council, becomes Thursday.

The president of the anarchists, a 'mountain of a man', as monumental as 'a statue deliberately carved as colossal', is Sunday (42). This massive, all-pervasive presence, the spectre haunting Europe, is apparently omnipotent. He is the master-mind, it is increasingly evident, behind the dreamlike events that ensue, a succession of ominous and at the same time ludicrous social games, conducted at a breakneck pace, involving reve-lations of concealed identities, violent duels, pitched battles and crazed chases across London and France. In the course of these episodes, in a series of mesmerizing, artfully calculated narrative displacements, it is successively revealed that, like Thursday, each of the anarchists on the Council is in fact a detective in disguise. It finally emerges that Sunday himself is none other than the police chief, who, quite as enigmatic and imposing as the arch-anarchist he has mimicked, has been responsible for recruiting this crack team of anti-terrorists. These disorientating revelations culminate, in the final chapter of the book, in a strange religious ritual, which involves all seven of the anarchists or detectives, who are dressed as the seven days of the Creation, and which is conducted before a vast audience, itself robed in elaborate, dreamlike costumes:

> For a long time – it seemed for hours – that huge masquerade of mankind swayed and stamped in front of them to marching and exultant music. Every couple dancing seemed a separate romance; it might be a fairy dancing with a pillar-box, or a peasant girl dancing with the moon; but in each case it was, somehow, as absurd as *Alice in Wonderland*, yet as grave and kind as a love story. (153)

The people participating in this carnival, to take a formulation from Chesterton's delightful book on Dickens, 'have seen the end of the End of the World'.[11] The identity of Sunday, however, the mischievous, semi-divine author of this metaphysical farce, remains elusive. Chesterton once intimated that Sunday was not so much God himself, as some commentators had claimed, as 'Nature as it appears to the pantheist whose pantheism is struggling out of pessimism.'[12] But this is at best half-helpful. He seems equally close to the gloriously paganistic image of Christ evoked by Chesterton at the end of *Orthodoxy*: a 'tremendous figure', who 'never concealed His tears' and 'never restrained His anger', but who nonetheless 'restrained something'; for 'there was in that shattering personality a thread that must be called shyness'.[13]

The plot of *The Man Who Was Thursday*, observed one contemporary critic of the book, in a doomed attempt to summarize its contents, 'and Mr Chesterton will excuse us for saying that the plot's the thing, turns on the discovery by a poet, who is also a detective, of a nest of Anarchists, each of whom appears to be trying to checkmate the others.'[14] But, although it positively mesmerizes the novel's reader, the plot is *not* the thing. This is not, for instance, *The Riddle of the Sands* (1903), Erskine Childers's naval adventure narrative about the discovery of

Germany's covert plans for an invasion of England. It is too anarchic, too confused even, to be memorable chiefly for the arc of its narrative. For that matter, Chesterton's novel is not even particularly interested in characterization, let alone in representing the convolutions of an individual's consciousness, the problem with which contemporaneous modernist novelists grappled. This is not Joseph Conrad's *The Secret Agent* (1907) either. Something else is going on beneath the novel's plot, beneath its characterization, something of seemingly immense philosophical or theological importance, though this remains impossible precisely to identify. Like Chesterton's Father Brown in 'The Sins of Prince Saradine' (1910), 'somehow [we have] not seen the real story, but some game or masque.'[15]

So is the plot an allegory, as a number of critics have suggested? No, not exactly. I suspect that the plot is a plot. That is, Chesterton's plot, which involves the anarchists' plot to overthrow order and the detectives' plot to overthrow disorder, is itself a form of plot; a sort of conspiratorial campaign against the complacent reader expecting adventure fiction. The revelations of this authorial plot, however, centre in the end not on the malign motives behind extraordinary events, but on what might be called the benign motivelessness of ordinary events. In his characteristically energetic, argumentative book about Browning, published in 1903, Chesterton had praised the poet's commitment to the commonplace and even the superficial; and it is to this almost sublime state of superficiality that he himself aspired: 'To the man who sees the marvellousness of all things, the surface of life is fully as strange and magical as its interior; clearness and plainness of life is fully as mysterious as its mysteries.'[16] The fiendishly complicated plot of *The Man Who Was Thursday* is a deliberate attempt to bamboozle his readers, and so to leave them, at the novel's climactic conclusion, both amazed and relieved at the divine simplicity of the universe, its grace and its gratuitousness.

Chesterton's novel vibrates and reverberates like 'one incessant carnival of insane and inspired improvisation', as he himself once said of Dickens's life.[17] It is uncontainable. In consequence, the first critics to review *The Man Who Was Thursday* channelled much of their energy into categorizing it generically. This is an activity that finally seems as futile as the central characters' attempt to capture Sunday atop his galloping elephant in Chapter 13. For the book comprises a riotously colourful patchwork of different genres, including the chivalric romance, the detective story, the dream poem, the dramatic farce, the dystopia, the fairy tale, the gothic fantasia, the allegorical masquerade, the melodrama, the nonsense tale, the novel of ideas, the political fable, the religious allegory, the spy thriller and the theological treatise; among other things. It consists of everything, in short, except the predictable conventions of the realist or naturalist novel. On the contrary, it is ostentatiously anti-realist, or 'irrealist'.[18] And in this respect it inhabits a tradition that Chesterton himself explored, in an essay entitled 'Dreams' (1901), a tradition of 'great works which mix up abstractions fit for an epic with fooleries not fit for a pantomime', and 'which present such a picture of literary chaos as might be produced if the characters of every book from *Paradise Lost* to *Pickwick Papers* broke from their covers and mingled in one mad romance'. Such books, this manifesto concludes, have 'the same unity that we find in dreams' – that is, nothing more than 'an absolute unity of emotion'.[19]

In 1908, the anonymous critic for the *Times Literary Supplement* was dismissive of *The Man Who Was Thursday*, precisely because, as a collage of all the non-realist forms imaginable, it proves so infuriatingly resistant to classification. 'As literature,' he expostulated, 'it is a hopeless *confusion de genres*; a scurrying, door-slamming farce that ends like a chapter in the Apocalypse.'[20] Others, like the reviewer for the *Hearth and Home* – possibly Frank Harris, the author of *The Bomb* (1908) – were more appreciative:

> The solemn men who read books for the London daily papers have conscientiously labelled, as best they could, *The Man Who Was Thursday*. It is a philosophy, a farce; a sermon, a practical joke; a newer 'New Arabian Nights', the dawning of a second Poe; an allegory, a brilliant bit of *blague*; in one word, it is everything!

'Mr Chesterton,' he added significantly, 'calls it "a nightmare".'[21] This emphasis demonstrated a penetration of which Chesterton probably approved. On more than one occasion, especially at the end of his life, he complained that readers of *The Man Who Was Thursday* had ignored its subtitle, 'A Nightmare', and consequently misunderstood the book. In *Autobiography*, for example, he impatiently pointed out 'that hardly anybody who looked at the title ever seems to have looked at the sub-title; which was "A Nightmare", and the answer to a good many critical questions.'[22] And in an article for the *Illustrated London News*, published the day before his death in 1936, Chesterton was equally peevish when he objected to 'that trick of missing the point of a story, or sometimes even the obvious sense of the very name of a story' (see Appendix, p. 159).

In the case of *The Man Who Was Thursday*, it could be contended, the sense of the name of the story is precisely that it is not sense. Or that it consists of sense and nonsense at once. The title is itself in this respect nightmarish. It is a cocktail – a Molotov Cocktail – of logic and the lunatic. 'The book was called *The Man Who Was Thursday: A Nightmare*,' Chesterton insisted; 'It was not intended to describe the real world as it was, or as I thought it was, even when my thoughts were considerably less settled than they are now' (159). The subtitle is equivalent to those his contemporaries used to identify other species of fantastic fiction – 'A Utopia', for example, or 'A Scientific Romance' – except that it refuses to offer its readers the clues needed to read and understand it. In its passionate fidelity to the truths that it pursues, and its committed refusal of realist forms as a means of communicating them, Chesterton's book deliberately mimics the anarchistic attitude that it mocks. In the *Observer*, Harrison perceptively noted that Chesterton had invested the narrative with 'his own Anarchic comprehension and incomprehensiveness.'[23]

So what precisely motivated the nightmare dramatized in *The Man Who Was Thursday*? The idea for this novel, as William Oddie has conclusively demonstrated, germinated in the early to mid-1890s, when Chesterton, a student at the Slade School of Art, experienced a psychological collapse of some description.[24]

The bad dream it depicts is 'the world of wild doubt and despair which the pessimists were generally describing at that date', as he himself put it in his final piece for the *Illustrated London News* (159). The book is in the first instance, then, an attack on the nihilism of the *fin de siècle*, which appears to have assumed an almost psychotic significance for Chesterton. Chesterton's time at the Slade, a time of intense emotional and intellectual confusion, was the moment at which, for one terrifying instant, and as if accidentally, he ingested the logic of his age. Momentarily, he became a pessimist. This precipitated an anaphylactic shock so dramatic that he spent the remaining decades of his life developing the philosophical and spiritual resources required to immunize him from it. In an article called 'The Nightmare' (1907), he subsequently reflected that 'nothing is so delightful as a nightmare – when you know it is a nightmare'. He added emphatically that 'sanity may play with insanity; but insanity must not be allowed to play with sanity.' During the 1890s, as he perceived it, the insanity of the epoch sported with his sanity. In a defiant slogan that still seems faintly defensive, this article concludes: 'I will ride on the Nightmare; but she shall not ride on me.'[25] At the *fin de siècle*, during his time at the Slade, the Nightmare rode on him. In effect, Chesterton therefore inscribed the same slogan, characteristically chivalric in tone, on the title page of *The Man Who Was Thursday*.

The form of philosophical pessimism that most appalled Chesterton at this time was Impressionism, as embodied above all by James McNeill Whistler, the Slade's presiding deity in the 1890s. In 1877, the art critic John Ruskin had famously accused Whistler – who promptly sued him – of 'flinging a pot of paint in the public's face' when he exhibited his 'Nocturne in Black and Gold: The Falling Rocket' (1874). A decade and a half later, Ruskin's sense of aesthetic shock, itself indisputably ethical in its implications, transformed into Chesterton's sense of philosophical and moral despair. The impact of that violent gesture, according to Chesterton, was far more corrosive and destructive than even Ruskin, himself terminally insane by this time, could have imagined. For, by the mid-1890s, Whistler had taught an entire generation of impressionable art students to be

Impressionists. This, as Chesterton explains in *Autobiography*, had a profound 'spiritual significance':

> I mean that it illustrated scepticism in the sense of subjectivism. Its principle was that if all that could be seen of a cow was a white line and a purple shadow, we should only render the line and the shadow; in a sense we should only believe in the line and the shadow, rather than in the cow. [. . .] Whatever may be the merits of this as a method of art, there is obviously something highly subjective and sceptical about it as a method of thought. It naturally lends itself to the metaphysical suggestion that things only exist as we perceive them, or that things do not exist at all. The philosophy of Impressionism is necessarily close to the philosophy of Illusion. And this atmosphere tended to contribute, however indirectly, to a certain mood of unreality and sterile isolation that settled at this time upon me; and I think upon many others.[26]

The pot of paint is packed, like a rocket, with explosives; and the Impressionist students that Chesterton encountered at the Slade are the aesthetic or intellectual equivalent of bomb throwers. It is anarchism in its philosophical form, rather than its political one, that is thus the object of his feverish polemic in *The Man Who Was Thursday*. As Samuel Hynes specified, 'the force of evil in [the novel] is not anarchism, but *anarchy*, the total dissolution of order.'[27] Like Shelley's poem of that name, it is a Masque of Anarchy.

Nihilism, and a generalized climate of pessimism, is then the real problem. This is abundantly evident from Chesterton's melancholic dedicatory verse, at the beginning of *The Man Who Was Thursday*, to his old school-friend, E. C. Bentley (see p. xxxvii). It is a description of the spiritual sclerosis that crippled the end of the nineteenth century: 'The world was very old indeed when you and I were young,' Chesterton intones, like a man who has himself aged prematurely because he has been contaminated by the climate of decadence. It is in this respect a reinscription of Matthew Arnold's 'Dover Beach' (1867), a poem which had mourned the retreating roar of the Sea of Faith on

the 'naked shingles of the world', and, in muted apocalyptic
tones, evoked 'a darkling plain / Swept with confused armies of
struggle and flight, / Where ignorant armies clash by night'. In
the opening lines of his dedication, Chesterton recalls the storm
cloud of the 1890s, and evokes an atmosphere of 'aimless gloom',
illuminated only by the ghastly luminescence of Whistler's
example. The prevailing mood of pessimism is 'a sick cloud upon
the soul'. The *fin de siècle* that the poem depicts – in which
'Science announced nonentity and art admired decay' – is a
nightmarish morality play in which Chesterton and Bentley have
become trapped. 'Crippled vices', among them Lust and Fear,
encircle these innocents 'in antic order'. 'This is a tale of those
old fears, even of those emptied hells', he continues. Nonetheless,
the dedication testifies to the fact that this nightmare has ended:
'We have found common things at last', including marriage and
a creed (these 'common things', though, are the most miraculous
things of all, according to Chesterton's creed). The truth about
the 1890s can in consequence be *safely* written and *safely* read,
he concludes – as if the process of composing the book had been
a protracted attempt to detonate an unexploded bomb, or to
conduct a kind of controlled explosion.

The Man Who Was Thursday is a record of Chesterton's dark
night of the soul. Indeed, its narrative is framed as a nocturne,
one painted not merely in black and gold but in all the colours
he could imagine. The dedication alludes to Chesterton and
Bentley roaming through the night, deep in discussion, in order
to overcome their sense of spiritual displacement: 'The doubts
that drove us through the night as we two talked amain, / And
day had broken on the streets e'er it broke upon the brain'
(xxxvii). The novel itself begins at sunset, a sunset that 'looked
like the end of the world', when Syme first encounters Gregory
in the streets of Saffron Park. Syme's appearance is so sudden,
the narrator intimates, that the other residents of the place
'looked at him as if he had that moment fallen out of that
impossible sky' (3). The 'attractive unreality' (2) of the fantastic
suburban setting thus starts to deepen. It is at the beginning of
Chapter 2 – when Syme and Gregory arrive outside a 'dreary
and greasy beershop', secretly bristling with insane incendiary

devices which look like 'the bulbs of iron plants, or the eggs of iron birds' (11, 13) – that the narrative plunges into nightmare. The plot only ceases to seem fantastical in the book's penultimate paragraph, when Syme gradually comes to full consciousness again and realizes that he has been 'walking along a country lane with an easy and conversational companion', namely his friend and rival, Gregory. Dawn is breaking, and Syme is surprised to discover 'rising all round him on both sides of the road the red, irregular buildings of Saffron Park' (158). They are back where they began, after restlessly walking throughout the night. The entire feverish narrative, then, has been a sort of psychotic episode, one apparently unnoticed by Syme's companion. In freeing himself from it, he feels as if he is 'in possession of some impossible good news, which made every other thing a triviality, but an adorable triviality' (158).

Chesterton talks in *Autobiography* about emerging from the pessimism of the *fin de siècle* and forging instead a philosophy of optimism:

> When I had been for some time in these, the darkest depths of the contemporary pessimism, I had a strong inward impulse to revolt; to dislodge this incubus or throw off this nightmare. But as I was still thinking the thing out by myself, with little help from philosophy and no real help from religion, I invented a rudimentary and makeshift mystical theory of my own. It was substantially this: that even mere existence, reduced to its most primary limits, was extraordinary enough to be exciting. Anything was magnificent as compared with nothing. Even if the very daylight were a dream, it was a day-dream; it was not a nightmare. The mere fact that one could wave one's arms and legs about (or those dubious external objects in the landscape which were called one's arms and legs) showed that it had not the mere paralysis of a nightmare. Or if it was a nightmare, it was an enjoyable nightmare.[28]

In the concluding paragraphs of *The Man Who Was Thursday*, Chesterton depicts a daylight in which, metaphorically speaking, Syme cautiously but triumphantly waves his arms and legs about, supremely grateful for the mere fact of existence. 'Syme could only feel an unnatural buoyancy in his body and a crystal simplicity in his mind that seemed to be superior to everything that he said or did', Chesterton writes (158). Syme has come out of the pessimism that he had slipped into like a coma, and finds himself susceptible at last to a spirit of optimism, which Chesterton defines as 'a sort of mystical minimum of gratitude'. 'At the back of our brains,' he affirms in the same paragraph of his *Autobiography*, 'there [is] a forgotten blaze or burst of astonishment at our own existence', and the 'object of the artistic and spiritual life [is] to dig for this submerged sunrise of wonder'.[29] It is this that inspired Chesterton, from the end of the nineteenth century, 'to write against the Decadents and Pessimists who ruled the culture of the age.'[30]

In *Orthodoxy*, composed at roughly the same time as *The Man Who Was Thursday*, Chesterton gives an important preliminary account of what he calls 'this elementary wonder', the principal function of which is to recall us, as in an artistic or spiritual epiphany, to a profound, beatified sense of being. In order to illustrate it, he sketches an archetypal subject – a modern, urban subject – who is condemned to live in a state of non-being:

> We have all read in scientific books, and, indeed, in all romances, the story of the man who has forgotten his name. This man walks about the streets and can see and appreciate everything; only he cannot remember who he is. Well, every man is that man in the story. Every man has forgotten who he is. [. . .] We are all under the same mental calamity; we have forgotten our names. We have all forgotten what we really are. All that we call common sense and rationality and practicality and positivism only means that for certain dead levels of our life we forget that we have forgotten. All that we call spirit and art and ecstasy only means that for one awful instant we remember that we forget.[31]

Who is the distinctly neurotic everyman, famous from 'scientific books' and romances alike, to whom Chesterton refers in this curious passage? I suspect that the 'story of the man who has forgotten his name', who roams the streets but cannot recall his identity, is that of the so-called 'mad traveller'. In 1887, a priest, who had abruptly disappeared from his home in Rhode Island a couple of months previously, reappeared in Pennsylvania under a different name. He had no memory of his former identity. In France, in the same year, another instance of 'ambulatory automatism', as some specialists named it, came to light; and, as a result of interest from the medical establishment, it quickly acquired the status of a specific mental disorder, sometimes called *fugue*. This initiated what Ian Hacking has diagnosed as 'the fugue epidemic of the 1890s'.[32] For Chesterton, psychologically traumatized as he had been in the 1890s, the man suffering from this apparently inexplicable form of amnesia is paradigmatic, because all individuals, in the times in which he lived, seemed oddly inured to the environment they inhabited. In this anaesthetic condition, 'we have all forgotten what we really are'. Everyday life is a constant state of forgetting, according to Chesterton; and art or spiritual ecstasy alone can for a moment make us forget that we have forgotten.

If Chesterton's protagonist, who himself experiences a form of ambulatory automatism as he roams about the suburbs of London at night, can be seen as a mad traveller, then he too is finally made to remember that he has forgotten who he really is. The name Thursday is, in this respect, not simply the pseudonym that he must adopt, when, as he falls into the depths of the nightmare, he is forced to assume the identity of an anarchist. It is his real name. It is the magic formula that, as in an incantation, brings his real identity into being. When Syme is forced to dress 'as Thursday' for the final biblical masquerade, at the end of the penultimate chapter, he experiences it as a relief, for 'though he affected to despise the mummey, he felt a curious freedom and naturalness in his movements as the blue and gold garment fell about him' (150). And his co-conspirators, from Monday through to Saturday, undergo the same epiphany, since 'these disguises did not disguise, but reveal' (150). As Slavoj Žižek has remarked of this passage, 'it is no longer "If you want to show your true self, tear off the mask!", but, on the contrary, "If you want to show your true self, put on the *right* mask!".'[33]

In becoming Thursday, he becomes himself; and it is the consciousness that he is secretly Thursday that makes Syme feel he is 'in possession of some impossible good news' when he resurfaces from the nightmare on a country lane at first light. In the terms provided by *Orthodoxy*, he is residually conscious of the fact that, for one awful instant, he remembered that he had forgotten who he is; and this is in itself enough to transfigure his everyday life. The deeper irony of the novel's title, then, is that this man is indeed Thursday. It is not simply some disguise that he temporarily assumed; it is the originary identity that he has managed to dig up. He is most himself when he finally becomes the man he pretended to be.

So *The Man Who Was Thursday* is framed in the form of an episode of mad travelling, a feverish tramp through the night in which Syme adopts the false identity that is in fact his true identity. The scene of his epiphany – though the reader is made to forget this until the final paragraphs of the book – is the road along which he has been walking through the night. For Chesterton, as the narrative frame emphasizes, the street is the supreme repository of poetry. 'Let us go through certain half-deserted streets', he appeals to his reader, like T. S. Eliot's Prufrock. But Chesterton's streets do not 'follow like a tedious argument / Of insidious intent'; they twist and gyrate with a mysterious, sometimes grotesque sense of joy. They are not meaningless, but pregnant with spiritual significance. In one of the most sinister and darkly comic passages in *The Man Who Was Thursday*, when Chesterton's urban fairy tale acquires a particularly demented force, Syme discovers to his horror that the ancient, death-like anarchist Professor de Worms, codenamed Friday, is stalking him through London's 'labyrinth of little streets' (61). For, although the Professor appears to be decrepit, he displays an athletic capacity for keeping up with Syme that is deeply disturbing. However much Syme accelerates, however much he deliberately loses himself in the maze of alleys and lanes that lie off the main thoroughfares, he continues to hear 'the clinking crutch and labouring feet of the infernal cripple' as he stops to catch his breath (62). Finally, in a state of desperation that is almost ecstatic, Syme has 'a new impulse to tear out the secret of this dancing, jumping and pursuing paralytic' (63), and he determines to turn and confront his pursuer. When he does so, the professor's form, outlined against a gas lamp, recalls 'that very imaginative figure in the nursery rhymes, "the crooked man who went a crooked mile".' 'He really looked,' the narrator adds, 'as if he had been twisted out of shape by the tortuous streets he had been threading.' (63) The Professor comes closer and closer; and Syme, 'remembering all the nightmares he had ever known', simply waits for him, 'as St George waited for the dragon, as a man waits for a final explanation or for death'. . .

It transpires, of course, that the Professor – his 'pale, grave' head grotesquely attached to a 'bounding body', 'like the head of a lecturer on the body of a harlequin' – is himself a heavily disguised police detective. The relief that the reader feels at this revelation, however, does not efface the indelible creepiness of the chase that Chesterton has so brilliantly described. The metropolitan city itself, after this episode, appears to be fatally haunted. On its streets, crisscrossed by both satanic and angelic energies, identities are ceaselessly made and unmade. Chesterton, the descendant of Dickens and Poe, is one of the great modernist poets of the city, even though he is generally classified neither as a modernist nor as a poet. His epiphanies take place on pavements. In *The Napoleon of Notting Hill* (1904), Chesterton's first novel, he describes in some detail a volume of poems by one of his most representative fictional characters, the pathologically eccentric Adam Wayne. The poems themselves are supposedly rather poor, but they are nonetheless remarkable for channelling all the spiritual passion of Romanticism from the countryside into the city, and for positing London as the supreme poetic subject. This poet, apparently, in one of the finer poems to apostrophize his muse, 'instead of saying that the rose and the lily contend in her complexion, says, with a purer modernism, that the red omnibus of Hammersmith and the white omnibus of Fulham fight there for the mastery!'[34] *The Man Who Was Thursday* is itself an instance of this 'purer modernism', which jams the most incongruous urban images up against one another in order to evoke the glorious chaos of being in a metropolitan city. The spectacular opening sight of the anarchists in Chapter

5, boisterously eating breakfast on the balcony overlooking Leicester Square, is an exemplary instance of this, because it concentrates Syme's 'eerie sensation of having strayed into a new world' (41). Chesterton's metropolitan city is an unstable, even at times explosive compound of the exotic and the everyday. It is in the same spirit that, in the opening chapter of *The Man Who Was Thursday*, Syme insists that, in so far as it embodies a kind of rapturous desire for order, the London Underground is 'the most poetical thing in the world' (4). Chesterton's modernism is a triumphant form of urban romanticism.

The narrator of *The Napoleon of Notting Hill* comments at one point that Adam Wayne 'was perhaps the first to realise how often the boundary of fairyland runs through a crowded city'.[35] He was of course far from the first to realize this. Chesterton was himself conscious that Dickens had been the poet laureate of the metropolitan city in the nineteenth century because he possessed, 'in the most sacred and serious sense of the term, the key of the street':

> Few of us understand the street. Even when we step into it, we step into it doubtfully, as into a house or room of strangers. Few of us see through the shining riddle of the street, the strange folk that belong to the street only [. . .]. Of the street at night many of us know even less. The street at night is a great house locked up. But Dickens had, if ever man had, the key of the street. His earth was the stones of the street; his stars were the lamps of the street; his hero was the man in the street.[36]

Chesterton too had the key to the street; and the proof of this is that, as he said of Dickens in the same book, 'he saw all his streets in fantastic perspectives'.[37] As *The Man Who Was Thursday* above all illustrates, Chesterton was supremely adept at defamiliarizing the mundane properties of the metropolitan city and making them seem miraculous. The image of the street lamp, to which he returned again and again in his fictional and non-fictional prose, is a good example of this, because it is an emblem of what, in *Orthodoxy*, Chesterton calls 'practical romance': it combines 'something that is strange with something that is secure', 'an idea of wonder and an idea of welcome'. Like other ordinary objects that only need to be estranged for a moment to seem extraordinary, it answers a 'double spiritual need, the need for that mixture of the familiar and the unfamiliar which Christendom has rightly named romance'.[38]

From its title on, *The Man Who Was Thursday* brings a fantastic perspective to bear on everyday life, and particularly the everyday life of the modern city. This fantastic perspective is of course informed by Chesterton's Christian faith, which became increasingly confident in the opening decade of the twentieth century, though he did not officially convert to Catholicism until 1922. I am however convinced that Hynes was right when, some time ago, he claimed that, in spite of the important scholarship on Chesterton by religious critics, 'above all, he needs secular attention'.[39] For Chesterton's commitment to estranging and transfiguring the commonplace is in literary terms consonant with the contemporaneous reaction against nineteenth-century realism. *The Man Who Was Thursday* is an incomparable instance of what might be called modernist romance. It uses some of the emergent techniques of modernism in order not to disenchant but to re-enchant everyday life. It takes the man who ambles about the streets but cannot remember his name and, in a gesture as anarchic as it is ecstatic, it spins him about in order to recall him abruptly to himself. Suddenly, this man inhabits a Wonderland in which, though nothing makes sense, everything makes sense. So too, as a blaze of astonishment flares up at the back of the brain, does Chesterton's reader.

NOTES

1. G. K. Chesterton, *Autobiography* (London: Hutchinson, 1936), p. 101.
2. Kingsley Amis, 'Introduction', *The Man Who Was Thursday* (Harmondsworth: Penguin, 1986), p. 4.
3. G. K. Chesterton, *Orthodoxy* (London: Bodley Head, 1908), pp. 80–81.
4. Chesterton, *Orthodoxy*, p. 132.

5. Oliver Sacks, *The Man Who Mistook His Wife for a Hat* (London: Picador, 1986), p. 9.
6. D. J. Conlon, ed., *G. K. Chesterton: The Critical Judgments* (Antwerp: Antwerp Studies in English Literature, 1976), p. 147.
7. Chesterton, *Autobiography*, pp. 101–2.
8. *The Defendant* (London: Dent, 1901), p. 69.
9. Conlon, ed., *G. K. Chesterton*, p. 145.
10. This is available at http://www.cse.dmu.ac.uk/~mward/gkc/ 380903.mp3
11. G. K. Chesterton, *Charles Dickens* (London: Methuen, 1906), p. 19.
12. Chesterton, *Autobiography*, p. 102.
13. Chesterton, *Orthodoxy*, p. 197.
14. Conlon, ed., *G. K. Chesterton*, p. 144.
15. G. K. Chesterton, *The Innocence of Father Brown* (Leipzig: Tauchnitz, 1911), p. 201.
16. G. K. Chesterton, *Robert Browning* (London: Macmillan, 1903), pp. 153, 111.
17. Chesterton, *Charles Dickens*, p. 213.
18. On 'irrealist' literature, see Michael Löwy, 'The Current of Critical Irrealism: A Moonlit Enchanted Night', in *Adventures in Realism*, ed. Matthew Beaumont (Oxford: Blackwell, 2007), pp. 193–206.
19. G. K. Chesterton, 'Dreams', in *The Coloured Lands* (London: Sheed & Ward, 1938), pp. 81–2.
20. Conlon, ed., *G. K. Chesterton*, p. 148.
21. Conlon, ed., *G. K. Chesterton*, p. 152.
22. Chesterton, *Autobiography*, p. 102.
23. Conlon, ed., *G. K. Chesterton*, p. 145. See also Heather Worthington, 'Identifying Anarchy in G. K. Chesterton's *The Man Who Was Thursday*', in *'To Hell with Culture': Anarchism and Twentieth-Century British Literature*, eds. H. Gustav Klaus and Stephen Knight (Cardiff: University of Wales Press, 2005), pp. 21–34.
24. See William Oddie, *Chesterton and the Romance of Orthodoxy: The Making of GKC, 1874–1908* (Oxford: Oxford University Press, 2008), pp. 84–125.
25. G. K. Chesterton, 'The Nightmare', in *Alarms and Discussions* (London: Methuen, 1910), pp. 17, 20.
26. Chesterton, *Autobiography*, pp. 91–2.
27. Samuel Hynes, 'The Chesterbelloc', in *Edwardian Occasions: Essays on English Writing in the Early Twentieth Century* (London: Routledge & Kegan Paul, 1972), p. 83.
28. Chesterton, *Autobiography*, pp. 93–4.

29. Chesterton, *Autobiography*, pp. 94–5.

30. Chesterton, *Autobiography*, p. 95.

31. Chesterton, *Orthodoxy*, pp. 80–81.

32. See Ian Hacking, *Mad Travellers: Reflections on the Reality of Transient Mental Illnesses* (Cambridge, Mass.: Harvard University Press, 1998), p. 12.

33. See Slavoj Žižek, 'Hegel – Chesterton: German Idealism and Christianity,' in *The Symptom* (http://www.lacan.com/zizhegche.htm).

34. Gilbert K. Chesterton, *The Napoleon of Notting Hill* (London: Bodley Head, 1904), p. 129.

35. Chesterton, *The Napoleon of Notting Hill*, p. 131.

36. Chesterton, *Charles Dickens*, pp. 44–5.

37. Chesterton, *Charles Dickens*, p. 144.

38. Chesterton, *Orthodoxy*, pp. 3–4.

39. Hynes, 'The Chesterbelloc', p. 80.

Further Reading

EDITIONS OF *THE MAN WHO WAS THURSDAY*

The Collected Works of G. K. Chesterton, Vol. 6: The Man Who Was Thursday, The Club of Queer Trades, The Napoleon of Notting Hill, The Ball and the Cross, ed. Denis J. Conlon (San Francisco: Ignatius Press, 1991).

The Man Who Was Thursday and Related Pieces, ed. Stephen Medcalf (Oxford: World's Classics, 1996).

The Annotated Thursday: G. K. Chesterton's Masterpiece, The Man Who Was Thursday, ed. Martin Gardner (San Francisco: Ignatius Press, 1999).

EDITIONS OF G. K. CHESTERTON

The Collected Works of G. K. Chesterton (San Francisco: Ignatius Press, 1986).

STUDIES OF G. K. CHESTERTON

Ahlquist, Dale, *G. K. Chesterton: The Apostle of Common Sense* (San Francisco: Ignatius Press, 2003).

Barker, Dudley, *G. K. Chesterton: A Biography* (London: Constable, 1973).

Belloc, Hilaire, *On the Place of Gilbert Chesterton in English Letters* (London: Sheed & Ward, 1940).

Boyd, Ian, *The Novels of G. K. Chesterton: A Study in Art and Propaganda* (London: Elek, 1975).

Canovan, Margaret, *G. K. Chesterton: A Radical Populist* (New York: Harcourt Brace Jovanovich, 1977).

Caserio, Robert L., 'G. K. Chesterton and the Terrorist God outside Modernism', in Lynne Hapgood and Nancy L. Paxton, eds., *Outside Modernism: In Pursuit of the English Novel, 1900–30* (Basingstoke: Macmillan, 2000: 63–82).

The Chesterton Review: A Newsletter of the G. K. Chesterton Society (1974–).

Clemens, Cyril, *Chesterton as Seen by His Contemporaries* (Webster Groves, Mo.: International Mark Twain Society, 1939).

Clipper, Lawrence J., *G. K. Chesterton* (New York: Twayne, 1974).

Coates, John D., *Chesterton and the Edwardian Cultural Crisis* (Hull: Hull University Press, 1984).

Coates, John, *G. K. Chesterton as Controversialist, Essayist, Novelist and Critic* (Lewiston, NY: E. Mellen Press, 2002).

Conlon, D. J., ed., *G. K. Chesterton: The Critical Judgments* (Antwerp: Antwerp Studies in English Literature, 1976).

Conlon, D. J., ed., *G. K. Chesterton: A Half Century of Views* (Oxford: Oxford University Press, 1987).

Coren, Michael, *Gilbert: The Man Who Was G. K. Chesterton* (London: Jonathan Cape, 1989).

Corrin, Jay P., *Chesterton and Hilaire Belloc: The Battle against Modernity* (Athens, Ohio: Ohio University Press, 1981).

Dale, Alzina Stone, *The Outline of Sanity: A Biography of G. K. Chesterton* (Grand Rapids, Mich.: Eerdmans, 1982).

Evans, Maurice, *G. K. Chesterton* (Cambridge: Cambridge University Press, 1939).

Finch, Michael, *G. K. Chesterton* (London: Harper Collins, 1986).

Hollis, Christopher, *The Mind of Chesterton* (London: Hollis & Carter, 1970).

Hunter, Lynette, *G. K. Chesterton: Explorations in Allegory* (London: Macmillan, 1979).

Hynes, Samuel, 'The Chesterbelloc', in *Edwardian Occasions:*

Essays on English Writing in the Early Twentieth Century (London: Routledge & Kegan Paul, 1972: 80–90).

Kenner, Hugh, *Paradox in Chesterton* (London: Sheed & Ward, 1948).

Oddie, William, *Chesterton and the Romance of Orthodoxy: The Making of GKC, 1874–1908* (Oxford: Oxford University Press, 2008).

Sullivan, John, ed., *G. K. Chesterton: A Centenary Appraisal* (London: Elek, 1974).

Sullivan, John, *G. K. Chesterton: A Bibliography* (London: University of London Press, 1958).

Ward, Maisie, *Gilbert Keith Chesterton* (New York: Sheed & Ward, 1943).

Ward, Maisie, *Return to Chesterton* (London: Sheed & Ward, 1952).

Wills, Gary, *Chesterton: Man and Mask* (New York: Sheed & Ward, 1961).

Worthington, Heather, 'Identifying Anarchy in G. K. Chesterton's *The Man Who Was Thursday*', in *'To Hell with Culture': Anarchism and Twentieth-Century British Literature*, eds. H. Gustav Klaus and Stephen Knight (Cardiff: University of Wales Press, 2005: 21-34).

Žižek, Slavoj, 'The "Thrilling Romance of Orthodoxy"', in *Theology and the Political: The New Debate*, eds. Creston Davis, John Milbank and Slavoj Žižek (Durham, NC: Duke University Press, 2005: 52-71).

OTHER STUDIES

Batchelor, John, *The Edwardian Novelists* (London: Duckworth, 1982).

Butterworth, Alex, *The World that Never Was: A True Story of Dreamers, Schemers, Anarchists and Secret Agents* (London: Bodley Head, 2010).

Carey, John, *The Intellectuals and the Masses: Pride and Prejudice among the Literary Intelligentsia, 1880-1939* (London: Faber & Faber, 1992).

Cole, Sarah, 'Dynamite, Violence and Literary Culture', *Modernism / Modernity* 16: 2 (2009): 301–28.

Freeman, Nicholas, *Conceiving the City: London, Literature, and Art 1870-1914* (Oxford: Oxford University Press, 2007).

Hanson, Gillian Mary, *City and Shore: The Function of Setting in the British Mystery* (Jefferson, NC: McFarland, 2004).

Hapgood, Lynne, *Margins of Desire: The Suburbs in Fiction and Culture 1880–1925* (Manchester: Manchester University Press, 2005).

Houen, Alex, *Terrorism and Modern Literature: From Joseph Conrad to Ciaran Carson* (Oxford: Oxford University Press, 2002).

Hunter, Jefferson, *Edwardian Fiction* (Cambridge, Mass.: Harvard University Press, 1982).

Hynes, Samuel, *The Edwardian Turn of Mind* (Princeton: Princeton University Press, 1968).

Keating, Paul, *The Haunted Study: A Social History of the English Novel 1875–1914* (London: Secker & Warburg, 1989).

Melchiori, Barbara Arnett, *Terrorism in the Late Victorian Novel* (Beckenham: Croom Helm, 1985).

Phillips, Wm. M., *Nightmares of Anarchy: Language and Cultural Change 1870–1914* (Lewisburg: Bucknell University Press, 2003).

Pykett, Lyn, *Engendering Fictions: The English Novel in the Early Twentieth Century* (London: Edward Arnold, 1995).

Wisnicki, Adrian S., *Conspiracy, Revolution, and Terrorism from Victorian Fiction to the Modern Novel* (London: Routledge, 2008).

Map

Police Courts

0   1 mile

0   1 km

To Edmund Clerihew Bentley[1]

A cloud was on the mind of men, and wailing went the weather,
Yea, a sick cloud upon the soul when we were boys together.
Science announced nonentity and art admired decay;
The world was old and ended: but you and I were gay.
Round us in antic order their crippled vices came –
Lust that had lost its laughter, fear that had lost its shame.
Like the white lock of Whistler,[2] that lit our aimless gloom.
Men showed their own white feather[3] as proudly as a plume.
Life was a fly that faded, and death a drone that stung;
The world was very old indeed when you and I were young.
They twisted even decent sin to shapes not to be named:
Men were ashamed of honour; but we were not ashamed.
Weak if we were and foolish, not thus we failed, not thus;
When that black Baal[4] blocked the heavens he had no hymns from us.
Children we were – our forts of sand were even as weak as we,
High as they went we piled them up to break that bitter sea.
Fools as we were in motley, all jangling and absurd,
When all church bells were silent our cap and bells were heard.

Not all unhelped we held the fort, our tiny flags unfurled;
Some giants laboured in that cloud to lift it from the world.
I find again the book we found, I feel the hour that flings
Far out of fish-shaped Paumanok[5] some cry of cleaner things;
And the Green Carnation[6] withered, as in forest fires that pass,
Roared in the wind of all the world ten million leaves of grass;[7]
Or sane and sweet and sudden as a bird sings in the rain –
Truth out of Tusitala[8] spoke and pleasure out of pain.
Yea, cool and clear and sudden as a bird sings in the grey,
Dunedin to Samoa spoke,[9] and darkness unto day.
But we were young; we lived to see God break their bitter charms,
God and the good Republic come riding back in arms:
We have seen the City of Mansoul,[10] even as it rocked, relieved –
Blessed are they who did not see, but being blind, believed.

This is a tale of those old fears, even of those emptied hells,
And none but you shall understand the true thing that it tells –
Of what colossal gods of shame could cow men and yet crash,
Of what huge devils hid the stars, yet fell at a pistol flash.
The doubts that were so plain to chase, so dreadful to withstand –
Oh, who shall understand but you: yea, who shall understand?
The doubts that drove us through the night as we two talked amain,
And day had broken on the streets e'er it broke upon the brain.
Between us, by the peace of God, such truth can now be told;
Yea, there is strength in striking root, and good in growing old.
We have found common things at last, and marriage and a creed,
And I may safely write it now, and you may safely read.

                                                          G. K. C.

The Man Who Was Thursday

I

The Two Poets of Saffron Park[1]

The suburb of Saffron Park lay on the sunset side of London, as red and ragged as a cloud of sunset. It was built of a bright brick throughout; its skyline was fantastic, and even its ground plan was wild. It had been the outburst of a speculative builder, faintly tinged with art, who called its architecture sometimes Elizabethan and sometimes Queen Anne, apparently under the impression that the two sovereigns were identical. It was described with some justice as an artistic colony, though it never in any definable way produced any art. But although its pretensions to be an intellectual centre were a little vague, its pretensions to be a pleasant place were quite indisputable. The stranger who looked for the first time at the quaint red houses could only think how very oddly shaped the people must be who could fit in to them. Nor when he met the people was he disappointed in this respect. The place was not only pleasant, but perfect, if once he could regard it not as a deception but rather as a dream. Even if the people were not 'artists', the whole was nevertheless artistic. That young man with the long, auburn hair and the impudent face – that young man was not really a poet; but surely he was a poem. That old gentleman with the wild, white beard and the wild, white hat – that venerable humbug was not really a philosopher; but at least he was the cause of philosophy in others. That scientific gentleman with the bald, egg-like head and the bare, bird-like neck had no real right to the airs of science that he assumed. He had not discovered anything new in biology; but what biological creature could he have discovered more singular than himself? Thus, and thus only, the whole place had properly to be regarded; it had to be considered not so much as a workshop for artists, but as a frail but finished work of art. A man who stepped into its social atmosphere felt as if he had stepped into a written comedy.

More especially this attractive unreality fell upon it about nightfall, when the extravagant roofs were dark against the afterglow and the whole insane village seemed as separate as a drifting cloud. This again was more strongly true of the many nights of local festivity, when the little gardens were often illuminated, and the big Chinese lanterns glowed in the dwarfish trees like some fierce and monstrous fruit. And this was strongest of all on one particular evening, still vaguely remembered in the locality, of which the auburn-haired poet was the hero. It was not by any means the only evening of which he was the hero. On many nights those passing by his little back garden might hear his high, didactic voice laying down the law to men and particularly to women. The attitude of women in such cases was indeed one of the paradoxes of the place. Most of the women were of the kind vaguely called emancipated, and professed some protest against male supremacy. Yet these new women[2] would always pay to a man the extravagant compliment which no ordinary woman ever pays to him, that of listening while he is talking. And Mr Lucian Gregory, the red-haired poet, was really (in some sense) a man worth listening to, even if one laughed at the end of it. He put the old cant of the lawlessness of art and the art of lawlessness with a certain impudent freshness which gave at least a momentary pleasure. He was helped in some degree by the arresting oddity of his appearance, which he worked, as the phrase goes, for all it was worth. His dark red hair parted in the middle was literally like a woman's, and curved into the slow curls of a virgin in a pre-Raphaelite picture.[3] From within this almost saintly oval, however, his face projected suddenly broad and brutal, the chin carried forward with a look of cockney contempt. This combination at once tickled and terrified the nerves of a neurotic population. He seemed like a walking blasphemy, a blend of the angel and the ape.

This particular evening, if it is remembered for nothing else, will be remembered in that place for its strange sunset. It looked like the end of the world.[4] All the heaven seemed covered with a quite vivid and palpable plumage; you could only say that the sky was full of feathers, and of feathers that almost brushed the face. Across the great part of the dome they were grey, with the strangest tints of violet and mauve and an unnatural pink or pale green; but towards the west the whole grew past description, transparent and passionate, and the last red-hot plumes of it covered up the sun like something too good to be seen. The whole was so close about the earth as to express nothing but a violent secrecy. The very empyrean seemed to be a secret. It expressed that splendid smallness which is the soul of local patriotism.[5] The very sky seemed small.

I say that there are some inhabitants who may remember the evening if only by that oppressive sky. There are others who may remember it because it marked the first appearance in the place of the second poet of Saffron Park. For a long time the red-haired revolutionary had reigned without a rival; it was upon the night of the sunset that his solitude suddenly ended. The new poet, who introduced himself by the name of Gabriel Syme,[6] was a very mild-looking mortal, with a fair, pointed beard and faint, yellow hair. But an impression grew that he was less meek than he looked. He signalized his entrance by differing with the established poet, Gregory, upon the whole nature of poetry. He said that he (Syme) was a poet of law, a poet of order; nay, he said he was a poet of respectability. So all the Saffron Parkers looked at him as if he had that moment fallen out of that impossible sky.

In fact, Mr Lucian Gregory, the anarchic poet, connected the two events.

'It may well be,' he said, in his sudden lyrical manner, 'it may well be on such a night of clouds and cruel colours that there is brought forth upon the earth such a portent as a respectable poet. You say you are a poet of law; I say you are a contradiction in terms. I only wonder there were not comets and earthquakes on the night you appeared in this garden.'

The man with the meek blue eyes and the pale, pointed beard endured these thunders with a certain submissive solemnity. The third party of the group, Gregory's sister Rosamond, who had her brother's braids of red hair, but a kindlier face underneath them, laughed with such mixture of admiration and disapproval as she gave commonly to the family oracle.

Gregory resumed in high oratorical good-humour.

'An artist is identical with an anarchist,' he cried. 'You might transpose the words anywhere. An anarchist is an artist. The man who throws a bomb is an artist, because he prefers a great moment to everything. He sees how much more valuable is one burst of blazing light, one peal of perfect thunder, than the mere common bodies of a few shapeless policemen. An artist disregards all governments, abolishes all conventions. The poet delights in disorder only. If it were not so, the most poetical thing in the world would be the Underground Railway.'[7]

'So it is,' said Mr Syme.

'Nonsense!' said Gregory, who was very rational when anyone else attempted paradox. 'Why do all the clerks and navvies in the railway trains look so sad and tired, so very sad and tired? I will tell you. It is because they know that the train is going right. It is because they know that whatever place they have taken a ticket for, that place they will reach. It is because after they have passed Sloane Square they know that the next station must be Victoria, and nothing but Victoria. Oh, their wild rapture! oh, their eyes like stars and their souls again in Eden, if the next station were unaccountably Baker Street!'

'It is you who are unpoetical,' replied the poet Syme. 'If what you say of clerks is true, they can only be as prosaic as your poetry. The rare, strange thing is to hit the mark; the gross, obvious thing is to miss it. We feel it is epical when man with one wild arrow strikes a distant bird. Is it not also epical when man with one wild engine strikes a distant station? Chaos is dull; because in chaos the train might indeed go anywhere, to Baker Street, or to Bagdad. But man is a magician, and his whole magic is in this, that he does say Victoria, and lo! it is Victoria. No, take your books of mere poetry and prose, let me read a time-table, with tears of pride. Take your Byron, who commemorates the defeats of man; give me Bradshaw[8] who commemorates his victories. Give me Bradshaw, I say!'

'Must you go?' inquired Gregory sarcastically.

'I tell you,' went on Syme with passion, 'that every time a

train comes in I feel that it has broken past batteries of besiegers, and that man has won a battle against chaos. You say contemptuously that when one has left Sloane Square one must come to Victoria. I say that one might do a thousand things instead, and that whenever I really come there I have the sense of hair-breadth escape. And when I hear the guard shout out the word "Victoria", it is not an unmeaning word. It is to me the cry of a herald announcing conquest. It is to me indeed "Victoria"; it is the victory of Adam.'

Gregory wagged his heavy, red head with a slow and sad smile.

'And even then,' he said, 'we poets always ask the question, "And what is Victoria now that you have got there?" You think Victoria is like the New Jerusalem. We know that the New Jerusalem will only be like Victoria. Yes, the poet will be discontented even in the streets of heaven. The poet is always in revolt.'

'There again,' said Syme irritably, 'what is there poetical about being in revolt? You might as well say that it is poetical to be sea-sick. Being sick is a revolt. Both being sick and being rebellious may be the wholesome thing on certain desperate occasions; but I'm hanged if I can see why they are poetical. Revolt in the abstract is – revolting. It's mere vomiting.'

The girl winced for a flash at the unpleasant word, but Syme was too hot to heed her.

'It is things going right,' he cried, 'that is poetical! Our digestions, for instance, going sacredly and silently right, that is the foundation of all poetry. Yes, the most poetical thing, more poetical than the flowers, more poetical than the stars – the most poetical thing in the world is not being sick.'

'Really,' said Gregory superciliously, 'the examples you choose—'

'I beg your pardon,' said Syme grimly, 'I thought we had abolished all conventions.'

For the first time a red patch appeared on Gregory's forehead.

'You don't expect me,' he said, 'to revolutionize society on this lawn?'

Syme looked straight into his eyes and smiled sweetly.

'No, I don't,' he said; 'but I suppose that if you were serious about your anarchism, that is exactly what you would do.'

Gregory's big bull's eyes blinked suddenly like those of an angry lion, and one could almost fancy that his red mane rose.

'Don't you think, then,' he said in a dangerous voice, 'that I am serious about my anarchism?'

'I beg your pardon?' said Syme.

'Am I not serious about my anarchism?' cried Gregory, with knotted fists.

'My dear fellow!' said Syme, and strolled away.

With surprise, but with a curious pleasure, he found Rosamond Gregory still in his company.

'Mr Syme,' she said, 'do the people who talk like you and my brother often mean what they say? Do you mean what you say now?'

Syme smiled.

'Do you?' he asked.

'What do you mean?' asked the girl, with grave eyes.

'My dear Miss Gregory,' said Syme gently, 'there are many kinds of sincerity. When you say "thank you" for the salt, do you mean what you say? No. When you say "the world is round", do you mean what you say? No. It is true, but you don't mean it. Now, sometimes a man like your brother really finds a thing he does mean. It may be only a half-truth, quarter-truth, tenth-truth; but then he says more than he means – from sheer force of meaning it.'

She was looking at him from under level brows; her face was grave and open, and there had fallen upon it the shadow of that unreasoning responsibility which is at the bottom of the most frivolous woman, the maternal watch which is as old as the world.

'Is he really an anarchist, then?' she asked.

'Only in that sense I speak of,' replied Syme; 'or if you prefer it, in that nonsense.'

She drew her broad brows together and said abruptly:

'He wouldn't really use – bombs or that sort of thing?'

Syme broke into a great laugh that seemed too large for his slight and somewhat dandified figure.

'Good Lord, no!' he said. 'That has to be done anonymously.'

And at that the corners of her own mouth broke into a smile, and she thought with a simultaneous pleasure of Gregory's absurdity and of his safety.

Syme strolled with her to a seat in the corner of the garden, and continued to pour out his opinions. For he was a sincere man, and in spite of his superficial airs and graces, at root a humble one. And it is always the humble man who talks too much; the proud man watches himself too closely. He defended respectability with violence and exaggeration. He grew passionate in his praise of tidiness and propriety. All the time there was a smell of lilac all round him. Once he heard very faintly in some distant street a barrel-organ begin to play, and it seemed to him that his heroic words were moving to a tiny tune from under or beyond the world.

He stared and talked at the girl's red hair and amused face for what seemed to be a few minutes; and then, feeling that the groups in such a place should mix, rose to his feet. To his astonishment, he discovered the whole garden empty. Everyone had gone long ago, and he went himself with a rather hurried apology. He left with a sense of champagne in his head, which he could not afterwards explain. In the wild events which were to follow, this girl had no part at all; he never saw her again until all his tale was over. And yet, in some indescribable way, she kept recurring like a motive in music through all his mad adventures afterwards, and the glory of her strange hair ran like a red thread through those dark and ill-drawn tapestries of the night. For what followed was so improbable that it might well have been a dream.

When Syme went out into the starlit street, he found it for the moment empty. Then he realized (in some odd way) that the silence was rather a living silence than a dead one. Directly outside the door stood a street lamp, whose gleam gilded the leaves of the tree that bent out over the fence behind him. About a foot from the lamp-post stood a figure almost as rigid and motionless as the lamp-post itself. The tall hat and long frock-coat were black; the face, in an abrupt shadow, was almost as dark. Only a fringe of fiery hair against the light, and also something aggressive in the attitude, proclaimed that it was the poet Gregory. He had something of the look of a masked bravo waiting sword in hand for his foe.

He made a sort of double salute, which Syme somewhat more formally returned.

'I was waiting for you,' said Gregory. 'Might I have a moment's conversation?'

'Certainly. About what?' asked Syme in a sort of weak wonder.

Gregory struck out with his stick at the lamp-post, and then at the tree.

'About *this* and *this*,' he cried; 'about order and anarchy. There is your precious order, that lean, iron lamp, ugly and barren; and there is anarchy, rich, living, reproducing itself – there is anarchy, splendid in green and gold.'

'All the same,' replied Syme patiently, 'just at present you only see the tree by the light of the lamp. I wonder when you would ever see the lamp by the light of the tree.' Then after a pause he said, 'But may I ask if you have been standing out here in the dark only to resume our little argument?'

'No,' cried Gregory, in a voice that rang down the street, 'I did not stand here to resume our argument, but to end it for ever.'

The silence fell again, and Syme, though he understood nothing, listened instinctively for something serious. Gregory began in a smooth voice and with a rather bewildering smile.

'Mr Syme,' he said, 'this evening you succeeded in doing something rather remarkable. You did something to me that no man born of woman[9] has ever succeeded in doing before.'

'Indeed!'

'Now I remember,' resumed Gregory reflectively, 'one other person succeeded in doing it. The captain of a penny steamer (if I remember correctly) at Southend. You have irritated me.'

'I am very sorry,' replied Syme with gravity.

'I am afraid my fury and your insult are too shocking to be wiped out even with an apology,' said Gregory very calmly. 'No duel could wipe it out. If I struck you dead I could not wipe it out. There is only one way by which that insult can be erased, and that way I choose. I am going, at the possible sacrifice of my life and honour, to *prove* to you that you were wrong in what you said.'

'In what I said?'

'You said I was not serious about being an anarchist.'

'There are degrees of seriousness,' replied Syme. 'I have never doubted that you were perfectly sincere in this sense, that you thought what you said well worth saying, that you thought a paradox might wake men up to a neglected truth.'

Gregory stared at him steadily and painfully.

'And in no other sense,' he asked, 'you think me serious? You think me a *flâneur*[10] who lets fall occasional truths. You do not think that in a deeper, a more deadly sense, I am serious.'

Syme struck his stick violently on the stones of the road.

'Serious!' he cried. 'Good Lord! is this street serious? Are these damned Chinese lanterns serious? Is the whole caboodle serious? One comes here and talks a pack of bosh, and perhaps some sense as well, but I should think very little of a man who didn't keep something in the background of his life that was more serious than all this talking – something more serious, whether it was religion or only drink.'

'Very well,' said Gregory, his face darkening, 'you shall see something more serious than either drink or religion.'

Syme stood waiting with his usual air of mildness until Gregory again opened his lips.

'You spoke just now of having a religion. Is it really true that you have one?'

'Oh,' said Syme with a beaming smile, 'we are all Catholics now.'

'Then may I ask you to swear by whatever gods or saints your religion involves that you will *not* reveal what I am now going to tell you to any son of Adam, and especially not to the police? Will you swear that! If you will take upon yourself this awful abnegation, if you will consent to burden your soul with a vow that you should never make and a knowledge you should never dream about, I will promise you in return—'

'You will promise me in return?' inquired Syme, as the other paused.

'I will promise you a very entertaining evening.'

Syme suddenly took off his hat.

'Your offer,' he said, 'is far too idiotic to be declined. You say that a poet is always an anarchist. I disagree; but I hope at least that he is always a sportsman. Permit me, here and now, to swear as a Christian, and promise as a good comrade and a fellow-artist, that I will not report anything of this, whatever it is, to the police. And now, in the name of Colney Hatch[11] what is it?'

'I think,' said Gregory, with placid irrelevancy, 'that we will call a cab.'

He gave two long whistles, and a hansom came rattling down the road. The two got into it in silence. Gregory gave through the trap the address of an obscure public-house on the Chiswick bank of the river. The cab whisked itself away again, and in it these two fantastics quitted their fantastic town.

2

The Secret of Gabriel Syme

The cab pulled up before a particularly dreary and greasy beer-shop, into which Gregory rapidly conducted his companion. They seated themselves in a close and dim sort of bar-parlour, at a stained wooden table with one wooden leg. The room was so small and dark, that very little could be seen of the attendant who was summoned, beyond a vague and dark impression of something bulky and bearded.

'Will you take a little supper?' asked Gregory politely. 'The *pâté de foie gras* is not good here, but I can recommend the game.'

Syme received the remark with stolidity, imagining it to be a joke. Accepting the vein of humour, he said with a well-bred indifference –

'Oh, bring me some lobster mayonnaise.'

To his indescribable astonishment, the man only said, 'Certainly, sir!' and went away apparently to get it.

'What will you drink?' resumed Gregory, with the same careless yet apologetic air. 'I shall only have a *crème de menthe*[1] myself; I have dined. But the champagne can really be trusted. Do let me start you with a half-bottle of Pommery at least?'

'Thank you!' said the motionless Syme. 'You are very good.'

His further attempts at conversation, somewhat disorganized in themselves, were cut short finally as by a thunderbolt by the actual appearance of the lobster. Syme tasted it, and found it particularly good. Then he suddenly began to eat with great rapidity and appetite.

'Excuse me if I enjoy myself rather obviously!' he said to Gregory, smiling. 'I don't often have the luck to have a dream like this. It is new to me for a nightmare to lead me to a lobster. It is commonly the other way.'

'You are not asleep, I assure you,' said Gregory. 'You are, on the contrary, close to the most actual and rousing moment of your existence. Ah, here comes your champagne! I admit that there may be a slight disproportion, let us say, between the inner arrangements of this excellent hotel and its simple and unpretentious exterior. But that is all our modesty. We are the most modest men that ever lived on earth.'

'And who are *we*?' asked Syme, emptying his champagne glass.

'It is quite simple,' replied Gregory. '*We* are the serious anarchists, in whom you do not believe.'

'Oh!' said Syme shortly. 'You do yourselves well in drinks.'

'Yes, we are serious about everything,' answered Gregory.

Then after a pause he added –

'If in a few moments this table begins to turn round a little, don't put it down to your inroads into the champagne. I don't wish you to do yourself an injustice.'

'Well, if I am not drunk, I am mad,' replied Syme with perfect calm; 'but I trust I can behave like a gentleman in either condition. May I smoke?'

'Certainly!' said Gregory, producing a cigar-case. 'Try one of mine.'

Syme took the cigar, clipped the end off with a cigar-cutter out of his waistcoat pocket, put it in his mouth, lit it slowly, and let out a long cloud of smoke. It is not a little to his credit that he performed these rites with so much composure, for almost before he had begun them the table at which he sat had begun to revolve, first slowly, and then rapidly, as if at an insane séance.

'You must not mind it,' said Gregory, 'it's a kind of screw.'

'Quite so,' said Syme placidly, 'a kind of screw![2] How simple that is!'

The next moment the smoke of his cigar, which had been wavering across the room in snaky twists, went straight up as if from a factory chimney, and the two, with their chairs and table, shot down through the floor as if the earth had swallowed them. They went rattling down a kind of roaring chimney as rapidly as a lift cut loose, and they came with an abrupt bump to the bottom. But when Gregory threw open a pair of doors and let in a red subterranean light, Syme was still smoking, with one leg thrown over the other, and had not turned a yellow hair.

Gregory led him down a low, vaulted passage, at the end of which was the red light. It was an enormous crimson lantern, nearly as big as a fireplace, fixed over a small but heavy iron door. In the door there was a sort of hatchway or grating; and on this Gregory struck five times. A heavy voice with a foreign accent asked him who he was. To this he gave the more or less unexpected reply, 'Mr Joseph Chamberlain'.[3] The heavy hinges began to move; it was obviously some kind of password.

Inside the doorway the passage gleamed as if it were lined with a network of steel. On a second glance, Syme saw that the glittering pattern was really made up of ranks and ranks of rifles and revolvers, closely packed or interlocked.

'I must ask you to forgive me all these formalities,' said Gregory; 'we have to be very strict here.'

'Oh, don't apologize,' said Syme. 'I know your passion for law and order,' and he stepped into the passage lined with the steel weapons. With his long, fair hair and rather foppish frock-coat, he looked a singularly frail and fanciful figure as he walked down that shining avenue of death.

They passed through several such passages, and came out at last into a queer steel chamber, with curved walls, almost spherical in shape, but presenting, with its tiers of benches, something of the appearance of a scientific lecture-theatre. There were no rifles or pistols in this apartment, but round the walls of it were hung more dubious and dreadful shapes, things that looked like the bulbs of iron plants, or the eggs of iron birds. They were bombs, and the very room itself seemed like the inside of a bomb. Syme knocked his cigar ash off against the wall, and went in.

'And now, my dear Mr Syme,' said Gregory, throwing himself in an expansive manner on the bench under the largest bomb, 'now we are quite cosy, so let us talk properly. Now, no human words can give you any notion of why I brought you here. It was one of those quite arbitrary emotions, like jumping off a

cliff or falling in love. Suffice it to say that you were an in-
expressibly irritating fellow, and, to do you justice, you are still.
I would break twenty oaths of secrecy for the pleasure of taking
you down a peg. That way you have of lighting a cigar would
make a priest break the seal of confession. Well, you have said
that you were quite certain I was not a serious anarchist. Does
this place strike you as being serious?'

'It does seem to have a moral under all its gaiety,' assented
Syme; 'but may I ask you two questions? You need not fear to
give me information, because, as you remember, you very wisely
extorted from me a promise not to tell the police, a promise I
shall certainly keep. So it is in mere curiosity that I make my
queries. First of all, what is it really all about? What is it you
object to? You want to abolish Government?'

'To abolish God!' said Gregory, opening the eyes of a fanatic.
'We do not only want to upset a few despotisms and police
regulations; that sort of anarchism does exist, but it is a mere
branch of the Nonconformists. We dig deeper and we blow you
higher. We wish to deny all those arbitrary distinctions of vice
and virtue, honour and treachery, upon which mere rebels base
themselves. The silly sentimentalists of the French Revolution
talked of the Rights of Man! We hate Rights and we hate Wrongs.
We have abolished Right and Wrong.'

'And Right and Left,' said Syme with a simple eagerness. 'I
hope you will abolish them too. They are much more trouble-
some to me.'

'You spoke of a second question,' snapped Gregory.

'With pleasure,' resumed Syme. 'In all your present acts and
surroundings there is a scientific attempt at secrecy. I have an
aunt who lived over a shop, but this is the first time I have found
people living for preference under a public-house. You have a
heavy iron door. You cannot pass it without submitting to the
humiliation of calling yourself Mr Chamberlain. You surround
yourself with steel instruments which make the place, if I may
say so, more impressive than homelike. May I ask why, after
taking all this trouble to barricade yourselves in the bowels of
the earth, you then parade your whole secret by talking about
anarchism to every silly woman in Saffron Park?'

Gregory smiled.

'The answer is simple,' he said. 'I told you I was a serious anarchist, and you did not believe me. Nor do *they* believe me. Unless I took them into this infernal room they would not believe me.'

Syme smoked thoughtfully, and looked at him with interest. Gregory went on.

'The history of the thing might amuse you,' he said. 'When first I became one of the New Anarchists,[4] I tried all kinds of respectable disguises. I dressed up as a bishop. I read up all about bishops in our anarchist pamphlets, in *Superstition the Vampire* and *Priests of Prey*. I certainly understood from them that bishops are strange and terrible old men keeping a cruel secret from mankind. I was misinformed. When on my first appearing in episcopal gaiters in a drawing-room I cried out in a voice of thunder "Down! Down! presumptuous human reason!" they found out in some way that I was not a bishop at all. I was nabbed at once. Then I made up as a millionaire; but I defended Capital with so much intelligence that a fool could see that I was quite poor. Then I tried being a major. Now, I am a humanitarian myself, but I have, I hope, enough intellectual breadth to understand the position of those who, like Nietzsche,[5] admire violence – the proud, mad war of Nature and all that, you know. I threw myself into the major. I drew my sword and waved it constantly. I called out "Blood!" abstractedly, like a man calling for wine. I often said, "Let the weak perish; it is the Law." Well, well, it seems majors don't do this. I was nabbed again. At last I went in despair to the President of the Central Anarchist Council,[6] who is the greatest man in Europe.'

'What is his name?' asked Syme.

'You would not know it,' answered Gregory. 'That is his greatness. Caesar and Napoleon put all their genius into being heard of, and they *were* heard of. He puts all his genius into not being heard of, and he is not heard of. But you cannot be for five minutes in the room with him without feeling that Caesar and Napoleon would have been children in his hands.'

He was silent and even pale for a moment, and, then resumed –

'But whenever he gives advice it is always something as startling as an epigram, and yet as practical as the Bank of England.
I said to him, "What disguise will hide me from the world? What
can I find more respectable than bishops and majors?" He looked
at me with his large but indecipherable face. "You want a safe
disguise, do you? You want a dress which will guarantee you
harmless; a dress in which no one would ever look for a bomb?"
I nodded. He suddenly lifted his lion's voice. "Why, then, dress
up as an *anarchist*, you fool!" he roared so that the room shook.
"Nobody will ever expect you to do anything dangerous then."
And he turned his broad back on me without another word. I
took his advice and have never regretted it. I preached blood
and murder to those women day and night, and – by God – they
would let me wheel their perambulators.'

Syme sat watching him with some respect in his large, blue
eyes.

'You took me in,' he said. 'It is really a smart dodge.'

Then after a pause he added –

'What do you call this tremendous President of yours?'

'We generally call him Sunday,' replied Gregory with simplicity.
'You see, there are seven members of the Central Anarchist
Council, and they are named after days of the week. He is called
Sunday, by some of his admirers Bloody Sunday.[7] It is curious
you should mention the matter, because the very night you have
dropped in (if I may so express it) is the night on which our
London branch, which assembles in this room, has to elect its
own deputy to fill a vacancy in the Council. The gentleman
who has for some time past played, with propriety and general
applause, the difficult part of Thursday, has died quite suddenly.
Consequently, we have called a meeting this very evening to elect
a successor.'

He got to his feet and strolled across the room with a sort of
smiling embarrassment.

'I feel somehow as if you were my mother, Syme,' he continued
casually, 'I feel that I can confide anything to you, as you have
promised to tell nobody. In fact, I will confide to you something
that I would not say in so many words to the anarchists who
will be coming to the room in about ten minutes. We shall, of

course, go through a form of election; but I don't mind telling you that it is practically certain what the result will be.' He looked down for a moment modestly. 'It is almost a settled thing that I am to be Thursday.'

'My dear fellow,' said Syme heartily, 'I congratulate you. A great career!'

Gregory smiled in deprecation, and walked across the room, talking rapidly.

'As a matter of fact, everything is ready for me on this table,' he said, 'and the ceremony will probably be the shortest possible.'

Syme also strolled across to the table, and found lying across it a walking-stick, which turned out on examination to be a sword-stick, a large Colt's revolver, a sandwich case, and a formidable flask of brandy. Over the chair, beside the table, was thrown a heavy-looking cape or cloak.

'I have only to get the form of election finished,' continued Gregory with animation, 'then I snatch up this cloak and stick, stuff these other things into my pocket, step out of a door in this cavern, which opens on the river, where there is a steam-tug already waiting for me, and then – then – oh, the wild joy of being Thursday!' And he clasped his hands.

Syme, who had sat down once more with his usual insolent languor, got to his feet with an unusual air of hesitation.

'Why is it,' he asked vaguely, 'that I think you are quite a decent fellow? Why do I positively like you, Gregory?' He paused a moment, and then added with a sort of fresh curiosity, 'Is it because you are such an ass?'

There was a thoughtful silence again, and then he cried out –

'Well, damn it all! this is the funniest situation I have ever been in in my life, and I am going to act accordingly. Gregory, I gave you a promise before I came into this place. That promise I would keep under red-hot pincers. Would you give me, for my own safety, a little promise of the same kind?'

'A promise?' asked Gregory, wondering.

'Yes,' said Syme, very seriously, 'a promise. I swore before God that I would not tell your secret to the police. Will you swear by Humanity, or whatever beastly thing you believe in, that you will not tell my secret to the anarchists?'

'Your secret?' asked the staring Gregory. 'Have you got a secret?'

'Yes,' said Syme, 'I have a secret.' Then after a pause, 'Will you swear?'

Gregory glared at him gravely for a few moments, and then said abruptly –

'You must have bewitched me, but I feel a furious curiosity about you. Yes, I will swear not to tell the anarchists anything you tell me. But look sharp, for they will be here in a couple of minutes.'

Syme rose to his feet and thrust his long white hands into his long, grey trousers' pockets. Almost as he did so there came five knocks on the outer grating, proclaiming the arrival of the first of the conspirators.

'Well,' said Syme slowly, 'I don't know how to tell you the truth more shortly than by saying that your expedient of dressing up as an aimless poet, is not confined to you or your President. We have known the dodge for some time at Scotland Yard.'

Gregory tried to spring up straight, but he swayed thrice.

'What do you say?' he asked in an inhuman voice.

'Yes,' said Syme simply, 'I am a police detective. But I think I hear your friends coming.'

From the doorway there came a murmur of 'Mr Joseph Chamberlain'. It was repeated twice and thrice, and then thirty times, and the crowd of Joseph Chamberlains (a solemn thought) could be heard trampling down the corridor.

3

The Man Who Was Thursday

Before one of the fresh faces could appear at the doorway, Gregory's stunned surprise had fallen from him. He was beside the table with a bound, and a noise in his throat like a wild beast. He caught up the Colt's revolver and took aim at Syme. Syme did not flinch, but he put up a pale and polite hand.

'Don't be such a silly man,' he said, with the effeminate dignity of a curate. 'Don't you see it's not necessary? Don't you see that we're both in the same boat? Yes, and jolly sea-sick.'

Gregory could not speak, but he could not fire either, and he looked his question.

'Don't you see we've checkmated each other?' cried Syme. 'I can't tell the police you are an anarchist. You can't tell the anarchists I'm a policeman. I can only watch you, knowing what you are; you can only watch me, knowing what I am. In short, it's a lonely, intellectual duel, my head against yours. I'm a policeman deprived of the help of the police. You, my poor fellow, are an anarchist deprived of the help of that law and organization which is so essential to anarchy. The one solitary difference is in your favour. You are not surrounded by inquisitive policemen; I am surrounded by inquisitive anarchists. I cannot betray you, but I might betray myself. Come, come: wait and see me betray myself. I shall do it so nicely.'

Gregory put the pistol slowly down, still staring at Syme as if he were a sea-monster.

'I don't believe in immortality,' he said at last, 'but if, after all this, you were to break your word, God would make a hell only for you, to howl in for ever.'

'I shall not break my word,' said Syme sternly, 'nor will you break yours. Here are your friends.'

The mass of the anarchists entered the room heavily, with a slouching and somewhat weary gait; but one little man, with a black beard and glasses – a man somewhat of the type of Mr Tim Healy[1] – detached himself, and bustled forward with some papers in his hand.

'Comrade Gregory,' he said, 'I suppose this man is a delegate?'

Gregory, taken by surprise, looked down and muttered the name of Syme; but Syme replied almost pertly –

'I am glad to see that your gate is well enough guarded to make it hard for anyone to be here who was not a delegate.'

The brow of the little man with the black beard was, however, still contracted with something like suspicion.

'What branch do you represent?' he asked sharply.

'I should hardly call it a branch,' said Syme, laughing. 'I should call it at the very least a root.'

'What do you mean?'

'The fact is,' said Syme serenely, 'the truth is I am a Sabbatarian.[2] I have been specially sent here to see that you show a due observance of Sunday.'

The little man dropped one of his papers, and a flicker of fear went over all the faces of the group. Evidently the awful President, whose name was Sunday, did sometimes send down such irregular ambassadors to such branch meetings.

'Well, comrade,' said the man with the papers after a pause, 'I suppose we'd better give you a seat in the meeting?'

'If you ask my advice as a friend,' said Syme with severe benevolence, 'I think you'd better.'

When Gregory heard the dangerous dialogue end, with a sudden safety for his rival, he rose abruptly and paced the floor in painful thought. He was, indeed, in an agony of diplomacy. It was clear that Syme's inspired impudence was likely to bring him out of all merely accidental dilemmas. Little was to be hoped from them. He could not himself betray Syme, partly from honour, but partly also because, if he betrayed him and for some reason failed to destroy him, the Syme who escaped would be a Syme freed from all obligation of secrecy, a Syme who would simply walk to the nearest police station. After all, it was only one night's discussion, and only one detective who would know of it. He would let out as little as possible of their plans at night, and then let Syme go, and chance it.

He strode across to the group of anarchists, which was already distributing itself along the benches.

'I think it is time we began,' he said; 'the steam-tug is waiting on the river already. I move that Comrade Buttons takes the chair.'

This being approved by a show of hands, the little man with the papers slipped into the presidential seat.

'Comrades,' he began, as sharp as a pistol-shot, 'our meeting tonight is important, though it need not be long. This branch has always had the honour of electing Thursdays for the Central European Council. We have elected many and splendid Thursdays. We all lament the sad decease of the heroic worker who occupied the post until last week. As you know, his services to the cause were considerable. He organized the great dynamite coup of Brighton, which, under happier circumstances, ought to have killed everybody on the pier. As you also know, his death was as self-denying as his life, for he died through his faith in a hygienic mixture of chalk and water as a substitute for milk, which beverage he regarded as barbaric, and as involving cruelty to the cow. Cruelty, or anything approaching to cruelty, revolted him always. But it is not to acclaim his virtues that we are met, but for a harder task. It is difficult properly to praise his qualities, but it is more difficult to replace them. Upon you, comrades, it devolves this evening to choose out of the company present the man who shall be Thursday. If any comrade suggests a name, I will put it to the vote. If no comrade suggests a name, I can only tell myself that that dear dynamiter, who is gone from us, has carried into the unknowable abysses the last secret of his virtues and his innocence.'

There was a stir of almost inaudible applause, such as is sometimes heard in church. Then a large old man, with a long and venerable white beard, perhaps the only real working-man present, rose lumberingly and said –

'I move that Comrade Gregory be elected Thursday,' and sat lumberingly down again.

'Does anyone second?' asked the chairman.

A little man with a velvet coat and pointed beard seconded.

'Before I put the matter to the vote,' said the chairman, 'I will call on Comrade Gregory to make a statement.'

Gregory rose amid a great rumble of applause. His face was deadly pale, so that by contrast his queer red hair looked almost scarlet. But he was smiling, and altogether at ease. He had made up his mind, and he saw his best policy quite plain in front of him like a white road. His best chance was to make a softened and ambiguous speech, such as would leave on the detective's mind the impression that the anarchist brotherhood was a very mild affair after all. He believed in his own literary power, his capacity for suggesting fine shades and picking perfect words. He thought that with care he could succeed in spite of all the people around him, in conveying an impression of the institution, subtly and delicately false. Syme had once thought that anarchists, under all their bravado, were only playing the fool. Could he not now, in the hour of peril, make Syme think so again?

'Comrades,' began Gregory, in a low but penetrating voice, 'it is not necessary for me to tell you what is my policy, for it is your policy also. Our belief has been slandered, it has been disfigured, it has been utterly confused and concealed, but it has never been altered. Those who talk about anarchism and its dangers go everywhere and anywhere to get their information, except to us, except to the fountain head. They learn about anarchists from sixpenny novels; they learn about anarchists from tradesmen's newspapers; they learn about anarchists from *Ally Sloper's Half-Holiday* and the *Sporting Times*.[3] They never learn about anarchists from anarchists. We have no chance of denying the mountainous slanders which are heaped upon our heads from one end of Europe to another. The man who has always heard that we are walking plagues has never heard our reply. I know that he will not hear it tonight, though my passion were to rend the roof. For it is deep, deep under the earth that the persecuted are permitted to assemble, as the Christians assembled in the Catacombs.[4] But if, by some incredible accident, there were here tonight a man who all his life had thus immensely misunderstood us, I would put this question to him: "When those Christians met in those Catacombs, what sort of moral reputation had they in the streets above? What tales were told of their atrocities by one educated Roman to another? Suppose" (I would say to him), "suppose that we are only repeating that still mysterious paradox of history. Suppose we seem as shocking as the Christians because we are really as harmless as the Christians. Suppose we seem as mad as the Christians because we are really as meek."'

The applause that had greeted the opening sentences had been gradually growing fainter, and at the last word it stopped suddenly. In the abrupt silence, the man with the velvet jacket said, in a high, squeaky voice –

'I'm not meek!'

'Comrade Witherspoon tells us,' resumed Gregory, 'that he is not meek. Ah, how little he knows himself! His words are, indeed, extravagant; his appearance is ferocious, and even (to an ordinary taste) unattractive. But only the eye of a friendship as deep and delicate as mine can perceive the deep foundation of solid meekness which lies at the base of him, too deep even for himself to see. I repeat, we are the true early Christians, only that we come too late. We are simple, as they were simple – look at Comrade Witherspoon. We are modest, as they were modest – look at me. We are merciful—'

'No, no!' called out Mr Witherspoon with the velvet jacket.

'I say we are merciful,' repeated Gregory furiously, 'as the early Christians were merciful. Yet this did not prevent their being accused of eating human flesh. We do not eat human flesh—'

'Shame!' cried Witherspoon. 'Why not?'

'Comrade Witherspoon,' said Gregory, with a feverish gaiety, 'is anxious to know why nobody eats him (laughter). In our society, at any rate, which loves him sincerely, which is founded upon love—'

'No, no!' said Witherspoon, 'down with love.'

'Which is founded upon love,' repeated Gregory, grinding his teeth, 'there will be no difficulty about the aims which we shall pursue as a body, or which I should pursue were I chosen as the representative of that body. Superbly careless of the slanders that represent us as assassins and enemies of human society, we shall pursue, with moral courage and quiet, intellectual pressure, the permanent ideals of brotherhood and simplicity.'

Gregory resumed his seat and passed his hand across his forehead. The silence was sudden and awkward, but the chairman rose like an automaton, and said in a colourless voice –

'Does anyone oppose the election of Comrade Gregory?'

The assembly seemed vague and subconsciously disappointed, and Comrade Witherspoon moved restlessly on his seat and muttered in his thick beard. By the sheer rush of routine, however, the motion would have been put and carried. But as the chairman was opening his mouth to put it, Syme sprang to his feet and said in a small and quiet voice –

'Yes, Mr Chairman, I oppose.'

The most effective fact in oratory is an unexpected change in the voice. Mr Gabriel Syme evidently understood oratory. Having said these first formal words in a moderated voice and with a brief simplicity, he made his next words ring and volley in the vault as if one of the guns had gone off.

'Comrades!' he cried, in a voice that made every man jump out of his boots, 'have we come here for this? Do we live underground like rats in order to listen to talk like this? This is talk we might listen to while eating buns at a Sunday School treat. Do we line these walls with weapons and bar that door with death lest anyone should come and hear Comrade Gregory saying to us, "Be good, and you will be happy", "Honesty is the best policy", and "Virtue is its own reward"? There was not a word in Comrade Gregory's address to which a curate could not have listened with pleasure (hear, hear). But I am not a curate (loud cheers), and I did not listen to it with pleasure (renewed cheers). The man who is fitted to make a good curate is not fitted to make a resolute, forcible, and efficient Thursday (hear, hear).

'Comrade Gregory has told us, in only too apologetic a tone, that we are not the enemies of society. But I say that we are the enemies of society, and so much the worse for society. We are the enemies of society, for society is the enemy of humanity, its oldest and its most pitiless enemy (hear, hear). Comrade Gregory has told us (apologetically again) that we are not murderers.

There I agree. We are not murderers, we are executioners (cheers).'

Ever since Syme had risen Gregory had sat staring at him, his face idiotic with astonishment. Now in the pause his lips of clay parted, and he said, with an automatic and lifeless distinctness –

'You damnable hypocrite!'

Syme looked straight into those frightful eyes with his own pale blue ones, and said with dignity –

'Comrade Gregory accuses me of hypocrisy. He knows as well as I do that I am keeping all my engagements and doing nothing but my duty. I do not mince words. I do not pretend to. I say that Comrade Gregory is unfit to be Thursday for all his amiable qualities. He is unfit to be Thursday because of his amiable qualities. We do not want the Supreme Council of Anarchy infected with a maudlin mercy (hear, hear). This is no time for ceremonial politeness, neither is it a time for ceremonial modesty. I set myself against Comrade Gregory as I would set myself against all the Governments of Europe, because the anarchist who has given himself to anarchy has forgotten modesty as much as he has forgotten pride (cheers). I am not a man at all. I am a cause (renewed cheers). I set myself against Comrade Gregory as impersonally and as calmly as I should choose one pistol rather than another out of that rack upon the wall; and I say that rather than have Gregory and his milk-and-water methods on the Supreme Council, I would offer myself for election—'

His sentence was drowned in a deafening cataract of applause. The faces, that had grown fiercer and fiercer with approval as his tirade grew more and more uncompromising, were now distorted with grins of anticipation or cloven with delighted cries. At the moment when he announced himself as ready to stand for the post of Thursday, a roar of excitement and assent broke forth, and became uncontrollable, and at the same moment Gregory sprang to his feet, with foam upon his mouth, and shouted against the shouting.

'Stop, you blasted madmen!' he cried, at the top of a voice that tore his throat. 'Stop, you—'

But louder than Gregory's shouting and louder than the roar

of the room came the voice of Syme, still speaking in a peal of pitiless thunder –

'I do not go to the Council to rebut that slander that calls us murderers; I go to earn it (loud and prolonged cheering). To the priest who says these men are the enemies of religion, to the judge who says these men are the enemies of law, to the fat parliamentarian who says these men are the enemies of order and public decency, to all these I will reply, "You are false kings, but you are true prophets. I am come to destroy you, and to fulfil your prophecies."'

The heavy clamour gradually died away, but before it had ceased Witherspoon had jumped to his feet, his hair and beard all on end, and had said –

'I move, as an amendment, that Comrade Syme be appointed to the post.'

'Stop all this, I tell you!' cried Gregory, with frantic face and hands. 'Stop it, it is all—'

The voice of the chairman clove his speech with a cold accent.

'Does anyone second this amendment?' he said.

A tall, tired man, with melancholy eyes and an American chin beard, was observed on the back bench to be slowly rising to his feet. Gregory had been screaming for some time past; now there was a change in his accent, more shocking than any scream.

'I end all this!' he said, in a voice as heavy as stone. 'This man cannot be elected. He is a—'

'Yes,' said Syme, quite motionless, 'what is he?'

Gregory's mouth worked twice without sound; then slowly the blood began to crawl back into his dead face.

'He is a man quite inexperienced in our work,' he said, and sat down abruptly.

Before he had done so, the long, lean man with the American beard was again upon his feet, and was repeating in a high American monotone –

'I beg to second the election of Comrade Syme.'

'The amendment will, as usual, be put first,' said Mr Buttons, the chairman, with mechanical rapidity. 'The question is that Comrade Syme—'

Gregory had again sprung to his feet, panting and passionate.

'Comrades,' he cried out, 'I am not a madman.'

'Oh, oh!' said Mr Witherspoon.

'I am not a madman,' reiterated Gregory, with a frightful sincerity which for a moment staggered the room, 'but I give you a counsel which you can call mad if you like. No, I will not call it a counsel, for I can give you no reason for it. I will call it a command. Call it a mad command, but act upon it. Strike, but hear me! Kill me! but obey me! Do not elect this man.'

Truth is so terrible, even in fetters, that for a moment Syme's slender and insane victory swayed like a reed. But you could not have guessed it from Syme's bleak blue eyes. He merely began –

'Comrade Gregory commands –'

Then the spell was snapped, and one anarchist called out to Gregory—

'Who are you? You are not Sunday'; and another anarchist added in a heavier voice, 'And you are not Thursday.'

'Comrades,' cried Gregory, in a voice like that of a martyr who in an ecstasy of pain has passed beyond pain, 'it is nothing to me whether you detest me as a tyrant or detest me as a slave. If you will not take my command, accept my degradation. I kneel to you. I throw myself at your feet. I implore you. Do not elect this man.'

'Comrade Gregory,' said the chairman after a painful pause, 'this is really not quite dignified.'

For the first time in the proceedings there was for a few seconds a real silence. Then Gregory fell back in his seat, a pale wreck of a man, and the chairman repeated, like a piece of clockwork suddenly started again –

'The question is that Comrade Syme be elected to the post of Thursday on the General Council.'

The roar rose like the sea, the hands rose like a forest, and three minutes afterwards Mr Gabriel Syme, of the Secret Police Service, was elected to the post of Thursday on the General Council of the Anarchists of Europe.

Everyone in the room seemed to feel the tug waiting on the river, the sword-stick and the revolver waiting on the table. The instant the election was ended and irrevocable, and Syme had received the paper proving his election, they all sprang to their feet, and the fiery groups moved and mixed in the room. Syme found himself, somehow or other, face to face with Gregory, who still regarded him with a stare of stunned hatred. They were silent for many minutes.

'You are a devil!' said Gregory at last.

'And you are a gentleman,' said Syme with gravity.

'It was you that entrapped me,' began Gregory, shaking from head to foot, 'entrapped me into—'

'Talk sense,' said Syme shortly. 'Into what sort of devils' parliament have you entrapped me, if it comes to that? You made me swear before I made you. Perhaps we are both doing what we think right. But what we think right is so damned different that there can be nothing between us in the way of concession. There is nothing possible between us but honour and death,' and he pulled the great cloak about his shoulders and picked up the flask from the table.

'The boat is quite ready,' said Mr Buttons, bustling up. 'Be good enough to step this way.'

With a gesture that revealed the shopwalker,[5] he led Syme down a short, iron-bound passage, the still agonized Gregory following feverishly at their heels. At the end of the passage was a door, which Buttons opened sharply, showing a sudden blue and silver picture of the moonlit river, that looked like a scene in a theatre. Close to the opening lay a dark, dwarfish steam-launch, like a baby dragon with one red eye.

Almost in the act of stepping on board, Gabriel Syme turned to the gaping Gregory.

'You have kept your word,' he said gently, with his face in shadow. 'You are a man of honour, and I thank you. You have kept it even down to a small particular. There was one special thing you promised me at the beginning of the affair, and which you have certainly given me by the end of it.'

'What do you mean?' cried the chaotic Gregory. 'What did I promise you?'

'A very entertaining evening,' said Syme, and he made a military salute with the sword-stick, as the steamboat slid away.

4

The Tale of a Detective

Gabriel Syme was not merely a detective who pretended to be a poet; he was really a poet who had become a detective. Nor was his hatred of anarchy hypocritical. He was one of those who are driven early in life into too conservative an attitude by the bewildering folly of most revolutionists. He had not attained it by any tame tradition. His respectability was spontaneous and sudden, a rebellion against rebellion. He came of a family of cranks, in which all the oldest people had all the newest notions. One of his uncles always walked about without a hat, and another had made an unsuccessful attempt to walk about with a hat and nothing else. His father cultivated art and self-realization; his mother went in for simplicity and hygiene. Hence the child, during his tenderer years, was wholly unacquainted with any drink between the extremes of absinthe and cocoa, of both of which he had a healthy dislike. The more his mother preached a more than Puritan abstinence the more did his father expand into a more than pagan latitude; and by the time the former had come to enforcing vegetarianism, the latter had pretty well reached the point of defending cannibalism.

Being surrounded with every conceivable kind of revolt from infancy, Gabriel had to revolt into something, so he revolted into the only thing left – sanity. But there was just enough in him of the blood of these fanatics to make even his protest for common sense a little too fierce to be sensible. His hatred of modern lawlessness had been crowned also by an accident. It happened that he was walking in a side street at the instant of a dynamite outrage. He had been blind and deaf for a moment, and then seen the smoke clearing, the broken windows and the bleeding faces. After that he went about as usual – quiet, courteous, rather gentle; but there was a spot on his mind that was not sane. He did not regard anarchists, as most of us do, as a handful of morbid men, combining ignorance with intellectualism. He regarded them as a huge and pitiless peril, like a Chinese invasion.[1]

He poured perpetually into newspapers and their waste-paper baskets a torrent of tales, verses, and violent articles, warning men of this deluge of barbaric denial. But he seemed to be getting no nearer this enemy, and, what was worse, no nearer a living. As he paced the Thames Embankment, bitterly biting a cheap cigar and brooding on the advance of Anarchy, there was no anarchist with a bomb in his pocket so savage or so solitary as he. Indeed, he always felt that Government stood alone and desperate, with its back to the wall. He was too quixotic to have cared for it otherwise.

He walked on the Embankment once under a dark red sunset. The red river reflected the red sky, and they both reflected his anger. The sky, indeed, was so swarthy, and the light on the river relatively so lurid, that the water almost seemed of fiercer flame than the sunset it mirrored. It looked like a stream of literal fire[2] winding under the vast caverns of the subterranean country.

Syme was shabby in those days. He wore an old-fashioned black chimney-pot hat; he was wrapped in a yet more old-fashioned cloak, black and ragged; and the combination gave him the look of the early villains in Dickens and Bulwer Lytton.[3] Also his yellow beard and hair were more unkempt and leonine than when they appeared long afterwards, cut and pointed, on the lawns of Saffron Park. A long, lean, black cigar, bought in Soho for twopence, stood out from between his tightened teeth, and altogether he looked a very satisfactory specimen of the anarchists upon whom he had vowed a holy war. Perhaps this was why a policeman on the Embankment spoke to him, and said 'Good evening'.

Syme, at a crisis of his morbid fears for humanity, seemed stung by the mere stolidity of the automatic official, a mere bulk of blue in the twilight

'A good evening, is it?' he said sharply. 'You fellows would call the end of the world a good evening. Look at that bloody red sun and that bloody river: I tell you that if that were literally human blood, spilt and shining, you would still be standing here as stolid as ever, looking out for some poor harmless tramp whom you could move on. You policemen are cruel to the poor, but I could forgive you even your cruelty if it were not for your calm.'

'If we are calm,' replied the policeman, 'it is the calm of organized resistance.'

'Eh?' said Syme, staring.

'The soldier must be calm in the thick of the battle,' pursued the policeman. 'The composure of an army is the anger of a nation.'

'Good God, the Board Schools!'[4] said Syme. 'Is this undenominational education?'

'No,' said the policeman sadly, 'I never had any of those advantages. The Board Schools came after my time. What education I had was very rough and old-fashioned, I am afraid.'

'Where did you have it?' asked Syme, wondering.

'Oh, at Harrow,'[5] said the policeman.

The class sympathies which, false as they are, are the truest things in so many men, broke out of Syme before he could control them.

'But, good Lord, man,' he said, 'you oughtn't to be a policeman!'

The policeman sighed and shook his head.

'I know,' he said solemnly, 'I know I am not worthy.'

'But why did you join the police?' asked Syme with rude curiosity.

'For much the same reason that you abused the police,' replied the other. 'I found that there was a special opening in the service for those whose fears for humanity were concerned rather with the aberrations of the scientific intellect than with the normal and excusable, though excessive, outbreaks of the human will. I trust I make myself clear.'

'If you mean that you make your opinion clear,' said Syme, 'I suppose you do. But as for making yourself clear, it is the last thing you do. How comes a man like you to be talking philosophy in a blue helmet on the Thames Embankment?'

'You have evidently not heard of the latest development in our police system,' replied the other. 'I am not surprised at it. We are keeping it rather dark from the educated class, because that class contains most of our enemies. But you seem to be exactly in the right frame of mind. I think you might almost join us.'

'Join you in what?' asked Syme.

'I will tell you,' said the policeman slowly. 'This is the situation. The head of one of our departments, one of the most celebrated detectives in Europe, has long been of opinion that a purely intellectual conspiracy would soon threaten the very existence of civilization. He is certain that the scientific and artistic worlds are silently bound in a crusade against the Family and the State. He has, therefore, formed a special corps of policemen, policemen who are also philosophers. It is their business to watch the beginnings of this conspiracy, not merely in a criminal but in a controversial sense. I am a democrat myself, and I am fully aware of the value of the ordinary man in matters of ordinary valour or virtue. But it would obviously be undesirable to employ the common policeman in an investigation which is also a heresy hunt.'

Syme's eyes were bright with a sympathetic curiosity.

'What do you do, then?' he said.

'The work of the philosophical policeman,' replied the man in blue, 'is at once bolder and more subtle than that of the ordinary detective. The ordinary detective goes to pot-houses[6] to arrest thieves; we go to artistic tea-parties to detect pessimists. The ordinary detective discovers from a ledger or a diary that a crime has been committed. We discover from a book of sonnets that a crime will be committed. We have to trace the origin of those dreadful thoughts that drive men on at last to intellectual fanaticism and intellectual crime. We were only just in time to prevent the assassination at Hartlepool, and that was entirely due to the fact that our Mr Wilks (a smart young fellow) thoroughly understood a triolet.'[7]

'Do you mean,' asked Syme, 'that there is really as much connexion between crime and the modern intellect as all that?'

'You are not sufficiently democratic,' answered the policeman, 'but you were right when you said just now that our ordinary treatment of the poor criminal was a pretty brutal business. I tell you I am sometimes sick of my trade when I see how perpetually it means merely a war upon the ignorant and the desperate. But this new movement of ours is a very different affair. We deny the snobbish English assumption that the un-educated are the dangerous criminals. We remember the Roman Emperors. We remember the great poisoning princes of the Renaissance. We say that the dangerous criminal is the educated criminal. We say that the most dangerous criminal now is the entirely lawless modern philosopher. Compared to him, burglars and bigamists are essentially moral men; my heart goes out to them. They accept the essential idea of man; they merely seek it wrongly. Thieves respect property. They merely wish the property to become their property that they may more perfectly respect it. But philosophers dislike property as property; they wish to destroy the very idea of personal possession. Bigamists respect marriage, or they would not go through the highly ceremonial and even ritualistic formality of bigamy. But philosophers despise marriage as marriage. Murderers respect human life; they merely wish to attain a greater fullness of human life in themselves by the sacrifice of what seems to them to be lesser lives. But philo-sophers hate life itself, their own as much as other people's.'

Syme struck his hands together.

'How true that is,' he said. 'I have felt it from my boyhood, but never could state the verbal antithesis. The common criminal is a bad man, but at least he is, as it were, a conditional good man. He says that if only a certain obstacle be removed – say a wealthy uncle – he is then prepared to accept the universe and to praise God. He is a reformer, but not an anarchist. He wishes to cleanse the edifice, but not to destroy it. But the evil philo-sopher is not trying to alter things, but to annihilate them. Yes, the modern world has retained all those parts of police work which are really oppressive and ignominious, the harrying of the poor, the spying upon the unfortunate. It has given up its more dignified work, the punishment of powerful traitors in the State and powerful heresiarchs in the Church. The moderns say we must not punish heretics. My only doubt is whether we have a right to punish anybody else.'

'But this is absurd!' cried the policeman, clasping his hands with an excitement uncommon in persons of his figure and costume, 'but this is intolerable! I don't know what you're doing, but you're wasting your life. You must, you shall, join our special army against anarchy. Their armies are on our frontiers. Their bolt is ready to fall. A moment more, and you may lose the glory of working with us, perhaps the glory of dying with the last heroes of the world.'

'It is a chance not to be missed, certainly,' assented Syme, 'but still I do not quite understand. I know as well as anybody that the modern world is full of lawless little men and mad little movements. But, beastly as they are, they generally have the one merit of disagreeing with each other. How can you talk of their leading one army or hurling one bolt? What is this anarchy?'

'Do not confuse it,' replied the constable, 'with those chance dynamite outbreaks from Russia or from Ireland, which are really the outbreaks of oppressed, if mistaken, men. This is a vast philosophic movement, consisting of an outer and inner ring. You might even call the outer ring the laity and the inner ring the priesthood. I prefer to call the outer ring the innocent section, the inner ring the supremely guilty section. The outer ring – the main mass of their supporters – are merely anarchists; that is, men who believe that rules and formulas have destroyed human happiness. They believe that all the evil results of human crime are the results of the system that has called it crime. They do not believe that the crime creates the punishment. They believe that the punishment has created the crime. They believe that if a man seduced seven women he would naturally walk away as blameless as the flowers of spring. They believe that if a man picked a pocket he would naturally feel exquisitely good. These I call the innocent section.'

'Oh!' said Syme.

'Naturally, therefore, these people talk about "a happy time coming"; "the paradise of the future"; "mankind freed from the bondage of vice and the bondage of virtue", and so on. And so also the men of the inner circle speak – the sacred priesthood. They also speak to applauding crowds of the happiness of the future, and of mankind freed at last. But in their mouths' – and the policeman lowered his voice – 'in their mouths these happy phrases have a horrible meaning. They are under no illusions; they are too intellectual to think that man upon this earth can ever be quite free of original sin and the struggle. And they mean death. When they say that mankind shall be free at last, they mean that mankind shall commit suicide. When they talk of a paradise without right or wrong, they mean the grave. They have but two objects, to destroy first humanity and then themselves. That is why they throw bombs instead of firing pistols. The innocent rank and file are disappointed because the bomb has not killed the king; but the high-priesthood are happy because it has killed somebody.'

'How can I join you?' asked Syme, with a sort of passion.

'I know for a fact that there is a vacancy at the moment,' said the policeman, 'as I have the honour to be somewhat in the confidence of the chief of whom I have spoken. You should really come and see him. Or rather, I should not say see him, nobody ever sees him; but you can talk to him if you like.'

'Telephone?' inquired Syme, with interest.

'No,' said the policeman placidly, 'he has a fancy for always sitting in a pitch-dark room. He says it makes his thoughts brighter. Do come along.'

Somewhat dazed and considerably excited, Syme allowed himself to be led to a side-door in the long row of buildings of Scotland Yard. Almost before he knew what he was doing, he had been passed through the hands of about four intermediate officials, and was suddenly shown into a room, the abrupt blackness of which startled him like a blaze of light. It was not the ordinary darkness, in which forms can be faintly traced; it was like going suddenly stone-blind.

'Are you the new recruit?' asked a heavy voice.

And in some strange way, though there was not the shadow of a shape in the gloom, Syme knew two things: first, that it came from a man of massive stature; and second, that the man had his back to him.

'Are you the new recruit?' asked the invisible chief, who seemed to have heard all about it. 'All right. You are engaged.'

Syme, quite swept off his feet, made a feeble fight against this irrevocable phrase.

'I really have no experience,' he began.

'No one has any experience,' said the other, 'of the battle of Armageddon.'

'But I am really unfit—'

'You are willing, that is enough,' said the unknown.

'Well, really,' said Syme, 'I don't know any profession of which mere willingness is the final test.'

'I do,' said the other – 'martyrs. I am condemning you to death. Good day.'

Thus it was that when Gabriel Syme came out again into the crimson light of evening, in his shabby black hat and shabby, lawless coat, he came out a member of the New Detective Corps for the frustration of the great conspiracy. Acting under the advice of his friend the policeman (who was professionally inclined to neatness), he trimmed his hair and beard, bought a good hat, clad himself in an exquisite summer suit of light blue-grey, with a pale yellow flower in the button-hole, and, in short, became that elegant and rather insupportable person whom Gregory had first encountered in the little garden of Saffron Park. Before he finally left the police premises his friend provided him with a small blue card, on which was written 'The Last Crusade', and a number, the sign of his official authority. He put this carefully in his upper waistcoat pocket, lit a cigarette, and went forth to track and fight the enemy in all the drawing-rooms of London. Where his adventure ultimately led him we have already seen. At about half past one on a February night he found himself steaming in a small tug up the silent Thames, armed with sword-stick and revolver, the duly elected Thursday of the Central Council of Anarchists.

When Syme stepped out on to the steam-tug he had a singular sensation of stepping out into something entirely new; not merely into the landscape of a new land, but even into the landscape of a new planet. This was mainly due to the insane yet solid decision of that evening, though partly also to an entire change in the weather and the sky since he entered the little tavern some two hours before. Every trace of the passionate plumage of the cloudy sunset had been swept away, and a naked moon stood in a naked sky. The moon was so strong and full, that (by a paradox often to be noticed) it seemed like a weaker sun. It gave, not the sense of bright moonshine, but rather of a dead daylight.

Over the whole landscape lay a luminous and unnatural discolouration, as of that disastrous twilight which Milton spoke of as shed by the sun in eclipse,[8] so that Syme fell easily into his first thought, that he was actually on some other and emptier planet, which circled round some sadder star. But the more he felt this glittering desolation in the moonlit land, the more his own chivalric folly glowed in the night like a great fire. Even the common things he carried with him – the food and the brandy and the loaded pistol – took on earth that concrete and material poetry which a child feels when he takes a gun upon a journey or a bun with him to bed. The sword-stick and the brandy-flask, though in themselves only the tools of morbid conspirators, became the expressions of his own more healthy romance. The sword-stick became almost the sword of chivalry, and the brandy the wine of the stirrup-cup.[9] For even the most dehumanized modern fantasies depend on some older and simpler figure; the adventures may be mad, but the adventurer must be sane. The dragon without St George would not even be grotesque. So this inhuman landscape was only imaginative by the presence of a man really human. To Syme's exaggerative mind the bright, bleak houses and terraces by the Thames looked as empty as the mountains of the moon. But even the moon is only poetical because there is a man in the moon.

The tug was worked by two men, and with much toil went comparatively slowly. The clear moon that had lit up Chiswick had gone down by the time that they passed Battersea, and when they came under the enormous bulk of Westminster day had already begun to break. It broke like the splitting of great bars of lead, showing bars of silver; and these had brightened like white fire when the tug, changing its onward course, turned inward to a large landing stage rather beyond Charing Cross.

The great stones of the Embankment seemed equally dark and gigantic as Syme looked up at them. They were big and black against the huge white dawn. They made him feel that he was landing on the colossal steps of some Egyptian palace,[10] and indeed the thing suited his mood, for he was, in his own mind, mounting to attack the solid thrones of horrible and heathen kings. He leapt out of the boat on to one slimy step, and stood, a dark and slender figure, amid the enormous masonry. The two men in the tug put her off again and turned up stream. They had never spoken a word.

5

The Feast of Fear

At first the large stone stair seemed to Syme as deserted as a pyramid; but before he reached the top he had realized that there was a man leaning over the parapet of the Embankment and looking out across the river. As a figure he was quite conventional, clad in a silk hat and frock-coat of the more formal type of fashion; he had a red flower in his button-hole. As Syme drew nearer to him step by step, he did not even move a hair; and Syme could come close enough to notice even in the dim, pale morning light that his face was long, pale, and intellectual, and ended in a small triangular tuft of dark beard at the very point of the chin, all else being clean-shaven. This scrap of hair almost seemed a mere oversight; the rest of the face was of the type that is best shaven – clear-cut, ascetic, and in its way noble. Syme drew closer and closer, noting all this, and still the figure did not stir.

At first an instinct had told Syme that this was the man whom he was meant to meet. Then, seeing that the man made no sign, he had concluded that he was not. And now again he had come back to a certainty that the man had something to do with his mad adventure. For the man remained more still than would have been natural if a stranger had come so close. He was as motionless as a waxwork, and got on the nerves somewhat in the same way. Syme looked again and again at the pale, dignified and delicate face, and the face still looked blankly across the river. Then he took out of his pocket the note from Buttons proving his election, and put it before that sad and beautiful face. Then the man smiled, and his smile was a shock, for it was all on one side, going up in the right cheek and down in the left.

There was nothing, rationally speaking, to scare anyone about this. Many people have this nervous trick of a crooked smile, and in many it is even attractive. But in all Syme's circumstances, with the dark dawn and the deadly errand and the loneliness on the great dripping stones, there was something unnerving in it. There was the silent river and the silent man, a man of even classic face. And there was the last nightmare touch that his smile suddenly went wrong.

The spasm of smile was instantaneous, and the man's face dropped at once into its harmonious melancholy. He spoke without further explanation or inquiry, like a man speaking to an old colleague.

'If we walk up towards Leicester Square,' he said, 'we shall just be in time for breakfast. Sunday always insists on an early breakfast. Have you had any sleep?'

'No,' said Syme.

'Nor have I,' answered the man in an ordinary tone. 'I shall try to get to bed after breakfast.'

He spoke with casual civility, but in an utterly dead voice that contradicted the fanaticism of his face. It seemed almost as if all friendly words were to him lifeless conveniences, and that his only life was hate. After a pause the man spoke again.

'Of course, the Secretary of the branch told you everything that can be told. But the one thing that can never be told is the last notion of the President, for his notions grow like a tropical forest. So in case you don't know, I'd better tell you that he is carrying out his notion of concealing ourselves by not concealing ourselves to the most extraordinary lengths just now. Originally, of course, we met in a cell underground, just as your branch does. Then Sunday made us take a private room at an ordinary restaurant. He said that if you didn't seem to be hiding nobody hunted you out. Well, he is the only man on earth, I know; but sometimes I really think that his huge brain is going a little mad in its old age. For now we flaunt ourselves before the public. We have our breakfast on a balcony – on a balcony, if you please – overlooking Leicester Square.'

'And what do the people say?' asked Syme.

'It's quite simple what they say,' answered his guide. 'They say we are a lot of jolly gentlemen who pretend they are anarchists.'

'It seems to me a very clever idea,' said Syme.

'Clever! God blast your impudence! Clever!' cried out the other in a sudden, shrill voice which was as startling and discordant as his crooked smile. 'When you've seen Sunday for a split second you'll leave off calling him clever.'

With this they emerged out of a narrow street, and saw the early sunlight filling Leicester Square.[1] It will never be known, I suppose, why this square itself should look so alien and in some ways so continental. It will never be known whether it was the foreign look that attracted the foreigners or the foreigners who gave it the foreign look. But on this particular morning the effect seemed singularly bright and clear. Between the open square and the sunlit leaves and the statue and the Saracenic outlines of the Alhambra,[2] it looked the replica of some French or even Spanish public place. And this effect increased in Syme the sensation, which in many shapes he had had through the whole adventure, the eerie sensation of having strayed into a new world. As a fact, he had bought bad cigars round Leicester Square ever since he was a boy. But as he turned that corner, and saw the trees and the Moorish cupolas, he could have sworn that he was turning into an unknown Place de something-or-other in some foreign town.

At one corner of the square there projected a kind of angle of a prosperous but quiet hotel, the bulk of which belonged to a street behind. In the wall there was one large French window, probably the window of a large coffee-room; and outside this window, almost literally overhanging the square, was a formidably buttressed balcony, big enough to contain a dining-table. In fact, it did contain a dining-table, or more strictly a breakfast-table; and round the breakfast-table, glowing in the sunlight and evident to the street, were a group of noisy and talkative men, all dressed in the insolence of fashion, and white waistcoats and expensive button-holes. Some of their jokes could almost be heard across the square. Then the grave Secretary gave his unnatural smile, and Syme knew that this boisterous breakfast party was the secret conclave of the European Dynamiters.

Then, as Syme continued to stare at them, he saw something that he had not seen before. He had not seen it literally because it was too large to see. At the nearest end of the balcony, blocking up a great part of the perspective, was the back of a great mountain of a man. When Syme had seen him, his first thought was that the weight of him must break down the balcony of stone. His vastness did not lie only in the fact that he was abnormally tall and quite incredibly fat. This man was planned enormously in his original proportions, like a statue carved deliberately as colossal. His head, crowned with white hair, as seen from behind looked bigger than a head ought to be. The ears that stood out from it looked larger than human ears. He was enlarged terribly to scale; and this sense of size was so staggering, that when Syme saw him all the other figures seemed quite suddenly to dwindle and become dwarfish. They were still sitting there as before with their flowers and frock-coats, but now it looked as if the big man was entertaining five children to tea.

As Syme and the guide approached the side door of the hotel, a waiter came out smiling with every tooth in his head.

'The gentlemen are up there, sare,' he said. 'They do talk and they do laugh at what they talk. They do say they will throw bombs at ze king.'

And the waiter hurried away with a napkin over his arm, much pleased with the singular frivolity of the gentlemen up-stairs.

The two men mounted the stairs in silence.

Syme had never thought of asking whether the monstrous man who almost filled and broke the balcony was the great President of whom the others stood in awe. He knew it was so, with an unaccountable but instantaneous certainty. Syme, indeed, was one of those men who are open to all the more nameless psychological influences in a degree a little dangerous to mental health. Utterly devoid of fear in physical dangers, he was a great deal too sensitive to the smell of spiritual evil. Twice already that night little unmeaning things had peeped out at him almost pruriently, and given him a sense of drawing nearer and nearer to the headquarters of hell. And this sense became overpowering as he drew nearer to the great President.

The form it took was a childish and yet hateful fancy. As he walked across the inner room towards the balcony, the large face of Sunday grew larger and larger; and Syme was gripped with fear that when he was quite close the face would be too big to be possible, and that he would scream aloud. He remembered that as a child he would not look at the mask of Memnon in the British Museum,[3] because it was a face, and so large.

By an effort braver than that of leaping over a cliff, he went to an empty seat at the breakfast-table and sat down. The men greeted him with good-humoured raillery as if they had always known him. He sobered himself a little by looking at their conventional coats and solid, shining coffee-pot; then he looked again at Sunday. His face was very large, but it was still possible to humanity.

In the presence of the President the whole company looked sufficiently commonplace; nothing about them caught the eye at first, except that by the President's caprice they had been dressed up with a festive respectability, which gave the meal the look of a wedding breakfast. One man indeed stood out at even a superficial glance. He at least was the common or garden Dynamiter. He wore, indeed, the high white collar and satin tie that were the uniform of the occasion; but out of this collar there sprang a head quite unmanageable and quite unmistakable, a bewildering bush of brown hair and beard that almost obscured the eyes like those of a Skye terrier. But the eyes did look out of the tangle, and they were the sad eyes of some Russian serf. The effect of this figure was not terrible like that of the President, but it had every diablerie[4] that can come from the utterly grotesque. If out of that stiff tie and collar there had come abruptly the head of a cat or a dog, it could not have been a more idiotic contrast.

The man's name, it seemed, was Gogol; he was a Pole, and in this circle of days he was called Tuesday. His soul and speech were incurably tragic; he could not force himself to play the prosperous and frivolous part demanded of him by President Sunday. And, indeed, when Syme came in the President, with that daring disregard of public suspicion which was his policy, was actually chaffing Gogol upon his inability to assume conventional graces.

'Our friend Tuesday,' said the President in a deep voice at once of quietude and volume, 'our friend Tuesday doesn't seem to grasp the idea. He dresses up like a gentleman, but he seems to be too great a soul to behave like one. He insists on the ways of the stage conspirator. Now if a gentleman goes about London in a top hat and a frock-coat, no one need know that he is an anarchist. But if a gentleman puts on a top hat and a frock-coat, and then goes about on his hands and knees – well, he may attract attention. That's what Brother Gogol does. He goes about on his hands and knees with such inexhaustible diplomacy, that by this time he finds it quite difficult to walk upright.'

'I am not good at gonzealment,' said Gogol sulkily, with a thick foreign accent; 'I am not ashamed of the cause.'

'Yes you are, my boy, and so is the cause of you,' said the President good-naturedly. 'You hide as much as anybody; but you can't do it, you see, you're such an ass! You try to combine two inconsistent methods. When a householder finds a man under his bed, he will probably pause to note the circumstance. But if he finds a man under his bed in a top hat, you will agree with me, my dear Tuesday, that he is not likely ever to forget it. Now when you were found under Admiral Biffin's bed—'

'I am not good at deception,' said Tuesday gloomily, flushing.

'Right, my boy, right,' said the President with a ponderous heartiness, 'you aren't good at anything.'

While this stream of conversation continued, Syme was looking more steadily at the men around him. As he did so, he gradually felt all his sense of something spiritually queer return.

He had thought at first that they were all of common stature and costume with the evident exception of the hairy Gogol. But as he looked at the others he began to see in each of them exactly what he had seen in the man by the river, a demoniac detail somewhere. That lop-sided laugh, which would suddenly disfigure the fine face of his original guide, was typical of all these types. Each man had something about him, perceived perhaps at the tenth or twentieth glance, which was not normal, and which seemed hardly human. The only metaphor he could think of was this, that they all looked as men of fashion and presence would look, with the additional twist given in a false and curved mirror.

Only the individual examples will express this half-concealed eccentricity. Syme's original cicerone[5] bore the title of Monday; he was the Secretary of the Council, and his twisted smile was regarded with more terror than anything, except the President's horrible, happy laughter. But now that Syme had more space and light to observe him, there were other touches. His fine face was so emaciated, that Syme thought it must be wasted with some disease; yet somehow the very distress of his dark eyes denied this. It was no physical ill that troubled him. His eyes were alive with intellectual torture, as if pure thought was pain.

He was typical of each of the tribe; each man subtly and differently wrong. Next to him sat Tuesday, the tousle-headed Gogol, a man more obviously mad. Next was Wednesday, a certain Marquis de St Eustache, a sufficiently characteristic figure. The first few glances found nothing unusual about him, except that he was the only man at table who wore the fashionable clothes as if they were really his own. He had a black French beard cut square and a black English frock-coat cut even squarer. But Syme, sensitive to such things, felt somehow that the man carried a rich atmosphere with him, a rich atmosphere that suffocated. It reminded one irrationally of drowsy odours and of dying lamps in the darker poems of Byron and Poe.[6] With this went a sense of his being clad, not in lighter colours, but in softer materials; his black seemed richer and warmer than the black shades about him, as if it were compounded of profound colour. His black coat looked as if it were only black by being too dense a purple. His black beard looked as if it were only black by being too deep a blue. And in the gloom and thickness of the beard his dark red mouth showed sensual and scornful. Whatever he was he was not a Frenchman; he might be a Jew; he might be something deeper yet in the dark heart of the East. In the bright coloured Persian tiles and pictures showing tyrants hunting, you may see just those almond eyes, those blue-black beards, those cruel, crimson lips.

Then came Syme, and next a very old man, Professor de Worms, who still kept the chair of Friday, though every day it was expected that his death would leave it empty. Save for his intellect, he was in the last dissolution of senile decay. His face was as grey as his long grey beard, his forehead was lifted and fixed finally in a furrow of mild despair. In no other case, not even that of Gogol, did the bridegroom brilliancy of the morning dress express a more painful contrast. For the red flower in his button-hole showed up against a face that was literally discoloured like lead; the whole hideous effect was as if some drunken dandies had put their clothes upon a corpse. When he rose or sat down, which was with long labour and peril, something worse was expressed than mere weakness, something indefinably connected with the horror of the whole scene. It did not express decrepitude merely, but corruption. Another hateful fancy crossed Syme's quivering mind. He could not help thinking that whenever the man moved a leg or arm might fall off.

Right at the end sat the man called Saturday, the simplest and the most baffling of all. He was a short, square man with a dark, square face clean shaven, a medical practitioner going by the name of Bull. He had that combination of *savoir-faire* with a sort of well-groomed coarseness which is not uncommon in young doctors. He carried his fine clothes with confidence rather than ease, and he mostly wore a set smile. There was nothing whatever odd about him, except that he wore a pair of dark, almost opaque spectacles. It may have been merely a crescendo of nervous fancy that had gone before, but those black discs were dreadful to Syme; they reminded him of half-remembered ugly tales, of some story about pennies being put on the eyes of the dead. Syme's eye always caught the black glasses and the blind grin. Had the dying Professor worn them, or even the pale Secretary, they would have been appropriate. But on the younger and grosser man they seemed only an enigma. They took away the key of the face. You could not tell what his smile or his gravity meant. Partly from this, and partly because he had a vulgar virility wanting in most of the others, it seemed to Syme that he might be the wickedest of all those wicked men. Syme even had the thought that his eyes might be covered up because they were too frightful to see.

6

The Exposure

Such were the six men who had sworn to destroy the world. Again and again Syme strove to pull together his common sense in their presence. Sometimes he saw for an instant that these notions were subjective, that he was only looking at ordinary men, one of whom was old, another nervous, another short-sighted. The sense of an unnatural symbolism always settled back on him again. Each figure seemed to be, somehow, on the borderland of things, just as their theory was on the borderland of thought. He knew that each one of these men stood at the extreme end, so to speak, of some wild road of reasoning. He could only fancy, as in some old-world fable, that if a man went westward to the end of the world he would find something – say a tree – that was more or less than a tree, a tree possessed by a spirit; and that if he went east to the end of the world he would find something else that was now wholly itself – a tower, perhaps, of which the very shape was wicked. So these figures seemed to stand up, violent, and unaccountable against an ultimate horizon, visions from the verge. The ends of the earth were closing in.

Talk had been going on steadily as he took in the scene; and not the least of the contrasts of that bewildering breakfast-table was the contrast between the easy and unobtrusive tone of talk and its terrible purport. They were deep in the discussion of an actual and immediate plot. The waiter downstairs had spoken quite correctly when he said that they were talking about bombs and kings. Only three days afterwards the Czar was to meet the President of the French Republic in Paris, and over their bacon and eggs upon their sunny balcony these beaming gentlemen had decided how both should die. Even the instrument was chosen; the black-bearded Marquis, it appeared, was to carry the bomb.

Ordinarily speaking, the proximity of this positive and objective crime would have sobered Syme, and cured him of all his merely mystical tremors. He would have thought of nothing but the need of saving at least two human bodies from being ripped in pieces with iron and roaring gas. But the truth was that by this time he had begun to feel a third kind of fear, more piercing and practical than either his moral revulsion or his social responsibility. Very simply, he had no fear to spare for the French President or the Czar; he had begun to fear for himself. Most of the talkers took little heed of him, debating now with their faces closer together, and almost uniformly grave, save when for an instant the smile of the Secretary ran aslant across his face as the jagged lightning runs aslant across the sky. But there was one persistent thing which first troubled Syme and at last terrified him. The President was always looking at him, steadily, and with a great and baffling interest. The enormous man was quite quiet, but his blue eyes stood out of his head. And they were always fixed on Syme.

Syme felt moved to spring up and leap over the balcony. When the President's eyes were on him he felt as if he were made of glass. He had hardly the shred of a doubt that in some silent and extraordinary way Sunday had found out that he was a spy. He looked over the edge of the balcony, and saw a policeman standing abstractedly just beneath, staring at the bright railings and the sunlit trees.

Then there fell upon him the great temptation that was to torment him for many days. In the presence of these powerful and repulsive men, who were the princes of anarchy, he had almost forgotten the frail and fanciful figure of the poet Gregory, the mere aesthete of anarchism. He even thought of him now with an old kindness, as if they had played together when children. But he remembered that he was still tied to Gregory by a great promise. He had promised never to do the very thing that he now felt himself almost in the act of doing. He had promised not to jump over that balcony and speak to that policeman. He took his cold hand off the cold stone balustrade.

His soul swayed in a vertigo of moral indecision. He had only to snap the thread of a rash vow made to a villainous society, and all his life could be as open and sunny as the square beneath him. He had, on the other hand, only to keep his antiquated honour, and be delivered inch by inch into the power of this great enemy of mankind, whose very intellect was a torture-chamber. Whenever he looked down into the square he saw the comfortable policeman, a pillar of common sense and common order. Whenever he looked back at the breakfast-table he saw the President still quietly studying him with big, unbearable eyes.

In all the torrent of his thought there were two thoughts that never crossed his mind. First, it never occurred to him to doubt that the President and his Council could crush him if he continued to stand alone. The place might be public, the project might seem impossible. But Sunday was not the man who would carry himself thus easily without having, somehow or somewhere, set open his iron trap. Either by anonymous poison or sudden street accident, by hypnotism or by fire from hell, Sunday could certainly strike him. If he defied the man he was probably dead, either struck stiff there in his chair or long afterwards as by an innocent ailment. If he called in the police promptly, arrested everyone, told all, and set against them the whole energy of England, he would probably escape; certainly not otherwise. They were a balconyful of gentlemen overlooking a bright and busy square; but he felt no more safe with them than if they had been a boatful of armed pirates overlooking an empty sea.

There was a second thought that never came to him. It never occurred to him to be spiritually won over to the enemy. Many moderns, inured to a weak worship of intellect and force, might have wavered in their allegiance under this oppression of a great personality. They might have called Sunday the super-man.[1] If any such creature be conceivable, he looked, indeed, somewhat like it, with his earth-shaking abstraction, as of a stone statue walking. He might have been called something above man, with his large plans, which were too obvious to be detected, with his large face, which was too frank to be understood. But this was a kind of modern meanness to which Syme could not sink even in his extreme morbidity. Like any man, he was coward enough to fear great force; but he was not quite coward enough to admire it.

The men were eating as they talked, and even in this they were typical. Dr Bull and the Marquis ate casually and conventionally of the best things on the table – cold pheasant or Strasbourg pie.[2] But the Secretary was a vegetarian, and he spoke earnestly of the projected murder over half a raw tomato and three-quarters of a glass of tepid water. The old Professor had such slops as suggested a sickening second childhood. And even in this President Sunday preserved his curious predominance of mere mass. For he ate like twenty men; he ate incredibly, with a frightful freshness of appetite, so that it was like watching a sausage factory. Yet continually, when he had swallowed a dozen crumpets or drunk a quart of coffee, he would be found with his great head on one side staring at Syme.

'I have often wondered,' said the Marquis, taking a great bite out of a slice of bread and jam, 'whether it wouldn't be better for me to do it with a knife. Most of the best things have been brought off with a knife. And it would be a new emotion to get a knife into a French President and wriggle it round.'

'You are wrong,' said the Secretary, drawing his black brows together. 'The knife was merely the expression of the old personal quarrel with a personal tyrant. Dynamite is not only our best tool, but our best method. It is as perfect a symbol of us as is incense of the prayers of the Christians. It expands; it only destroys because it broadens; even so, thought only destroys because it broadens. A man's brain is a bomb,' he cried out, loosening suddenly his strange passion and striking his own skull with violence. 'My brain feels like a bomb, night and day. It must expand! It must expand! A man's brain must expand, if it breaks up the universe.'

'I don't want the universe broken up just yet,' drawled the Marquis. 'I want to do a lot of beastly things before I die. I thought of one yesterday in bed.'

'No, if the only end of the thing is nothing,' said Dr Bull with his sphinx-like smile, 'it hardly seems worth doing.'

The old Professor was staring at the ceiling with dull eyes.

'Every man knows in his heart,' he said, 'that nothing is worth doing.'

There was a singular silence, and then the Secretary said –

'We are wandering, however, from the point. The only question is how Wednesday is to strike the blow. I take it we should all agree with the original notion of a bomb. As to the actual arrangements, I should suggest that tomorrow morning he should go first of all to—'

The speech was broken off short under a vast shadow. President Sunday had risen to his feet, seeming to fill the sky above them.

'Before we discuss that,' he said in a small, quiet voice, 'let us go into a private room. I have something very particular to say.'

Syme stood up before any of the others. The instant of choice had come at last, the pistol was at his head. On the pavement below he could hear the policeman idly stir and stamp, for the morning, though bright, was cold.

A barrel-organ in the street suddenly sprang with a jerk into a jovial tune. Syme stood up taut, as if it had been a bugle before the battle. He found himself filled with a supernatural courage that came from nowhere. The jingling music seemed full of the vivacity, the vulgarity, and the irrational valour of the poor, who in all those unclean streets were all clinging to the decencies and the charities of Christendom. His youthful prank of being a policeman had faded from his mind; he did not think of himself as the representative of the corps of gentlemen turned into fancy constables, or of the old eccentric who lived in the dark room. But he did feel himself as the ambassador of all these common and kindly people in the street, who every day marched into battle to the music of the barrel-organ. And this high pride in being human had lifted him unaccountably to an infinite height above the monstrous men around him. For an instant, at least, he looked down upon all their sprawling eccentricities from the starry pinnacle of the commonplace. He felt towards them all that unconscious and elementary superiority that a brave man feels over powerful beasts or a wise man over powerful errors. He knew that he had neither the intellectual nor the physical strength of President Sunday, but in that moment he minded it no more than the fact that he had not the muscles of a tiger or a horn on his nose like a rhinoceros. All was swallowed up in an ultimate certainty that the President was wrong and that the barrel-organ was right. There clanged in his mind that unanswerable and terrible truism in the song of Roland –

'Païens ont tort et Chrétiens ont droit,'[3]

which in the old nasal French has the clang and groan of great iron. This liberation of his spirit from the load of his weakness went with a quite clear decision to embrace death. If the people of the barrel-organ could keep their old-world obligations, so could he. This very pride in keeping his word was that he was keeping it to miscreants. It was his last triumph over these lunatics to go down into their dark room and die for something that they could not even understand. The barrel-organ seemed to give the marching tune with the energy and the mingled noises of a whole orchestra; and he could hear deep and rolling, under all the trumpets of the pride of life, the drums of the pride of death.

The conspirators were already filing through the open window and into the rooms behind. Syme went last, outwardly calm, but with all his brain and body throbbing with romantic rhythm. The President led them down an irregular side stair, such as might be used by servants, and into a dim, cold, empty room, with a table and benches, like an abandoned board-room. When they were all in, he closed and locked the door.

The first to speak was Gogol, the irreconcilable, who seemed bursting with inarticulate grievance.

'Zso! Zso!' he cried, with an obscure excitement, his heavy Polish accent becoming almost impenetrable. 'You zay you nod 'ide. You zay you show himselves. It is all nuzzinks. Ven you vant talk importance you run yourselves in a dark box!'

The President seemed to take the foreigner's incoherent satire with entire good humour.

'You can't get hold of it yet, Gogol,' he said in a fatherly way. 'When once they have heard us talking nonsense on that balcony they will not care where we go afterwards. If we had come here first, we should have had the whole staff at the keyhole. You don't seem to know anything about mankind.'

'I die for zem,' cried the Pole in thick excitement, 'and I slay zare oppressors. I care not for these games of gonzealment. I would zmite ze tyrant in ze open square.'

'I see, I see,' said the President, nodding kindly as he seated himself at the top of a long table. 'You die for mankind first, and then you get up and smite their oppressors. So that's all right. And now may I ask you to control your beautiful sentiments, and sit down with the other gentlemen at this table. For the first time this morning something intelligent is going to be said.'

Syme, with the perturbed promptitude he had shown since the original summons, sat down first. Gogol sat down last, grumbling in his brown beard about gombromise. No one except Syme seemed to have any notion of the blow that was about to fall. As for him, he had merely the feeling of a man mounting the scaffold with the intention, at any rate, of making a good speech.

'Comrades,' said the President, suddenly rising, 'we have spun out this farce long enough. I have called you down here to tell you something so simple and shocking that even the waiters upstairs (long inured to our levities) might hear some new seriousness in my voice. Comrades, we were discussing plans and naming places. I propose, before saying anything else, that those plans and places should not be voted by this meeting, but should be left wholly in the control of some one reliable member. I suggest Comrade Saturday, Dr Bull.'

They all stared at him; then they all started in their seats, for the next words, though not loud, had a living and sensational emphasis. Sunday struck the table.

'Not one word more about the plans and places must be said at this meeting. Not one tiny detail more about what we mean to do must be mentioned in this company.'

Sunday had spent his life in astonishing his followers; but it seemed as if he had never really astonished them until now. They all moved feverishly in their seats, except Syme. He sat stiff in his, with his hand in his pocket, and on the handle of his loaded revolver. When the attack on him came he would sell his life dear. He would find out at least if the President was mortal.

Sunday went on smoothly:

'You will probably understand that there is only one possible motive for forbidding free speech at this festival of freedom. Strangers overhearing us matters nothing. They assume that we are joking. But what would matter, even unto death, is this, that there should be one actually among us who is not of us, who knows our grave purpose, but does not share it, who—'

The Secretary screamed out suddenly like a woman.

'It can't be!' he cried, leaping. 'There can't —'

The President flapped his large flat hand on the table like the fin of some huge fish.

'Yes,' he said slowly, 'there is a spy in this room. There is a traitor at this table. I will waste no more words. His name—'

Syme half rose from his seat, his finger firm on the trigger.

'His name is Gogol,' said the President. 'He is that hairy humbug over there who pretends to be a Pole.'

Gogol sprang to his feet, a pistol in each hand. With the same flash three men sprang at his throat. Even the Professor made an effort to rise. But Syme saw little of the scene, for he was blinded with a beneficent darkness; he had sunk down into his seat shuddering in a palsy of passionate relief.

7

The Unaccountable Conduct of Professor De Worms

'Sit down!' said Sunday in a voice that he used once or twice in his life, a voice that made men drop drawn swords.

The three who had risen fell away from Gogol, and that equivocal person himself resumed his seat.

'Well, my man,' said the President briskly, addressing him as one addresses a total stranger, 'will you oblige me by putting your hand in your upper waistcoat pocket and showing me what you have there?'

The alleged Pole was a little pale under his tangle of dark hair, but he put two fingers into the pocket with apparent coolness and pulled out a blue strip of card. When Syme saw it lying on the table, he woke up again to the world outside him. For although the card lay at the other extreme of the table, and he could read nothing of the inscription on it, it bore a startling resemblance to the blue card in his own pocket, the card which had been given to him when he joined the anti-anarchist constabulary.

'Pathetic Slav,' said the President, 'tragic child of Poland, are you prepared in the presence of that card to deny that you are in this company – shall we say, *de trop*?'[1]

'Right oh!' said the late Gogol. It made everyone jump to hear a clear, commercial, and somewhat Cockney voice coming out of that forest of foreign hair. It was irrational, as if a Chinaman had suddenly spoken with a Scotch accent.

'I gather that you fully understand your position,' said Sunday.

'You bet,' answered the Pole. 'I see it's a fair cop. All I say is, I don't believe any Pole could have imitated my accent like I did his.'

'I concede the point,' said Sunday. 'I believe your own accent to be inimitable, though I shall practise it in my bath. Do you mind leaving your beard with your card?'

'Not a bit,' answered Gogol; and with one finger he ripped off the whole of his shaggy head-covering, emerging with thin red hair and a pale, pert face. 'It was hot,' he added.

'I will do you the justice to say,' said Sunday, not without a sort of brutal admiration, 'that you seem to have kept pretty cool under it. Now listen to me. I like you. The consequence is that it would annoy me for just about two and a half minutes if I heard that you had died in torments. Well, if you ever tell the police or any human soul about us, I shall have that two and a half minutes of discomfort. On your discomfort I will not dwell. Good day. Mind the step.'

The red-haired detective who had masqueraded as Gogol rose to his feet without a word, and walked out of the room with an air of perfect nonchalance. Yet the astonished Syme was able to realize that this ease was suddenly assumed; for there was a slight stumble outside the door, which showed that the departing detective had not minded the step.

'Time is flying,' said the President in his gayest manner, after glancing at his watch, which like everything about him seemed bigger than it ought to be. 'I must go off at once; I have to take the chair at a Humanitarian meeting.'

The Secretary turned to him with working eyebrows.

'Would it not be better,' he said a little sharply, 'to discuss further the details of our project, now that the spy has left us?'

'No, I think not,' said the President with a yawn like an unobtrusive earthquake. 'Leave it as it is. Let Saturday settle it. I must be off. Breakfast here next Sunday.'

But the late loud scenes had whipped up the almost naked nerves of the Secretary. He was one of those men who are conscientious even in crime.

'I must protest, President, that the thing is irregular,' he said. 'It is a fundamental rule of our society that all plans shall be debated in full council. Of course, I fully appreciate your fore-thought when in the actual presence of a traitor—'

'Secretary,' said the President seriously, 'if you'd take your head home and boil it for a turnip it might be useful. I can't say. But it might.'

The Secretary reared in a kind of equine anger.

'I really fail to understand—' he began in high offence.

'That's it, that's it,' said the President, nodding a great many times. 'That's where you fail right enough. You fail to understand. Why, you dancing donkey,' he roared, rising, 'you didn't want to be overheard by a spy, did you? How do you know you aren't overheard now?'

And with these words he shouldered his way out of the room, shaking with incomprehensible scorn.

Four of the men left behind gaped after him without any apparent glimmering of his meaning. Syme alone had even a glimmering, and such as it was it froze him to the bone. If the last words of the President meant anything, they meant that he had not after all passed unsuspected. They meant that while Sunday could not denounce him like Gogol, he still could not trust him like the others.

The other four got to their feet grumbling more or less, and betook themselves elsewhere to find lunch, for it was already well past midday. The Professor went last, slowly and painfully. Syme sat long after the rest had gone, revolving his strange position. He had escaped a thunderbolt, but he was still under a cloud. At last he rose and made his way out of the hotel into Leicester Square. The bright, cold day had grown increasingly colder, and when he came out into the street he was surprised by a few flakes of snow. While he still carried the sword-stick and the rest of Gregory's portable luggage, he had thrown the cloak down and left it somewhere, perhaps on the steam-tug, perhaps on the balcony. Hoping, therefore, that the snow-shower might be slight, he stepped back out of the street for a moment and stood up under the doorway of a small and greasy hairdresser's shop, the front window of which was empty, except for a sickly wax lady in evening dress.

Snow, however, began to thicken and fall fast; and Syme, having found one glance at the wax lady quite sufficient to depress his spirits, stared out instead into the white and empty street. He was considerably astonished to see, standing quite still outside the shop and staring into the window, a man. His top hat was loaded with snow like the hat of Father Christmas, the white drift was rising round his boots and ankles; but it seemed as if nothing could tear him away from the contemplation of the colourless wax doll in dirty evening dress. That any human being should stand in such weather looking into such a shop was a matter of sufficient wonder to Syme; but his idle wonder turned suddenly into a personal shock; for he realized that the man standing there was the paralytic old Professor de Worms. It scarcely seemed the place for a person of his years and infirmities.

Syme was ready to believe anything about the perversions of this dehumanized brotherhood; but even he could not believe that the Professor had fallen in love with that particular wax lady. He could only suppose that the man's malady (whatever it was) involved some momentary fits of rigidity or trance. He was not inclined, however, to feel in this case any very compassionate concern. On the contrary, he rather congratulated himself that the Professor's stroke and his elaborate and limping walk would make it easy to escape from him and leave him miles behind. For Syme thirsted first and last to get clear of the whole poisonous atmosphere, if only for an hour. Then he could collect his thoughts, formulate his policy, and decide finally whether he should or should not keep faith with Gregory.

He strolled away through the dancing snow, turned up two or three streets, down through two or three others, and entered a small Soho restaurant for lunch. He partook reflectively of four small and quaint courses, drank half a bottle of red wine, and ended up over black coffee and a black cigar, still thinking. He had taken his seat in the upper room of the restaurant, which was full of the chink of knives and the chatter of foreigners. He remembered that in old days he had imagined that all these harmless and kindly aliens were anarchists. He shuddered, remembering the real thing. But even the shudder had the delightful shame of escape. The wine, the common food, the familiar place, the faces of natural and talkative men, made him almost feel as if the Council of the Seven Days had been a bad dream; and although he knew it was nevertheless an objective reality, it was at least a distant one. Tall houses and populous streets lay between him and his last sight of the shameful seven; he was free in free London, and drinking wine among the free. With a somewhat easier action, he took his hat and stick and strolled down the stair into the shop below.

When he entered that lower room he stood stricken and rooted to the spot. At a small table, close up to the blank window and the white street of snow, sat the old anarchist Professor over a glass of milk, with his lifted vivid face and pendent eyelids. For an instant Syme stood as rigid as the stick he leant upon. Then with a gesture as of blind hurry, he brushed past the Professor, dashing open the door and slamming it behind him, and stood outside in the snow.

'Can that old corpse be following me?' he asked himself, biting his yellow moustache. 'I stopped too long up in that room, so that even such leaden feet could catch me up. One comfort is, with a little brisk walking I can put a man like that as far away as Timbuctoo.[2] Or am I too fanciful? Was he really following me? Surely Sunday would not be such a fool as to send a lame man?'

He set off at a smart pace, twisting and whirling his stick, in the direction of Covent Garden. As he crossed the great market the snow increased, growing blinding and bewildering as the afternoon began to darken. The snowflakes tormented him like a swarm of silver bees. Getting into his eyes and beard, they added their unremitting futility to his already irritated nerves; and by the time that he had come at a swinging pace to the beginning of Fleet Street, he lost patience, and finding a Sunday tea shop, turned into it to take shelter. He ordered another cup of black coffee as an excuse. Scarcely had he done so, when Professor de Worms hobbled heavily into the shop, sat down with difficulty and ordered a glass of milk.

Syme's walking-stick had fallen from his hand with a great clang, which confessed the concealed steel. But the Professor did not look round. Syme, who was commonly a cool character, was literally gaping as a rustic gapes at a conjuring trick. He had seen no cab following; he had heard no wheels outside the shop; to all mortal appearances the man had come on foot. But the old man could only walk like a snail, and Syme had walked like the wind. He started up and snatched his stick, half crazy with the contradiction in mere arithmetic, and swung out of the swinging doors, leaving his coffee untasted. An omnibus going to the Bank went rattling by with an unusual rapidity. He had a violent run of a hundred yards to reach it; but he managed to spring, swaying upon the splash-board,[3] and pausing for an instant to pant, he climbed on to the top. When he had been seated for about half a minute, he heard behind him a sort of heavy and asthmatic breathing.

Turning sharply, he saw rising gradually higher and higher up the omnibus steps a top hat soiled and dripping with snow, and under the shadow of its brim the short-sighted face and shaky shoulders of Professor de Worms. He let himself into a seat with characteristic care, and wrapped himself up to the chin in the mackintosh rug.

Every movement of the old man's tottering figure and vague hands, every uncertain gesture and panic-stricken pause, seemed to put it beyond question that he was helpless, that he was in the last imbecility of the body. He moved by inches, he let himself down with little gasps of caution. And yet, unless the philosophical entities called time and space have no vestige even of a practical existence, it appeared quite unquestionable that he had run after the omnibus.

Syme sprang erect upon the rocking car, and after staring wildly at the wintry sky, that grew gloomier every moment, he ran down the steps. He had repressed an elemental impulse to leap over the side.

Too bewildered to look back or to reason, he rushed into one of the little courts at the side of Fleet Street as a rabbit rushes into a hole. He had a vague idea, if this incomprehensible old Jack-in-the-box was really pursuing him, that in that labyrinth of little streets he could soon throw him off the scent. He dived in and out of those crooked lanes, which were more like cracks than thoroughfares; and by the time that he had completed about twenty alternate angles and described an unthinkable polygon, he paused to listen for any sound of pursuit. There was none; there could not in any case have been much, for the little streets were thick with the soundless snow. Somewhere behind Red Lion Court, however, he noticed a place where some energetic citizen had cleared away the snow for a space of about twenty yards, leaving the wet, glistening cobble-stones. He thought little of this as he passed it, only plunging into yet another arm of the maze. But when a few hundred yards farther on he stood still again to listen, his heart stood still also, for he heard from that space of rugged stones the clinking crutch and labouring feet of the infernal cripple.

The sky above was loaded with the clouds of snow, leaving London in a darkness and oppression premature for that hour of the evening. On each side of Syme the walls of the alley were blind and featureless; there was no little window or any kind of eye. He felt a new impulse to break out of this hive of houses, and to get once more into the open and lamplit street. Yet he rambled and dodged for a long time before he struck the main thoroughfare. When he did so, he struck it much farther up than he had fancied. He came out into what seemed the vast and void of Ludgate Circus, and saw St Paul's Cathedral sitting in the sky.

At first he was startled to find these great roads so empty, as if a pestilence had swept through the city. Then he told himself that some degree of emptiness was natural; first because the snow-storm was even dangerously deep, and secondly because it was Sunday. And at the very word Sunday he bit his lip; the word was henceforth for him like some indecent pun. Under the white fog of snow high up in the heaven the whole atmosphere of the city was turned to a very queer kind of green twilight, as of men under the sea. The sealed and sullen sunset behind the dark dome of St Paul's had in it smoky and sinister colours – colours of sickly green, dead red, or decaying bronze, that were just bright enough to emphasize the solid whiteness of the snow. But right up against these dreary colours rose the black bulk of the cathedral; and upon the top of the cathedral was a random splash and great stain of snow, still clinging as to an Alpine peak. It had fallen accidentally, but just so fallen as to half drape the dome from its very topmost point, and to pick out in perfect silver the great orb and the cross.[4] When

Syme saw it he suddenly straightened himself, and made with his sword-stick an involuntary salute.

He knew that that evil figure, his shadow, was creeping quickly or slowly behind him, and he did not care. It seemed a symbol of human faith and valour that while the skies were darkening that high place of the earth was bright. The devils might have captured heaven, but they had not yet captured the cross. He had a new impulse to tear out the secret of this dancing, jumping, and pursuing paralytic; and at the entrance of the court as it opened upon the Circus he turned, stick in hand, to face his pursuer.

Professor de Worms came slowly round the corner of the irregular alley behind him, his unnatural form outlined against a lonely gas-lamp, irresistibly recalling that very imaginative figure in the nursery rhymes, 'the crooked man who went a crooked mile'. He really looked as if he had been twisted out of shape by the tortuous streets he had been threading. He came nearer and nearer, the lamplight shining on his lifted spectacles, his lifted, patient face. Syme waited for him as St George waited for the dragon, as a man waits for a final explanation or for death. And the old Professor came right up to him and passed him like a total stranger, without even a blink of his mournful eyelids.

There was something in this silent and unexpected innocence that left Syme in a final fury. The man's colourless face and manner seemed to assert that the whole following had been an accident. Syme was galvanized with an energy that was something between bitterness and a burst of boyish derision. He made a wild gesture as if to knock the old man's hat off, called out something like 'Catch me if you can', and went racing away across the white, open Circus. Concealment was impossible now; and looking back over his shoulder he could see the black figure of the old gentleman coming after him with long, swinging strides like a man winning a mile race. But the head upon that bounding body was still pale, grave, and professional, like the head of a lecturer upon the body of a harlequin.

This outrageous chase sped across Ludgate Circus, up Ludgate Hill, round St Paul's Cathedral, along Cheapside, Syme remembering all the nightmares he had ever known. Then Syme broke away towards the river, and ended almost down by the docks. He saw the yellow panes of a low, lighted public-house, flung himself into it, and ordered beer. It was a foul tavern, sprinkled with foreign sailors, a place where opium might be smoked or knives drawn.

A moment later Professor de Worms entered the place, sat down carefully, and asked for a glass of milk.

8

The Professor Explains

When Gabriel Syme found himself finally established in a chair, and opposite to him, fixed and final also, the lifted eyebrows and leaden eyelids of the Professor, his fears fully returned. This incomprehensible man from the fierce council, after all, had certainly pursued him. If the man had one character as a paralytic and another character as a pursuer, the antithesis might make him more interesting, but scarcely more soothing. It would be a very small comfort that he could not find the Professor out, if by some serious accident the Professor should find him out. He emptied a whole pewter pot of ale before the Professor had touched his milk.

One possibility, however, kept him hopeful and yet helpless. It was just possible that this escapade signified something other than even a slight suspicion of him. Perhaps it was some regular form or sign. Perhaps the foolish scamper was some sort of friendly signal that he ought to have understood. Perhaps it was a ritual. Perhaps the new Thursday was always chased along Cheapside, as the new Lord Mayor is always escorted along it. He was just selecting a tentative inquiry, when the old Professor opposite suddenly and simply cut him short. Before Syme could ask the first diplomatic question, the old anarchist had asked suddenly, without any sort of preparation –

'Are you a policeman?'

Whatever else Syme had expected, he had never expected anything so brutal and actual as this. Even his great presence of mind could only manage a reply with an air of rather blundering jocularity.

'A policeman?' he said, laughing vaguely. 'Whatever made you think of a policeman in connexion with me?'

'The process was simple enough,' answered the Professor patiently. 'I thought you looked like a policeman. I think so now.'

'Did I take a policeman's hat by mistake out of the restaurant?' asked Syme, smiling wildly. 'Have I by any chance got a number stuck on to me somewhere? Have my boots got that watchful look? Why must I be a policeman? Do, do let me be a postman.'

The old Professor shook his head with a gravity that gave no hope, but Syme ran on with a feverish irony.

'But perhaps I misunderstood the delicacies of your German philosophy. Perhaps policeman is a relative term. In an evolutionary sense, sir, the ape fades so gradually into the policeman, that I myself can never detect the shade. The monkey is only the policeman that may be. Perhaps a maiden lady on Clapham Common is only the policeman that might have been. I don't mind being the policeman that might have been. I don't mind being anything in German thought.'

'Are you in the police service?' said the old man, ignoring all Syme's improvised and desperate raillery. 'Are you a detective?'

Syme's heart turned to stone, but his face never changed.

'Your suggestion is ridiculous,' he began. 'Why on earth—'

The old man struck his palsied hand passionately on the rickety table, nearly breaking it.

'Did you hear me ask a plain question, you paltering spy?' he shrieked in a high, crazy voice. 'Are you, or are you not, a police detective?'

'No!' answered Syme, like a man standing on the hangman's drop.

'You swear it?' said the old man, leaning across to him, his dead face becoming as it were loathsomely alive. 'You swear it? You swear it? If you swear falsely, will you be damned? Will you be sure that the devil dances at your funeral? Will you see that the nightmare sits on your grave? Will there really be no mistake? You are an anarchist, you are a dynamiter? Above all, you are not in any sense a detective? You are not in the British police?'

He leant his angular elbow far across the table, and put his large loose hand like a flap to his ear.

'I am not in the British police,' said Syme with insane calm.

Professor de Worms fell back in his chair with a curious air of kindly collapse.

'That's a pity,' he said, 'because I am.'

Syme sprang up straight, sending back the bench behind him with a crash.

'Because you are what?' he said thickly. 'You are what?'

'I am a policeman,' said the Professor with his first broad smile, and beaming through his spectacles. 'But as you think policemen only a relative term, of course I have nothing to do with you. I am in the British police force; but as you tell me you are not in the British police force, I can only say that I met you in a dynamiters' club. I suppose I ought to arrest you.' And with these words he laid on the table before Syme an exact facsimile of the blue card which Syme had in his own waistcoat pocket, the symbol of his power from the police.

Syme had for a flash the sensation that the cosmos had turned exactly upside down, that all the trees were growing downwards and that all stars were under his feet. Then came slowly the opposite conviction. For the last twenty-four hours the cosmos had really been upside down, but now the capsized universe had come right side up again. The devil from whom he had been fleeing all day was only an elder brother of his own house, who on the other side of the table lay back and laughed at him. He did not for the moment ask any questions of detail; he only knew the happy and silly fact that his shadow, which had pursued him with an intolerable oppression of peril, was only the shadow of a friend trying to catch him up. He knew simultaneously that he was a fool and a free man. For with any recovery from morbidity there must go a certain healthy humiliation. There comes a certain point in such conditions when only three things are possible; first a perpetuation of Satanic pride, secondly tears, and thirdly laughter. Syme's egotism held hard to the first course for a few seconds, and then suddenly adopted the third. Taking his own blue police ticket from his own waistcoat pocket, he tossed it on to the table; then he flung his head back until his

spike of yellow beard almost pointed at the ceiling, and shouted
with a barbaric laughter.

Even in that close den, perpetually filled with the din of knives,
plates, cans, clamorous voices, sudden struggles and stampedes,
there was something Homeric in Syme's mirth which made many
half-drunken men look round.

'What yer laughing at, guv'nor?' asked one wondering
labourer from the docks.

'At myself,' answered Syme, and went off again into the agony
of his ecstatic reaction.

'Pull yourself together,' said the Professor, 'or you'll get
hysterical. Have some more beer. I'll join you.'

'You haven't drunk your milk,' said Syme.

'My milk!' said the other, in tones of withering and unfathomable contempt, 'my milk! Do you think I'd look at the
beastly stuff when I'm out of sight of the bloody anarchists?
We're all Christians in this room, though perhaps,' he added,
glancing around at the reeling crowd, 'not strict ones. Finish
my milk? Great blazes! yes, I'll finish it right enough!' and he
knocked the tumbler off the table, making a crash of glass and
a splash of silver fluid.

Syme was staring at him with a happy curiosity.

'I understand now,' he cried; 'of course, you're not an old man
at all.'

'I can't take my face off here,' replied Professor de Worms.
'It's rather an elaborate make-up. As to whether I'm an old man,
that's not for me to say. I was thirty-eight last birthday.'

'Yes, but I mean,' said Syme impatiently, 'there's nothing the
matter with you.'

'Yes,' answered the other dispassionately. 'I am subject to
colds.'

Syme's laughter at all this had about it a wild weakness of relief.
He laughed at the idea of the paralytic Professor being really a
young actor dressed up as if for foot-lights. But he felt that he
would have laughed as loudly if a pepper-pot had fallen over.

The false Professor drank and wiped his false beard.

'Did you know,' he asked, 'that this man Gogol was one of
us?'

'I? No, I didn't know it,' answered Syme in some surprise. 'But didn't you?'

'I knew no more than the dead,' replied the man who called himself de Worms. 'I thought the President was talking about me, and I rattled in my boots.'

'And I thought he was talking about me,' said Syme, with his rather reckless laughter. 'I had my hand on my revolver all the time.'

'So had I,' said the Professor grimly; 'so had Gogol evidently.'

Syme struck the table with an exclamation.

'Why, there were three of us there!' he cried. 'Three out of seven is a fighting number. If we had only known that we were three!'

The face of Professor de Worms darkened, and he did not look up.

'We were three,' he said. 'If we had been three hundred we could still have done nothing.'

'Not if we were three hundred against four?' asked Syme, jeering rather boisterously.

'No,' said the Professor with sobriety, 'not if we were three hundred against Sunday.'

And the mere name struck Syme cold and serious; his laughter had died in his heart before it could die on his lips. The face of the unforgettable President sprang into his mind as startling as a coloured photograph, and he remarked this difference between Sunday and all his satellites, that their faces, however fierce or sinister, became gradually blurred by memory like other human faces, whereas Sunday's seemed almost to grow more actual during absence, as if a man's painted portrait should slowly come alive.

They were both silent for a measure of moments, and then Syme's speech came with a rush, like the sudden foaming of champagne.

'Professor,' he cried, 'it is intolerable. Are you afraid of this man?'

The Professor lifted his heavy lids, and gazed at Syme with large, wide-open, blue eyes of an almost ethereal honesty.

'Yes, I am,' he said mildly. 'So are you.'

Syme was dumb for an instant. Then he rose to his feet erect, like an insulted man, and thrust the chair away from him.

'Yes,' he said in a voice indescribable, 'you are right. I am afraid of him. Therefore I swear by God that I will seek out this man whom I fear until I find him, and strike him on the mouth. If heaven were his throne and the earth his footstool,[1] I swear that I would pull him down.'

'How?' asked the staring Professor. 'Why?'

'Because I am afraid of him,' said Syme; 'and no man should leave in the universe anything of which he is afraid.'

De Worms blinked at him with a sort of blind wonder. He made an effort to speak, but Syme went on in a low voice, but with an undercurrent of inhuman exaltation:

'Who would condescend to strike down the mere things he does not fear? Who would debase himself to be merely brave, like any common prize-fighter? Who would stoop to be fearless – like a tree? Fight the thing that you fear. You remember the old tale of the English clergyman who gave the last rites to the brigand of Sicily, and how on his death-bed the great robber said, "I can give you no money, but I can give you advice for a lifetime: your thumb on the blade, and strike upwards." So I say to you, strike upwards, if you strike at the stars.'

The other looked at the ceiling, one of the tricks of his pose.

'Sunday is a fixed star,' he said.

'You shall see him a falling star,' said Syme, and put on his hat.

The decision of his gesture drew the Professor vaguely to his feet.

'Have you any idea,' he asked, with a sort of benevolent bewilderment, 'exactly where you are going?'

'Yes,' replied Syme shortly, 'I am going to prevent this bomb being thrown in Paris.'

'Have you any conception how?' inquired the other.

'No,' said Syme with equal decision.

'You remember, of course,' resumed the soi-disant de Worms, pulling his beard and looking out of the window, 'that when we broke up rather hurriedly the whole arrangements for the atrocity were left in the private hands of the Marquis and Dr

Bull. The Marquis is by this time probably crossing the Channel. But where he will go and what he will do it is doubtful whether even the President knows; certainly we don't. The only man who does know is Dr Bull.'

'Confound it!' cried Syme. 'And we don't know where he is.'

'Yes,' said the other in his curious, absent-minded way, 'I know where he is myself.'

'Will you tell me?' asked Syme with eager eyes.

'I will take you there,' said the Professor, and took down his own hat from a peg.

Syme stood looking at him with a sort of rigid excitement.

'What do you mean?' he asked sharply. 'Will you join me? Will you take the risk?'

'Young man,' said the Professor pleasantly, 'I am amused to observe that you think I am a coward. As to that I will say only one word, and that shall be entirely in the manner of your own philosophical rhetoric. You think that it is impossible to pull down the President. I know that it is impossible, and I am going to try it,' and opening the tavern door, which let in a blast of bitter air, they went out together into the dark streets by the docks.

Most of the snow was melted or trampled to mud, but here and there a clot of it still showed grey rather than white in the gloom. The small streets were sloppy and full of pools, which reflected the flaming lamps irregularly, and by accident, like fragments of some other and fallen world. Syme felt almost dazed as he stepped through this growing confusion of lights and shadows; but his companion walked on with a certain briskness towards where, at the end of the street, an inch or two of the lamp-lit river looked like a bar of flame.

'Where are you going?' Syme inquired.

'Just now,' answered the Professor, 'I am going just round the corner to see whether Dr Bull has gone to bed. He is hygienic, and retires early.'

'Dr Bull!' exclaimed Syme. 'Does he live round the corner?'

'No,' answered his friend. 'As a matter of fact he lives some way off, on the other side of the river, but we can tell from here whether he has gone to bed.'

Turning the corner as he spoke, and facing the dim river, flecked with flame, he pointed with his stick to the other bank. On the Surrey side at this point there ran out into the Thames, seeming almost to overhang it, a bulk and cluster of those tall tenements, dotted with lighted windows, and rising like factory chimneys to an almost insane height. Their special poise and position made one block of buildings especially look like a Tower of Babel[2] with a hundred eyes. Syme had never seen any of the sky-scraping buildings in America, so he could only think of the buildings in a dream.

Even as he stared, the highest light in this innumerably lighted turret abruptly went out, as if this black Argus[3] had winked at him with one of his innumerable eyes.

Professor de Worms swung round on his heel, and struck his stick against his boot.

'We are too late,' he said, 'the hygienic Doctor has gone to bed.'

'What do you mean?' asked Syme. 'Does he live over there, then?'

'Yes,' said de Worms, 'behind that particular window which you can't see. Come along and get some dinner. We must call on him tomorrow evening.'

Without further parley, he led the way through several byways until they came out into the flare and clamour of the East India Dock Road. The Professor, who seemed to know his way about the neighbourhood, proceeded to a place where the line of lighted shops fell back into a sort of abrupt twilight and quiet, in which an old white inn, all out of repair, stood back some twenty feet from the road.

'You can find good English inns left by accident everywhere, like fossils,' exclaimed the Professor. 'I once found a decent place in the West End.'

'I suppose,' said Syme, smiling, 'that this is the corresponding decent place in the East End?'

'It is,' said the Professor reverently, and went in.

In that place they dined and slept, both very thoroughly. The beans and bacon, which these unaccountable people cooked well, the astonishing emergence of Burgundy from their cellars, crowned Syme's sense of a new comradeship and comfort.

Through all this ordeal his root horror had been isolation, and there are no words to express the abyss between isolation and having one ally. It may be conceded to the mathematicians that four is twice two. But two is not twice one; two is two thousand times one. That is why, in spite of a hundred disadvantages, the world will always return to monogamy.

Syme was able to pour out for the first time the whole of his outrageous tale, from the time when Gregory had taken him to the little tavern by the river. He did it idly and amply, in a luxuriant monologue, as a man speaks with very old friends. On his side also, the man who had impersonated Professor de Worms was not less communicative. His own story was almost as silly as Syme's.

'That's a good get-up of yours,' said Syme, draining a glass of Mâcon;[4] 'a lot better than old Gogol's. Even at the start I thought he was a bit too hairy.'

'A difference of artistic theory,' replied the Professor pensively. 'Gogol was an idealist. He made up the abstract or platonic ideal of an anarchist. But I am a realist. I am a portrait painter. But, indeed, to say that I am a portrait painter is an inadequate expression. I am a portrait.'

'I don't understand you,' said Syme.

'I'm a portrait,' repeated the Professor. 'I am a portrait of the celebrated Professor de Worms, who is, I believe, in Naples.'

'You mean you are made up like him,' said Syme. 'But doesn't he know that you are taking his nose in vain?'

'He knows it right enough,' replied his friend cheerfully.

'Then why doesn't he denounce you?'

'I have denounced him,' answered the Professor.

'Do explain yourself,' said Syme.

'With pleasure, if you don't mind hearing my story,' replied the eminent foreign philosopher. 'I am by profession an actor, and my name is Wilks. When I was on the stage I mixed with all sorts of Bohemian and blackguard company. Sometimes I touched the edge of the turf, sometimes the riff-raff of the arts, and occasionally the political refugee. In some den of exiled dreamers I was introduced to the great German Nihilist philosopher, Professor de Worms. I did not gather much about him beyond his appearance, which was very disgusting, and which I studied carefully. I understood that he had proved that the destructive principle in the universe was God; hence he insisted on the need for a furious and incessant energy, rending all things in pieces. Energy, he said, was the All. He was lame, short-sighted, and partially paralytic. When I met him I was in a frivolous mood, and I disliked him so much that I resolved to imitate him. If I had been a draughtsman I would have drawn a caricature. I was only an actor, I could only act a caricature. I made myself up into what was meant for a wild exaggeration of the old Professor's dirty old self. When I went into the room full of his supporters I expected to be received with a roar of laughter, or (if they were too far gone) with a roar of indignation at the insult. I cannot describe the surprise I felt when my entrance was received with a respectful silence, followed (when I had first opened my lips) with a murmur of admiration. The curse of the perfect artist had fallen upon me. I had been too subtle, I had been too true. They thought I really was the great Nihilist Professor. I was a healthy-minded young man at the time, and I confess that it was a blow. Before I could fully recover, however, two or three of these admirers ran up to me radiating indignation, and told me that a public insult had been put upon me in the next room. I inquired its nature. It seemed that an impertinent fellow had dressed himself up as a preposterous parody of myself. I had drunk more champagne than was good for me, and in a flash of folly I decided to see the situation through. Consequently it was to meet the glare of the company and my own lifted eyebrows and freezing eyes that the real Professor came into the room.

I need hardly say there was a collision. The pessimists all round me looked anxiously from one Professor to the other Professor to see which was really the more feeble. But I won. An old man in poor health, like my rival, could not be expected to be so impressively feeble as a young actor in the prime of life. You see, he really had paralysis, and, working within this definite limitation, he couldn't be so jolly paralytic as I was. Then he tried to blast my claims intellectually. I countered that by a very simple dodge. Whenever he said something that nobody but he could understand, I replied with something which I could not even understand myself. "I don't fancy," he said, "that you could have worked out the principle that evolution is only negation, since there inheres in it the introduction of lacunae, which are an essential of differentiation." I replied quite scornfully, "You read all that up in Pinckwerts; the notion that involution functioned eugenically was exposed long ago by Glumpe." It is unnecessary for me to say that there never were such people as Pinckwerts and Glumpe. But the people all round (rather to my surprise) seemed to remember them quite well, and the Professor, finding that the learned and mysterious method left him rather at the mercy of an enemy slightly deficient in scruples, fell back upon a more popular form of it. "I see," he sneered, "you prevail like the false pig in Aesop.'⁵ "And you fail," I answered, smiling, "like the hedgehog in Montaigne." 'Need I say that there is no hedgehog in Montaigne. "Your clap-trap comes off," he said; "so would your beard." I had no intelligent answer to this, which was quite true and rather witty. But I laughed heartily, answered, "Like the Pantheist's boots," at random, and turned on my heel with the honours of victory. The real Professor was thrown out, but not with violence, though one man tried very patiently to pull off his nose. He is now, I believe, received everywhere in Europe as a delightful impostor. His apparent earnestness and anger, you see, make him all the more entertaining.'

'Well,' said Syme, 'I can understand your putting on his dirty old beard for a night's practical joke, but I don't understand you never taking it off again.'

'That is the rest of the story,' said the impersonator. 'When I myself left the company, followed by reverent applause, I went limping down the dark street, hoping that I should soon be far enough away to be able to walk like a human being. To my astonishment, as I was turning the corner, I felt a touch on the shoulder, and, turning round, found myself under the shadow of an enormous policeman. He told me I was wanted. I struck a sort of paralytic attitude, and cried in a high German accent, "Yes, I am wanted – by the oppressed of the world. You are arresting me on the charge of being the great anarchist Professor de Worms." The policeman impassively consulted a paper in his

hand. "No, sir," he said civilly, "at least, not exactly, sir. I am
arresting you on the charge of not being the celebrated anarchist,
Professor de Worms." This charge, if it was criminal at all, was
certainly the lighter of the two, and I went along with the man,
doubtful, but not greatly dismayed. I was shown into a number
of rooms, and eventually into the presence of a police officer,
who explained that a serious campaign had been opened against
the centres of anarchy, and that this, my successful masquerade,
might be of considerable value to the public safety. He offered
me a good salary and this little blue card. Though our conversation was short, he struck me as a man of very massive common
sense and humour; but I cannot tell you much about him
personally, because—'

Syme laid down his knife and fork.

'I know,' he said, 'because you talked to him in a dark room.'

Professor de Worms nodded and drained his glass.

9

The Man in Spectacles

Burgundy is a jolly thing,' said the Professor sadly, as he set his glass down.

'You don't look as if it were,' said Syme; 'you drink as if it were medicine.'

'You must excuse my manner,' said the Professor dismally, 'my position is rather a curious one. Inside I am really bursting with boyish merriment; but I acted the paralytic Professor so well, that now I can't leave off. So that when I am among friends, and have no need at all to disguise myself, I still can't help speaking slow and wrinkling my forehead – just as if it were my forehead. I can be quite happy, you understand, but only in a paralytic sort of way. The most buoyant exclamations leap up in my heart, but they come out of my mouth quite different. You should hear me say, "Buck up, old cock!" It would bring tears to your eyes.'

'It does,' said Syme; 'but I cannot help thinking that apart from all that you are really a bit worried.'

The Professor started a little and looked at him steadily.

'You are a very clever fellow,' he said, 'it is a pleasure to work with you. Yes, I have rather a heavy cloud in my head. There is a great problem to face,' and he sank his bald brow in his two hands.

Then he said in a low voice:

'Can you play the piano?'

'Yes,' said Syme in simple wonder, 'I'm supposed to have a good touch.'

Then, as the other did not speak, he added:

'I trust the great cloud is lifted.'

After a long silence, the Professor said out of the cavernous shadow of his hands:

'It would have done just as well if you could work a typewriter.'

'Thank you,' said Syme, 'you flatter me.'

'Listen to me,' said the other, 'and remember whom we have to see tomorrow. You and I are going tomorrow to attempt something which is very much more dangerous than trying to steal the Crown Jewels out of the Tower. We are trying to steal a secret from a very sharp, very strong, and very wicked man. I believe there is no man, except the President, of course, who is so seriously startling and formidable as that little grinning fellow in goggles. He has not perhaps the white-hot enthusiasm unto death, the mad martyrdom for anarchy, which marks the Secretary. But then that very fanaticism in the Secretary had a human pathos, and is almost a redeeming trait. But the little Doctor has a brutal sanity that is more shocking than the Secretary's disease. Don't you notice his detestable virility and vitality? He bounces like an india-rubber ball. Depend on it, Sunday was not asleep (I wonder if he ever sleeps?) when he locked up all the plans of this outrage in the round, black head of Dr Bull.'

'And you think,' said Syme, 'that this unique monster will be soothed if I play the piano to him?'

'Don't be an ass,' said his mentor. 'I mentioned the piano because it gives one quick and independent fingers. Syme, if we are to go through this interview and come out sane or alive, we must have some code of signals between us that this brute will not see. I have made a rough alphabetical cipher corresponding to the five fingers – like this, see,' and he rippled with his fingers on the wooden table – 'B A D, bad, a word we may frequently require.'

Syme poured himself out another glass of wine, and began to study the scheme. He was abnormally quick with his brains at puzzles, and with his hands at conjuring, and it did not take him long to learn how he might convey simple messages by what would seem to be idle taps upon a table or knee. But wine and companionship had always the effect of inspiring him to a farcical ingenuity, and the Professor soon found himself struggling

with the too-vast energy of the new language, as it passed
through the heated brain of Syme.

'We must have several word-signs,' said Syme seriously –
'words that we are likely to want, fine shades of meaning. My
favourite word is "coeval". What's yours?'

'Do stop playing the goat,' said the Professor plaintively. 'You
don't know how serious this is.'

'"Lush", too,' said Syme, shaking his head sagaciously. 'We
must have "lush" – word applied to grass, don't you know?'

'Do you imagine,' asked the Professor furiously, 'that we are
going to talk to Dr Bull about grass?'

'There are several ways in which the subject could be approached,' said Syme reflectively, 'and the word introduced
without appearing forced. We might say, "Dr Bull, as a revo-
lutionist, you remember that a tyrant once advised us to eat
grass,[1] and indeed many of us, looking on the fresh lush grass
of summer—"'

'Do you understand,' said the other, 'that this is a tragedy?'

'Perfectly,' replied Syme; 'always be comic in a tragedy. What
the deuce else can you do? I wish this language of ours had a wider
scope. I suppose we could not extend it from the fingers to the
toes? That would involve pulling off our boots and socks during
the conversation, which, however unobtrusively performed—'

'Syme,' said his friend with a stern simplicity, 'go to bed!'

Syme, however, sat up in bed for a considerable time mastering
the new code. He was awakened next morning while the east
was still sealed with darkness, and found his grey-bearded ally
standing like a ghost beside his bed.

Syme sat up in bed blinking; then slowly collected his thoughts,
threw off the bed-clothes, and stood up. It seemed to him in
some curious way that all the safety and sociability of the night
before fell with the bed-clothes off him, and he stood up in an
air of cold danger. He still felt an entire trust and loyalty towards
his companion; but it was the trust between two men going to
the scaffold.

'Well,' said Syme, with a forced cheerfulness as he pulled on
his trousers. 'I dreamt of that alphabet of yours. Did it take you
long to make it up?'

The Professor made no answer, but gazed in front of him with eyes the colour of a wintry sea; so Syme repeated his question.

'I say, did it take you long to invent all this? I'm considered good at these things, and it was a good hour's grind. Did you learn it all on the spot?'

The Professor was silent; his eyes were wide open, and he wore a fixed but a very small smile.

'How long did it take you?'

The Professor did not move.

'Confound you, can't you answer?' called out Syme, in a sudden anger that had something like fear underneath. Whether or not the Professor could answer, he did not.

Syme stood staring back at the stiff face like parchment and the blank, blue eyes. His first thought was that the Professor had gone mad, but his second thought was more frightful. After all, what did he know about this queer creature whom he had heedlessly accepted as a friend? What did he know, except that the man had been at the anarchist breakfast and had told him a ridiculous tale? How improbable it was that there should be another friend there beside Gogol! Was this man's silence a sensational way of declaring war? Was this adamantine stare after all only the awful sneer of some threefold traitor, who had turned for the last time? He stood and strained his ears in this heartless silence. He almost fancied he could hear dynamiters come to capture him shifting softly in the corridor outside.

Then his eye strayed downwards, and he burst out laughing. Though the Professor himself stood there as voiceless as a statue, his five dumb fingers were dancing alive upon the dead table. Syme watched the twinkling movements of the talking hand, and read clearly the message –

'I will only talk like this. We must get used to it.'

He rapped out the answer with the impatience of relief.

'All right. Let's get out to breakfast.'

They took their hats and sticks in silence; but as Syme took his sword-stick, he held it hard.

They paused for a few minutes only to stuff down coffee and coarse, thick sandwiches at a coffee-stall, and then made their way across the river, which under the grey and growing light looked as desolate as Acheron.[2] They reached the bottom of the huge block of buildings which they had seen from across the river, and began in silence to mount the naked and numberless stone steps, only pausing now and then to make short remarks on the rail of the banister. At about every other flight they passed a window; each window showed them a pale and tragic dawn lifting itself laboriously over London. From each the innumerable roofs of slate looked like the leaden surges of a grey, troubled sea after rain. Syme was increasingly conscious that his new adventure had somehow a quality of cold sanity worse than the wild adventures of the past. Last night, for instance, the tall tenements had seemed to him like a tower in a dream. As he now went up the weary and perpetual steps, he was daunted and bewildered by their almost infinite series. But it was not the hot horror of a dream or of anything that might be exaggeration or delusion. Their infinity was more like the empty infinity of arithmetic, something unthinkable, yet necessary to thought. Or it was like the stunning statements of astronomy about the distance of the fixed stars. He was ascending the house of reason, a thing more hideous than unreason itself.

By the time they reached Dr Bull's landing, a last window showed them a harsh, white dawn edged with banks of a coarse red, more like red clay than red cloud. And when they entered Dr Bull's bare garret it was full of light.

Syme had been haunted by a half historic memory in connexion with these empty rooms and that austere daybreak. The moment he saw the garret and Dr Bull sitting writing at a table, he remembered what the memory was – the French Revolution. There should have been the black outline of a guillotine against that heavy red and white of the morning. Dr Bull was in his white shirt and black breeches only; his cropped, dark head might well have just come out of its wig; he might have been Marat or a more slipshod Robespierre.[3]

Yet when he was seen properly, the French fancy fell away. The Jacobins[4] were idealists; there was about this man a murderous materialism. The strong, white light of morning coming from one side creating sharp shadows, made him seem both more pale and more angular than he had looked at the breakfast on the balcony. Thus the two black glasses that encased his eyes might really have been black cavities in his skull, making him look like a death's-head. And, indeed, if ever Death sat writing at a wooden table, it might have been he.

He looked up and smiled brightly enough as the men came in, and rose with the resilient rapidity of which the Professor had spoken. He set chairs for both of them, and, going to a peg behind the door, proceeded to put on a coat and waistcoat of rough, dark tweed; he buttoned it up neatly, and came back to sit down at his table.

The quiet good humour of his manner left his two opponents helpless. It was with some momentary difficulty that the Professor broke silence and began, 'I'm sorry to disturb you so early, comrade,' said he, with a careful resumption of the slow de Worms manner. 'You have no doubt made all the arrangements for the Paris affair?' Then he added with infinite slowness, 'We have information which renders intolerable anything in the nature of a moment's delay.'

Dr Bull smiled again, but continued to gaze on them without speaking. The Professor resumed, a pause before each weary word –

'Please do not think me excessively abrupt; but I advise you to alter those plans, or if it is too late for that, to follow your agent with all the support you can get for him. Comrade Syme and I have had an experience which it would take more time to recount than we can afford, if we are to act on it. I will, however, relate the occurrence in detail, even at the risk of losing time, if you really feel that it is essential to the understanding of the problem we have to discuss.'

He was spinning out his sentences, making them intolerably long and lingering, in the hope of maddening the practical little Doctor into an explosion of impatience which might show his hand. But the little Doctor continued only to stare and smile, and the monologue was uphill work. Syme began to feel a new sickness and despair. The Doctor's smile and silence were not at all like the cataleptic stare and horrible silence which he had confronted in the Professor half an hour before. About the Professor's make-up and all his antics there was always something

merely grotesque, like a golliwog.[5] Syme remembered those wild
woes of yesterday as one remembers being afraid of Bogy[6] in
childhood. But here was daylight; here was a healthy square-
shouldered man in tweeds, not odd save for the accident of his
ugly spectacles, not glaring or grinning at all, but smiling steadily
and not saying a word. The whole had a sense of unbearable
reality. Under the increasing sunlight the colours of the Doctor's
complexion, the pattern of his tweeds, grew and expanded
outrageously, as such things grow too important in a realistic
novel. But his smile was quite slight, the pose of his head polite;
the only uncanny thing was his silence.

'As I say,' resumed the Professor, like a man toiling through
heavy sand, 'the incident that has occurred to us and has led us
to ask for information about the Marquis is one which you may
think it better to have narrated; but as it came in the way of
Comrade Syme rather than me—'

His words he seemed to be dragging out like words in an
anthem; but Syme, who was watching, saw his long fingers rattle
quickly on the edge of the crazy table. He read the message, 'You
must go on. This devil has sucked me dry!'

Syme plunged into the breach with that bravado of improvisation which always came to him when he was alarmed.

'Yes, the thing really happened to me,' he said hastily. 'I had
the good fortune to fall into conversation with a detective who
took me, thanks to my hat, for a respectable person. Wishing to
clinch my reputation for respectability, I took him and made
him very drunk at the Savoy.[7] Under this influence he became
friendly, and told me in so many words that within a day or two
they hope to arrest the Marquis in France. So unless you or I
can get on his track—'

The Doctor was still smiling in the most friendly way, and his
protected eyes were still impenetrable. The Professor signalled
to Syme that he would resume his explanation, and he began
again with the same elaborate calm.

'Syme immediately brought this information to me, and we
came here together to see what use you would be inclined to
make of it. It seems to me unquestionably urgent that—'

All this time Syme had been staring at the Doctor almost as

steadily as the Doctor stared at the Professor, but quite without the smile. The nerves of both comrades-in-arms were near snapping under that strain of motionless amiability, when Syme suddenly leant forward and idly tapped the edge of the table. His message to his ally ran, 'I have an intuition.'

The Professor, with scarcely a pause in his monologue, signalled back, 'Then sit on it.'

Syme telegraphed, 'It is quite extraordinary!'

The other answered, 'Extraordinary rot!'

Syme said, 'I am a poet.'

The other retorted, 'You are a dead man.'

Syme had gone quite red up to his yellow hair, and his eyes were burning feverishly. As he said, he had an intuition, and it had risen to a sort of light-headed certainty. Resuming his symbolic taps, he signalled to his friend, 'You scarcely realize how poetic my intuition is. It has that sudden quality we sometimes feel in the coming of spring.'

He then studied the answer on his friend's fingers. The answer was, 'Go to hell!'

The Professor then resumed his merely verbal monologue addressed to the Doctor.

'Perhaps I should rather say,' said Syme on his fingers, 'that it resembles that sudden smell of the sea which may be found in the heart of lush woods.'

His companion disdained to reply.

'Or yet again,' tapped Syme, 'it is positive, as is the passionate red hair of a beautiful woman.'

The Professor was continuing his speech, but in the middle of it Syme decided to act. He leant across the table, and said in a voice that could not be neglected –

'Dr Bull!'

The Doctor's sleek and smiling head did not move, but they could have sworn that under his dark glasses his eyes darted towards Syme.

'Dr Bull,' said Syme, in a voice peculiarly precise and courteous, 'would you do me a small favour? Would you be so kind as to take off your spectacles?'

The Professor swung round on his seat, and stared at Syme

with a sort of frozen fury of astonishment. Syme, like a man who has thrown his life and fortune on the table, leant forward with a fiery face. The Doctor did not move.

For a few seconds there was a silence in which one could hear a pin drop, split once by the single hoot of a distant steamer on the Thames. Then Dr Bull rose slowly, still smiling, and took off his spectacles.

Syme sprang to his feet, stepping backwards a little, like a chemical lecturer from a successful explosion. His eyes were like stars, and for an instant he could only point without speaking.

The Professor had also started to his feet, forgetful of his supposed paralysis. He leant on the back of the chair and stared doubtfully at Dr Bull, as if the Doctor had been turned into a toad before his eyes. And indeed it was almost as great a transformation scene.

The two detectives saw sitting in the chair before them a very boyish-looking young man, with very frank and happy hazel eyes, an open expression, Cockney clothes like those of a city clerk, and an unquestionable breath about him of being very good and rather commonplace. The smile was still there, but it might have been the first smile of a baby.

'I knew I was a poet,' cried Syme in a sort of ecstasy. 'I knew my intuition was as infallible as the Pope. It was the spectacles that did it! It was all the spectacles! Given those beastly black eyes, and all the rest of him, his health and his jolly looks, made him a live devil among dead ones.'

'It certainly does make a queer difference,' said the Professor shakily. 'But as regards the project of Dr Bull—'

'Project be damned!' roared Syme, beside himself. 'Look at him! Look at his face, look at his collar, look at his blessed boots! You don't suppose, do you, that that thing's an anarchist?'

'Syme!' cried the other in an apprehensive agony.

'Why, by God,' said Syme, 'I'll take the risk of that myself! Dr Bull, I am a police officer. There's my card,' and he flung down the blue card upon the table.

The Professor still feared that all was lost; but he was loyal. He pulled out his own official card and put it beside his friend's.

Then the third man burst out laughing, and for the first time that morning they heard his voice.

'I'm awfully glad you chaps have come so early,' he said, with a sort of schoolboy flippancy, 'for we can all start for France together. Yes, I'm in the force right enough,' and he flicked a blue card towards them lightly as a matter of form.

Clapping a brisk bowler on his head and resuming his goblin glasses, the Doctor moved so quickly towards the door that the others instinctively followed him. Syme seemed a little distrait, and as he passed under the doorway he suddenly struck his stick on the stone passage so that it rang.

'But Lord God Almighty,' he cried out, 'if this is all right, there were more damned detectives than there were damned dynamiters at the damned Council!'

'We might have fought easily,' said Bull; 'we were four against three.'

The Professor was descending the stairs, but his voice came up from below.

'No,' said the voice, 'we were not four against three – we were not so lucky. We were four against One.'

The others went down the stairs in silence.

The young man called Bull, with an innocent courtesy characteristic of him, insisted on going last until they reached the street; but there his own robust rapidity asserted itself unconsciously, and he walked quickly on ahead towards a railway inquiry office, talking to the others over his shoulder.

'It is jolly to get some pals,' he said. 'I've been half dead with the jumps, being quite alone. I nearly flung my arms round Gogol and embraced him, which would have been imprudent. I hope you won't despise me for having been in a blue funk.'

'All the blue devils in blue hell,'[8] said Syme, 'contributed to my blue funk! But the worst devil was you and your infernal goggles.'

The young man laughed delightedly.

'Wasn't it a rag?' he said. 'Such a simple idea – not my own. I haven't got the brains. You see, I wanted to go into the detective service, especially the anti-dynamite business. But for that purpose they wanted someone to dress up as a dynamiter; and they all swore by blazes that I could never look like a dynamiter. They said my walk was very respectable, and that seen from behind I looked like the British Constitution.[9] They said I looked too healthy and too optimistic, and too reliable and benevolent; they called me all sorts of names at Scotland Yard. They said that if I had been a criminal, I might have made my fortune by looking so like an honest man; but as I had the misfortune to be an honest man, there was not even the remotest chance of my assisting them by ever looking like a criminal. But at last I was brought before some old josser[10] who was high up in the force, and who seemed to have no end of a head on his shoulders. And there the others all talked hopelessly. One asked whether a bushy beard would hide my nice smile; another said that if they blacked my face I might look like a Negro anarchist; but this old chap chipped in with a most extraordinary remark. "A pair of smoked spectacles will do it," he said positively. "Look at him now; he looks like an angelic office boy. Put him on a pair of smoked spectacles, and children will scream at the sight of him." And so it was, by George! When once my eyes were covered all the rest, smile and big shoulders and short hair, made me look a perfect little devil. As I say, it was simple enough when it was done, like miracles; but that wasn't the really miraculous part of it. There was one really staggering thing about the business, and my head still turns at it.'

'What was that?' asked Syme.

'I'll tell you,' answered the man in spectacles. 'This big pot in the police who sized me up so that he knew how the goggles would go with my hair and socks – by God, he never saw me at all!'

Syme's eyes suddenly flashed on him.

'How was that?' he asked. 'I thought you talked to him.'

'So I did,' said Bull brightly; 'but we talked in a pitch-dark room like a coal cellar. There, you would never have guessed that.'

'I could not have conceived it,' said Syme gravely.

'It is indeed a new idea,' said the Professor.

Their new ally was in practical matters a whirlwind. At the inquiry office he asked with businesslike brevity about the trains for Dover. Having got his information, he bundled the company into a cab, and put them and himself inside a railway carriage before they had properly realized the breathless process. They were already on the Calais boat before conversation flowed freely.

'I had already arranged,' he explained, 'to go to France for my lunch; but I am delighted to have someone to lunch with me. You see, I had to send that beast, the Marquis, over with his bomb, because the President had his eye on me, though God knows how. I'll tell you the story some day. It was perfectly choking. Whenever I tried to slip out of it I saw the President somewhere, smiling out of the bow-window of a club or taking off his hat to me from the top of an omnibus. I tell you, you can say what you like, that fellow has sold himself to the devil; he can be in six places at once.'

'So you sent the Marquis off, I understand,' asked the Professor. 'Was it long ago? Shall we be in time to catch him?'

'Yes,' answered the new guide. 'I've timed it all. He'll still be at Calais when we arrive.'

'But when we do catch him at Calais,' said the Professor, 'what are we going to do?'

At this question the countenance of Dr Bull fell for the first time. He reflected a little, and then said –

'Theoretically, I suppose, we ought to call the police.'

'Not I,' said Syme. 'Theoretically I ought to drown myself first. I promised a poor fellow who was a real modern pessimist, on my word of honour not to tell the police. I'm no hand at casuistry, but I can't break my word to a modern pessimist. It's like breaking one's word to a child.'

'I'm in the same boat,' said the Professor. 'I tried to tell the police, and I couldn't because of some silly oath I took. You see, when I was an actor I was a sort of all-round beast. Perjury or treason is the only crime I haven't committed. If I did that I shouldn't know the difference between right and wrong.'

'I've been through all that,' said Dr Bull, 'and I've made up my mind. I gave my promise to the Secretary – you know him, man who smiles upside down. My friends, that man is the most utterly unhappy man that was ever human. It may be his

digestion, or his conscience, or his nerves, or his philosophy of
the universe, but he's damned, he's in hell! Well, I can't turn on
a man like that, and hunt him down. It's like whipping a leper.
I may be mad, but that's how I feel; and there's jolly well the
end of it.'

'I don't think you're mad,' said Syme. 'I knew you would
decide like that when first you—'

'Eh?' said Dr Bull.

'When you first took off your spectacles.'

Dr Bull smiled a little, and strolled across the deck to look at
the sunlit sea. Then he strolled back again, kicking his heels
carelessly, and a companionable silence fell between the three
men.

'Well,' said Syme, 'it seems that we have all the same kind of
morality or immorality, so we had better face the fact that comes
of it.'

'Yes,' assented the Professor, 'you're quite right; and we must
hurry up, for I can see the Grey Nose[11] standing out from France.'

'The fact that comes of it,' said Syme seriously, 'is this, that
we three are alone on this planet. Gogol has gone, God knows
where; perhaps the President has smashed him like a fly. On the
Council we are three men against three, like the Romans who
held the bridge.[12] But we are worse off than that, first because
they can appeal to their organization and we cannot appeal to
ours, and second because—'

'Because one of those other three men,' said the Professor, 'is
not a man.'

Syme nodded and was silent for a second or two, then he said:

'My idea is this. We must do something to keep the Marquis
in Calais till tomorrow midday. I have turned over twenty
schemes in my head. We cannot denounce him as a dynamiter;
that is agreed. We cannot get him detained on some trivial charge,
for we should have to appear; he knows us, and he would smell
a rat. We cannot pretend to keep him on anarchist business; he
might swallow much in that way, but not the notion of stopping
in Calais while the Czar went safely through Paris. We might
try to kidnap him, and lock him up ourselves; but he is a well-
known man here. He has a whole bodyguard of friends; he is

very strong and brave, and the event is doubtful. The only thing I can see to do is actually to take advantage of the very things that are in the Marquis's favour. I am going to profit by the fact that he is a highly respected nobleman. I am going to profit by the fact that he has many friends and moves in the best society.'

'What the devil are you talking about?' asked the Professor.

'The Symes are first mentioned in the fourteenth century,' said Syme; 'but there is a tradition that one of them rode behind Bruce at Bannockburn.[13] Since 1350 the tree is quite clear.'

'He's gone off his head,' said the little Doctor, staring.

'Our bearings,' continued Syme calmly, 'are "argent a chevron gules charged with three cross crosslets of the field".[14] The motto varies.'

The Professor seized Syme roughly by the waistcoat.

'We are just inshore,' he said. 'Are you seasick or joking in the wrong place?'

'My remarks are almost painfully practical,' answered Syme, in an unhurried manner. 'The house of St Eustache also is very ancient. The Marquis cannot deny that he is a gentleman. He cannot deny that I am a gentleman. And in order to put the matter of my social position quite beyond a doubt, I propose at the earliest opportunity to knock his hat off. But here we are in the harbour.'

They went on shore under the strong sun in a sort of daze. Syme, who had now taken the lead as Bull had taken it in London, led them along a kind of marine parade until he came to some cafés, embowered in a bulk of greenery and overlooking the sea. As he went before them his step was slightly swaggering, and he swung his stick like a sword. He was making apparently for the extreme end of the line of cafés, but he stopped abruptly. With a sharp gesture he motioned them to silence, but he pointed with one gloved finger to a café table under a bank of flowering foliage at which sat the Marquis de St Eustache, his teeth shining in his thick, black beard, and his bold, brown face shadowed by a light yellow straw hat and outlined against the violet sea.

10

The Duel

Syme sat down at a café table with his companions, his blue eyes sparkling like the bright sea below, and ordered a bottle of Saumur[1] with a pleased impatience. He was for some reason in a condition of curious hilarity. His spirits were already unnaturally high; they rose as the Saumur sank, and in half an hour his talk was a torrent of nonsense. He professed to be making out a plan of the conversation which was going to ensue between himself and the deadly Marquis. He jotted it down wildly with a pencil. It was arranged like a printed catechism, with questions and answers, and was delivered with an extraordinary rapidity of utterance.

'I shall approach. Before taking off his hat, I shall take off my own. I shall say, "The Marquis de Saint Eustache, I believe." He will say, "The celebrated Mr Syme, I presume." He will say in the most exquisite French, "How are you?" I shall reply in the most exquisite Cockney, "Oh, just the Syme."'

'Oh, shut it,' said the man in spectacles. 'Pull yourself together, and chuck away that bit of paper. What are you really going to do?'

'But it was a lovely catechism,' said Syme pathetically. 'Do let me read it you. It has only forty-three questions and answers, and some of the Marquis's answers are wonderfully witty. I like to be just to my enemy.'

'But what's the good of it all?' asked Dr Bull in exasperation.

'It leads up to my challenge, don't you see,' said Syme, beaming. 'When the Marquis has given the thirty-ninth reply, which runs—'

'Has it by any chance occurred to you,' asked the Professor, with a ponderous simplicity, 'that the Marquis may not say all the forty-three things you have put down for him? In that case, I understand, your own epigrams may appear somewhat more forced.'

Syme struck the table with a radiant face.

'Why, how true that is,' he said, 'and I never thought of it. Sir, you have an intellect beyond the common. You will make a name.'

'Oh, you're as drunk as an owl!' said the Doctor.

'It only remains,' continued Syme quite unperturbed, 'to adopt some other method of breaking the ice (if I may so express it) between myself and the man I wish to kill. And since the course of a dialogue cannot be predicted by one of its parties alone (as you have pointed out with such recondite acumen), the only thing to be done, I suppose, is for the one party, as far as possible, to do all the dialogue by himself. And so I will, by George!' And he stood up suddenly, his yellow hair blowing in the slight sea breeze.

A band was playing in a *café chantant*[2] hidden somewhere among the trees, and a woman had just stopped singing. On Syme's heated head the bray of the brass band seemed like the jar and jingle of that barrel-organ in Leicester Square, to the tune of which he had once stood up to die. He looked across to the little table where the Marquis sat. The man had two companions now, solemn Frenchmen in frock-coats and silk hats, one of them with the red rosette of the Legion of Honour,[3] evidently people of a solid social position. Beside these black, cylindrical costumes, the Marquis, in his loose straw hat and light spring clothes, looked Bohemian and even barbaric; but he looked the Marquis. Indeed, one might say that he looked the king, with his animal elegance, his scornful eyes, and his proud head lifted against the purple sea. But he was no Christian king, at any rate; he was, rather, some swarthy despot, half Greek, half Asiatic, who in the days when slavery seemed natural looked down on the Mediterranean, on his galley and his groaning slaves. Just so, Syme thought, would the brown-gold face of such a tyrant have shown against the dark green olives and the burning blue.

'Are you going to address the meeting?' asked the Professor peevishly, seeing that Syme still stood up without moving.

Syme drained his last glass of sparkling wine.

'I am,' he said, pointing across to the Marquis and his companions, 'that meeting. That meeting displeases me. I am going to pull that meeting's great ugly, mahogany-coloured nose.'

He stepped across swiftly, if not quite steadily. The Marquis, seeing him, arched his black Assyrian eyebrows in surprise, but smiled politely.

'You are Mr Syme, I think,' he said.

Syme bowed.

'And you are the Marquis de Saint Eustache,' he said, gracefully. 'Permit me to pull your nose.'

He leant over to do so, but the Marquis started backwards, upsetting his chair, and the two men in top hats held Syme back by the shoulders.

'This man has insulted me!' said Syme, with gestures of explanation.

'Insulted you?' cried the gentleman with the red rosette. 'When?'

'Oh, just now,' said Syme recklessly. 'He insulted my mother.'

'Insulted your mother!' exclaimed the gentleman incredulously.

'Well, anyhow,' said Syme, conceding a point, 'my aunt.'

'But how can the Marquis have insulted your aunt just now?' said the second gentleman with some legitimate wonder. 'He has been sitting here all the time.'

'Ah, it was what he said!' said Syme darkly.

'I said nothing at all,' said the Marquis, 'except something about the band. I only said that I liked Wagner played well.'

'It was an allusion to my family,' said Syme firmly. 'My aunt played Wagner badly. It was a painful subject. We are always being insulted about it.'

'This seems most extraordinary,' said the gentleman who was décoré,[4] looking doubtfully at the Marquis.

'Oh, I assure you,' said Syme earnestly, 'the whole of your conversation was simply packed with sinister allusions to my aunt's weaknesses.'

'This is nonsense!' said the second gentleman. 'I for one have

said nothing for half an hour except that I liked the singing of
that girl with black hair.'

'Well, there you are again!' said Syme indignantly. 'My aunt's
was red.'

'It seems to me,' said the other, 'that you are simply seeking
a pretext to insult the Marquis.'

'By George!' said Syme, facing round and looking at him.
'What a clever chap you are!'

The Marquis started up with eyes flaming like a tiger's.

'Seeking a quarrel with me!' he cried. 'Seeking a fight with
me! By God! there was never a man who had to seek long. These
gentlemen will perhaps act for me. There are still four hours of
daylight. Let us fight this evening.'

Syme bowed with a beautiful graciousness.

'Marquis,' he said, 'your action is worthy of your fame and
blood. Permit me to consult for a moment with the gentlemen
in whose hands I shall place myself.'

In three long strides he rejoined his companions, and they,
who had seen his champagne-inspired attack and listened to his
idiotic explanations, were quite startled at the look of him. For
now that he came back to them he was quite sober, a little pale,
and he spoke in a low voice of passionate practicality.

'I have done it,' he said hoarsely. 'I have fixed a fight on the
beast. But look here, and listen carefully. There is no time for
talk. You are my seconds, and everything must come from you.
Now you must insist, and insist absolutely, on the duel coming
off after seven tomorrow, so as to give me the chance of pre-
venting him from catching the 7.45 for Paris. If he misses that
he misses his crime. He can't refuse to meet you on such a small
point of time and place. But this is what he will do. He will
choose a field somewhere near a wayside station, where he can
pick up the train. He is a very good swordsman, and he will
trust to killing me in time to catch it. But I can fence well too,
and I think I can keep him in play, at any rate, until the train
is lost. Then perhaps he may kill me to console his feelings.
You understand! Very well, then, let me introduce you to some
charming friends of mine,' and leading them quickly across the
parade, he presented them to the Marquis's seconds by two

very aristocratic names of which they had not previously heard.

Syme was subject to spasms of singular common sense, not otherwise a part of his character. They were (as he said of his impulse about the spectacles) poetic intuitions, and they sometimes rose to the exaltation of prophecy.

He had correctly calculated in this case the policy of his opponent. When the Marquis was informed by his seconds that Syme could only fight in the morning, he must fully have realized that an obstacle had suddenly arisen between him and his bomb-throwing business in the capital. Naturally he could not explain this objection to his friends, so he chose the course which Syme had predicted. He induced his seconds to settle on a small meadow not far from the railway, and he trusted to the fatality of the first engagement.

When he came down very coolly to the field of honour, no one could have guessed that he had any anxiety about a journey; his hands were in his pockets, his straw hat on the back of his head, his handsome face brazen in the sun. But it might have struck a stranger as odd that there appeared in his train, not only his seconds carrying the sword-case, but two of his servants carrying a portmanteau and a luncheon basket.

Early as was the hour, the sun soaked everything in warmth, and Syme was vaguely surprised to see so many spring flowers burning gold and silver in the tall grass in which the whole company stood almost knee-deep.

With the exception of the Marquis, all the men were in sombre and solemn morning-dress, with hats like black chimney-pots; the little Doctor especially, with the addition of his black spectacles, looked like an undertaker in a farce. Syme could not help feeling a comic contrast between this funereal church parade of apparel and the rich and glistening meadow, growing wild flowers everywhere. But, indeed, this comic contrast between the yellow blossoms and the black hats was but a symbol of the tragic contrast between the yellow blossoms and the black business. On his right was a little wood; far away to his left lay the long curve of the railway line which he was, so to speak, guarding from the Marquis, whose goal and escape it was. In front of him, behind the black groups of his opponents, he could see, like a tinted cloud, a small almond bush in flower against the faint line of the sea.

The member of the Legion of Honour, whose name it seemed was Colonel Ducroix, approached the Professor and Dr Bull with great politeness, and suggested that the play should terminate with the first considerable hurt.

Dr Bull, however, having been carefully coached by Syme upon this point of policy, insisted, with great dignity and in very bad French, that it should continue until one of the combatants was disabled. Syme had made up his mind that he could avoid disabling the Marquis and prevent the Marquis from disabling him for at least twenty minutes. In twenty minutes the Paris train would have gone by.

'To a man of the well-known skill and valour of Monsieur de St Eustache,' said the Professor solemnly, 'it must be a matter of indifference which method is adopted, and our principal has strong reasons for demanding the longer encounter, reasons the delicacy of which prevent me from being explicit, but for the just and honourable nature of which I can—'

'*Peste!*'[5] broke from the Marquis behind, whose face had suddenly darkened, 'let us stop talking and begin,' and he slashed off the head of a tall flower with his stick.

Syme understood his rude impatience, and instinctively looked over his shoulder to see whether the train was coming in sight. But there was no smoke on the horizon.

Colonel Ducroix knelt down and unlocked the case, taking out a pair of twin swords, which took the sunlight and turned to two streaks of white fire. He offered one to the Marquis, who snatched it without ceremony, and another to Syme, who took it, bent it, and poised it with as much delay as was consistent with dignity. Then the Colonel took out another pair of blades, and taking one himself and giving another to Dr Bull, proceeded to place the men.

Both combatants had thrown off their coats and waistcoats and stood sword in hand. The seconds stood on each side of the line of fight with drawn swords also, but still sombre in their dark frock-coats and hats. The principals saluted. The Colonel said quietly, 'Engage!' and the two blades touched and tingled.

When the jar of the joined iron ran up Syme's arm, all the fantastic fears that had been the subject of this story fell from him like dreams from a man waking up in bed. He remembered them clearly and in order as mere delusions of the nerves – how the fear of the Professor had been the fear of the tyrannic accidents of nightmare, and how the fear of the Doctor had been the fear of the airless vacuum of science. The first was the old fear that any miracle might happen, the second the more hopeless modern fear that no miracle can ever happen. But he saw that these fears were fancies, for he found himself in the presence of the great fact of the fear of death, with its coarse and pitiless common sense. He felt like a man who had dreamed all night of falling over precipices, and had woken up on the morning when he was to be hanged. For as soon as he had seen the sunlight run down the channel of his foe's foreshortened blade, and as soon as he had felt the two tongues of steel touch, vibrating like two living things, he knew that his enemy was a terrible fighter, and that probably his last hour had come.

He felt a strange and vivid value in all the earth around him, in the grass under his feet; he felt the love of life in all living things. He could almost fancy that he heard the grass growing; he could almost fancy that even as he stood fresh flowers were springing up and breaking into blossom in the meadow – flowers blood-red and burning gold and blue, fulfilling the whole pageant of the spring. And whenever his eyes strayed for a flash from the calm, staring, hypnotic eyes of the Marquis, they saw the little tuft of almond tree against the skyline. He had the feeling that if by some miracle he escaped he would be ready to sit for ever before that almond tree, desiring nothing else in the world.

But while earth and sky and everything had the living beauty of a thing lost, the other half of his head was as clear as glass, and he was parrying his enemy's point with a kind of clockwork skill of which he had hardly supposed himself capable. Once his enemy's point ran along his wrist, leaving a slight streak of blood, but it either was not noticed or was tacitly ignored. Every now and then he *riposted*, and once or twice he could almost fancy that he felt his point go home, but as there was no blood on

blade or shirt he supposed he was mistaken. Then came an
interruption and a change.

At the risk of losing all, the Marquis, interrupting his quiet
stare, flashed one glance over his shoulder at the line of railway
on his right. Then he turned on Syme a face transfigured to that
of a fiend, and began to fight as if with twenty weapons. The
attack came so fast and furious that the one shining sword
seemed a shower of shining arrows. Syme had no chance to look
at the railway; but also he had no need. He could guess the
reason of the Marquis's sudden madness of battle – the Paris
train was in sight.

But the Marquis's morbid energy overreached itself. Twice
Syme, parrying, knocked his opponent's point far out of the
fighting circle; and the third time his *riposte* was so rapid that
there was no doubt about the hit this time. Syme's sword actually
bent under the weight of the Marquis's body, which it had
pierced. Syme was as certain that he had stuck his blade into his
enemy as a gardener that he has stuck his spade into the ground.
Yet the Marquis sprang back from the stroke without a stagger,
and Syme stood staring at his own sword-point like an idiot.
There was no blood on it at all.

There was an instant of rigid silence, and then Syme in his
turn fell furiously on the other, filled with a flaming curiosity.
The Marquis was probably, in a general sense, a better fencer
than he, as he had surmised at the beginning, but at the moment
the Marquis seemed distraught and at a disadvantage. He fought
wildly and even weakly, and he constantly looked away at the
railway line, almost as if he feared the train more than the
pointed steel. Syme, on the other hand, fought fiercely but still
carefully, in an intellectual fury, eager to solve the riddle of his
own bloodless sword. For this purpose, he aimed less at the
Marquis's body, and more at his throat and head. A minute and
a half afterwards he felt his point enter the man's neck below
the jaw. It came out clean. Half mad, he thrust again, and made
what should have been a bloody scar on the Marquis's cheek.
But there was no scar.

For one moment the heaven of Syme again grew black with
supernatural terrors. Surely the man had a charmed life. But this

new spiritual dread was a more awful thing than had been the
mere spiritual topsy-turvydom symbolized by the paralytic who
pursued him. The Professor was only a goblin; this man was a
devil – perhaps he was the Devil! Anyhow, this was certain, that
three times had a human sword been driven into him and made
no mark. When Syme had that thought he drew himself up, and
all that was good in him sang high up in the air as a high wind
sings in the trees. He thought of all the human things in his story
– of the Chinese lanterns in Saffron Park, of the girl's red hair
in the garden, of the honest, beer-swilling sailors down by the
dock, of his loyal companions standing by. Perhaps he had been
chosen as a champion of all these fresh and kindly things to
cross swords with the enemy of all creation. 'After all,' he said
to himself, 'I am more than a devil; I am a man. I can do the one
thing which Satan himself cannot do – I can die,' and as the
word went through his head, he heard a faint and far-off hoot,
which would soon be the roar of the Paris train.

He fell to fighting again with a supernatural levity, like a
Mohammedan panting for Paradise. As the train came nearer
and nearer he fancied he could see people putting up the floral
arches in Paris; he joined in the growing noise and the glory of
the great Republic whose gate he was guarding against Hell. His
thoughts rose higher and higher with the rising roar of the train,
which ended, as if proudly, in a long and piercing whistle. The
train stopped.

Suddenly, to the astonishment of everyone, the Marquis sprang
back quite out of sword reach and threw down his sword. The
leap was wonderful, and not the less wonderful because Syme
had plunged his sword a moment before into the man's thigh.

'Stop!' said the Marquis in a voice that compelled a momentary
obedience. 'I want to say something.'

'What is the matter?' asked Colonel Ducroix, staring. 'Has
there been foul play?'

'There has been foul play somewhere,' said Dr Bull, who was
a little pale. 'Our principal has wounded the Marquis four times
at least, and he is none the worse.'

The Marquis put up his hand with a curious air of ghastly
patience.

'Please let me speak,' he said. 'It is rather important. Mr Syme,' he continued, turning to his opponent, 'we are fighting today, if I remember right, because you expressed a wish (which I thought irrational) to pull my nose. Would you oblige me by pulling my nose now as quickly as possible? I have to catch a train.'

'I protest that this is most irregular,' said Dr Bull indignantly.

'It is certainly somewhat opposed to precedent,' said Colonel Ducroix, looking wistfully at his principal. 'There is, I think, one case on record (Captain Bellegarde and the Baron Zumpt) in which the weapons were changed in the middle of the encounter at the request of one of the combatants. But one can hardly call one's nose a weapon.'

'Will you or will you not pull my nose?' said the Marquis in exasperation. 'Come, come, Mr Syme! You wanted to do it; do it! You can have no conception of how important it is to me. Don't be selfish! Pull my nose at once, when I ask you!' and he bent slightly forward with a fascinating smile. The Paris train, panting and groaning, had grated into a little station behind the neighbouring hill.

Syme had the feeling he had more than once had in these adventures – the sense that a horrible and sublime wave lifted to heaven was just toppling over. Walking in a world he half understood, he took two paces forward and seized the Roman nose of this remarkable nobleman. He pulled it hard, and it came off in his hand.

He stood for some seconds with a foolish solemnity, with the pasteboard proboscis still between his fingers, looking at it, while the sun and the clouds and the wooden hills looked down upon this imbecile scene.

The Marquis broke the silence in a loud and cheerful voice.

'If anyone has any use for my left eyebrow,' he said, 'he can have it. Colonel Ducroix, do accept my left eyebrow! It's the kind of thing that might come in useful any day,' and he gravely tore off one of his swarthy Assyrian brows, bringing about half his brown forehead with it, and politely offered it to the Colonel, who stood crimson and speechless with rage.

'If I had known,' he spluttered, 'that I was acting for a poltroon who pads himself to fight—'

'Oh, I know, I know!' said the Marquis, recklessly throwing various parts of himself right and left about the field. 'You are making a mistake; but it can't be explained just now. I tell you the train has come into the station!'

'Yes,' said Dr Bull fiercely, 'and the train shall go out of the station. It shall go out without you. We know well enough for what devil's work—'

The mysterious Marquis lifted his hands with a desperate gesture. He was a strange scarecrow, standing there in the sun with half his old face peeled off, and half another face glaring and grinning from underneath.

'Will you drive me mad?' he cried. 'The train—'

'You shall not go by the train,' said Syme firmly, and grasped his sword.

The wild figure turned towards Syme, and seemed to be gathering itself for a sublime effort before speaking.

'You great fat, blasted, blear-eyed, blundering, thundering, brainless, God-forsaken, doddering, damned fool!' he said without taking breath. 'You great silly, pink-faced tow-headed turnip! You—'

'You shall not go by this train,' repeated Syme.

'And why the infernal blazes,' roared the other, 'should I want to go by this train?'

'We know all,' said the Professor sternly. 'You are going to Paris to throw a bomb!'

'Going to Jericho to throw a Jabberwock!'[6] cried the other, tearing his hair, which came off easily. 'Have you all got softening of the brain, that you don't realize what I am? Did you really think I wanted to catch that train? Twenty Paris trains might go by for me. Damn Paris trains!'

'Then what did you care about?' began the Professor.

'What did I care about? I didn't care about catching the train; I cared about whether the train caught me, and now, by God! it has caught me.'

'I regret to inform you,' said Syme with restraint, 'that your remarks convey no impression to my mind. Perhaps if you were to remove the remains of your original forehead and some portions of what was once your chin, your meaning would become clearer. Mental lucidity fulfils itself in many ways. What do you mean by saying that the train has caught you? It may be my literary fancy, but somehow I feel that it ought to mean something.'

'It means everything,' said the other, 'and the end of everything. Sunday has us now in the hollow of his hand.'

'Us!' repeated the Professor, as if stupefied. 'What do you mean by "us"?'

'The police, of course!' said the Marquis, and tore off his scalp and half his face.

The head which emerged was the blond, well-brushed, smooth-haired head which is common in the English contabulary, but the face was terribly pale.

'I am Inspector Ratcliffe,' he said, with a sort of haste that verged on harshness. 'My name is pretty well known to the police, and I can see well enough that you belong to them. But if there is any doubt about my position, I have a card –' and he began to pull a blue card from his pocket.

The Professor gave a tired gesture.

'Oh, don't show it us,' he said wearily; 'we've got enough of them to equip a paper-chase.'[7]

The little man named Bull had, like many men who seem to be of a mere vivacious vulgarity, sudden movements of good taste. Here he certainly saved the situation. In the midst of this staggering transformation scene he stepped forward with all the gravity and responsibility of a second, and addressed the two seconds of the Marquis.

'Gentlemen,' he said, 'we all owe you a serious apology; but I assure you that you have not been made the victims of such a low joke as you imagine, or indeed of anything undignified in a man of honour. You have not wasted your time; you have helped to save the world. We are not buffoons, but very desperate men at war with a vast conspiracy. A secret society of anarchists is hunting us like hares; not such unfortunate madmen as may here or there throw a bomb through starvation or German philosophy but a rich and powerful and fanatical church, a church of eastern pessimism, which holds it holy to destroy mankind like vermin. How hard they hunt us you can gather from the fact that we are driven to such disguises as those for which I apologize, and to such pranks as this one by which you suffer.'

The younger second of the Marquis, a short man with a black moustache, bowed politely, and said:

'Of course, I accept the apology; but you will in your turn forgive me if I decline to follow you further into your difficulties, and permit myself to say good morning! The sight of an acquaintance and distinguished fellow-townsman coming to pieces in the open air is unusual, and, upon the whole, sufficient for one day. Colonel Ducroix, I would in no way influence your actions, but if you feel with me that our present society is a little abnormal, I am now going to walk back to the town.'

Colonel Ducroix moved mechanically, but then tugged abruptly at his white moustache and broke out:

'No, by George, I won't! If these gentlemen are really in a mess with a lot of low wreckers like that, I'll see them through it. I have fought for France, and it is hard if I can't fight for civilization.'

Dr Bull took off his hat and waved it, cheering as at a public meeting.

'Don't make too much noise,' said Inspector Ratcliffe, 'Sunday may hear you.'

'Sunday!' cried Bull, and dropped his hat.

'Yes,' retorted Ratcliffe, 'he may be with them.'

'With whom?' asked Syme.

'With the people out of that train,' said the other.

'What you say seems utterly wild,' began Syme. 'Why, as a matter of fact – But, my God,' he cried out suddenly, like a man who sees an explosion a long way off, 'by God! if this is true the whole bally lot of us on the Anarchist Council were against anarchy! Every born man was a detective except the President and his personal secretary. What can it mean?'

'Mean!' said the new policeman with incredible violence. 'It means that we are struck dead! Don't you know Sunday? Don't you know that his jokes are always so big and simple that one had never thought of them? Can you think of anything more like Sunday than this, that he should put all his powerful enemies on the Supreme Council, and then take care that it was not supreme? I tell you he has bought every trust, he has captured every cable, he has control of every railway line – especially of that railway line!' and he pointed a shaking finger towards the small wayside station. 'The whole movement was controlled by him; half the world was ready to rise for him. But there were just five people, perhaps, who would have resisted him . . . and the old devil put them on the Supreme Council, to waste their time in watching each other. Idiots that we are, he planned the whole of our idiocies! Sunday knew that the Professor would chase Syme through London, and that Syme would fight me in France. And he was combining great masses of capital, and seizing great lines of telegraphy, while we idiots were running after each other like a lot of confounded babies playing blind man's buff.'[8]

'Well!' asked Syme with a sort of steadiness,

'Well,' replied the other with sudden serenity, 'he has found us playing blind man's buff today in a field of great rustic beauty and extreme solitude. He has probably captured the world; it only remains to him to capture this field and all the fools in it. And since you really want to know what was my objection to the arrival of that train, I will tell you. My objection was that Sunday or his Secretary has just this moment got out of it.'

Syme uttered an involuntary cry, and they all turned their eyes towards the far-off station. It was quite true that a considerable bulk of people seemed to be moving in their direction. But they were too distant to be distinguished in any way.

'It was a habit of the late Marquis de St Eustache,' said the new policeman, producing a leather case, 'always to carry a pair of opera glasses. Either the President or the Secretary is coming after us with that mob. They have caught us in a nice quiet place where we are under no temptations to break our oaths by calling the police. Dr Bull, I have a suspicion that you will see better through these than through your own highly decorative spectacles.'

He handed the field-glasses to the Doctor, who immediately took off his spectacles and put the apparatus to his eyes.

'It cannot be as bad as you say,' said the Professor, somewhat shaken. 'There are a good number of them certainly, but they may easily be ordinary tourists.'

'Do ordinary tourists,' asked Bull, with the field-glass to his eyes, 'wear black masks half-way down the face?'

Syme almost tore the glasses out of his hand, and looked through them. Most men in the advancing mob really looked ordinary enough; but it was quite true that two or three of the leaders in front wore black half-masks almost down to their mouths. This disguise is very complete, especially at such a distance, and Syme found it impossible to conclude anything from the clean-shaven jaws and chins of the men talking in the front. But presently as they talked they all smiled, and one of them smiled on one side.

11

The Criminals Chase the Police

Syme put the field-glass from his eyes with an almost ghastly relief.

'The President is not with them, anyhow,' he said, and wiped his forehead.

'But surely they are right away on the horizon,' said the bewildered Colonel, blinking and but half recovered from Bull's hasty though polite explanation. 'Could you possibly know your President among all those people?'

'Could I know a white elephant among all those people!' answered Syme, somewhat irritably. 'As you very truly say, they are on the horizon; but if he were walking with them ... by God! I believe this ground would shake.'

After an instant's pause the new man called Ratcliffe said with gloomy decision:

'Of course the President isn't with them. I wish to Gemini he were. Much more likely the President is riding in triumph through Paris, or sitting on the ruins of St Paul's Cathedral.'

'This is absurd!' said Syme. 'Something may have happened in our absence: but he cannot have carried the world with a rush like that. It is quite true,' he added, frowning dubiously at the distant fields that lay towards the little station, 'it is certainly true that there seems to be a crowd coming this way; but they are not all the army that you make out.'

'Oh, they,' said the new detective contemptuously; 'no, they are not a very valuable force. But let me tell you frankly that they are precisely calculated to our value – we are not much, my boy, in Sunday's universe. He has got hold of all the cables and telegraphs himself. But to kill the Supreme Council he regards as a trivial matter, like a postcard; it may be left to his private secretary,' and he spat on the grass.

Then he turned to the others and said somewhat austerely:

'There is a great deal to be said for death; but if anyone has any preference for the other alternative, I strongly advise him to walk after me.'

With those words, he turned his broad back and strode with silent energy towards the wood. The others gave one glance over their shoulders, and saw that the dark cloud of men had detached itself from the station and was moving with a mysterious discipline across the plain. They saw already, even with the naked eye, black dots on the foremost faces, which marked the masks they wore. They turned and followed their leader, who had already struck the wood, and disappeared among the twinkling trees.

The sun on the grass was dry and hot. So in plunging into the wood they had a cool shock of shadow, as of divers who plunge into a dim pool. The inside of the wood was full of shattered sunlight and shaken shadows. They made a sort of shuddering veil, almost recalling the dizziness of a cinematograph.[1] Even the solid figures walking with him Syme could hardly see for the patterns of sun and shade that danced upon them. Now a man's head was lit as with a light of Rembrandt, leaving all else obliterated; now again he had strong and staring white hands with the face of a Negro. The ex-Marquis had pulled the old straw hat over his eyes, and the black shade of the brim cut his face so squarely in two that it seemed to be wearing one of the black half-masks of their pursuers. The fancy tinted Syme's overwhelming sense of wonder. Was he wearing a mask? Was anyone wearing a mask? Was anyone anything? This wood of witchery, in which men's faces turned black and white by turns, in which their figures first swelled into sunlight and then faded into formless night, this mere chaos of chiaroscuro (after the clear daylight outside) seemed to Syme a perfect symbol of the world in which he had been moving for three days, this world where men took off their beards and their spectacles and their noses, and turned into other people. That tragic self-confidence which he had felt when he believed that the Marquis was a devil had strangely disappeared now that he knew that the Marquis

was a friend. He felt almost inclined to ask after all these be-
wilderments what was a friend and what an enemy. Was there
anything that was apart from what it seemed? The Marquis had
taken off his nose and turned out to be a detective. Might he
not just as well take off his head and turn out to be a hobgoblin?
Was not everything, after all, like this bewildering woodland,
this dance of dark and light? Everything only a glimpse, the
glimpse always unforeseen, and always forgotten. For Gabriel
Syme had found in the heart of that sun-splashed wood what
many modern painters had found there. He had found the thing
which the modern people call Impressionism,[2] which is another
name for that final scepticism which can find no floor to the
universe.

As a man in an evil dream strains himself to scream and wake,
Syme strove with a sudden effort to fling off this last and worst
of his fancies. With two impatient strides he overtook the man
in the Marquis's straw hat, the man whom he had come to
address as Ratcliffe. In a voice exaggeratively loud and cheerful,
he broke the bottomless silence and made conversation.

'May I ask,' he said, 'where on earth we are all going to?'

So genuine had been the doubts of his soul that he was quite
glad to hear his companion speak in an easy human voice.

'We must get down through the town of Lancy[3] to the sea,'
he said, 'I think that part of the country is least likely to be with
them.'

'What can you mean by all this?' cried Syme. 'They can't be
running the real world in that way. Surely not many working
men are anarchists, and surely, if they were, mere mobs could
not beat modern armies and police!'

'Mere mobs!' repeated his new friend with a snort of scorn.
'So you talk about mobs and the working classes as if they
were the question. You've got that eternal idiotic idea that if
anarchy came it would come from the poor. Why should it?
The poor have been rebels, but they have never been anarchists:
they have more interest than anyone else in there being some
decent government. The poor man really has a stake in the
country. The rich man hasn't; he can go away to New Guinea
in a yacht. The poor have sometimes objected to being governed

badly; the rich have always objected to being governed at all. Aristocrats were always anarchists, as you can see from the barons' wars.'[4]

'As a lecture on English history for the little ones,' said Syme, 'this is all very nice, but I have not yet grasped its application.'

'Its application is,' said his informant, 'that most of old Sunday's right-hand men are South African and American millionaires. That is why he has got hold of the communications; and that is why the last four champions of the anti-anarchist police force are running through a wood like rabbits.'

'Millionaires I can understand,' said Syme thoughtfully, 'they are nearly all mad. But getting hold of a few wicked old gentlemen with hobbies is one thing; getting hold of great Christian nations is another. I would bet the nose off my face (forgive the allusion) that Sunday would stand perfectly helpless before the task of converting any ordinary healthy person anywhere.'

'Well,' said the other, 'it rather depends what sort of person you mean.'

'Well, for instance,' said Syme, 'we could never convert that person,' and he pointed straight in front of him.

They had come to an open space of sunlight, which seemed to express to Syme the final return of his own good sense; and in the middle of this forest clearing was a figure that might well stand for that common sense in an almost awful actuality. Burnt by the sun and stained with perspiration, and grave with the bottomless gravity of small necessary toils, a heavy French peasant was cutting wood with a hatchet. His cart stood a few yards off, already full of timber; and the horse that cropped the grass was, like his master, valorous but not desperate; like his master, he was even prosperous, but yet was almost sad. The man was a Norman, taller than the average of the French and very angular; and his swarthy figure stood dark against a square of sunlight, almost like some allegoric figure of labour frescoed on a ground of gold.

'Mr Syme is saying,' called out Ratcliffe to the French Colonel, 'that this man, at least, will never be an anarchist.'

'Mr Syme is right enough there,' answered Colonel Ducroix, laughing, 'if only for the reason that he has plenty of property

to defend. But I forgot that in your country you are not used to
peasants being wealthy.'

'He looks poor,' said Dr Bull doubtfully.

'Quite so,' said the Colonel; 'that is why he is rich.'

'I have an idea,' called out Dr Bull suddenly; 'how much would
he take to give us a lift in his cart? Those dogs are all on foot,
and we could soon leave them behind.'

'Oh, give him anything!' said Syme eagerly. 'I have piles of
money on me.'

'That will never do,' said the Colonel; 'he will never have any
respect for you unless you drive a bargain.'

'Oh, if he haggles!' began Bull impatiently.

'He haggles because he is a free man,' said the other. 'You do
not understand; he would not see the meaning of generosity. He
is not being tipped.'

And even while they seemed to hear the very feet of their
strange pursuers behind them, they had to stand and stamp while
the French Colonel talked to the French woodcutter with all the
leisurely badinage and bickering of market-day. At the end of
four minutes, however, they saw that the Colonel was right, for
the woodcutter entered into their plans, not with the vague
servility of a tout too well paid, but with the seriousness of a
solicitor who had been paid the proper fee. He told them that
the best thing they could do was to make their way down to the
little inn on the hills above Lancy, where the innkeeper, an old
soldier who had become *dévot*⁵ in his latter years, would be
certain to sympathize with them, and even to take risks in their
support. The whole company, therefore, piled themselves on top
of the stacks of wood, and went rocking in the rude cart down
the other and steeper side of the woodland. Heavy and ram-
shackle as was the vehicle, it was driven quickly enough,
and they soon had the exhilarating impression of distancing
altogether those, whoever they were, who were hunting them.
For, after all, the riddle as to where the anarchists had got all
these followers was still unsolved. One man's presence had
sufficed for them; they had fled at the first sight of the deformed
smile of the Secretary. Syme every now and then looked back
over his shoulder at the army on their track.

As the wood grew first thinner and then smaller with distance, he could see the sunlit slopes beyond it and above it; and across these was still moving the square black mob like one monstrous beetle. In the very strong sunlight and with his own very strong eyes, which were almost telescopic, Syme could see this mass of men quite plainly. He could see them as separate human figures; but he was increasingly surprised by the way in which they moved as one man. They seemed to be dressed in dark clothes and plain hats, like any common crowd out of the streets; but they did not spread and sprawl and trail by various lines to the attack, as would be natural in an ordinary mob. They moved with a sort of dreadful and wicked woodenness, like a staring army of automatons.

Syme pointed this out to Ratcliffe.

'Yes,' replied the policeman, 'that's discipline. That's Sunday. He is perhaps five hundred miles off, but the fear of him is on all of them, like the finger of God. Yes, they are walking regularly; and you bet your boots that they are talking regularly, yes, and thinking regularly. But the one important thing for us is that they are disappearing regularly.'

Syme nodded. It was true that the black patch of the pursuing men was growing smaller and smaller as the peasant belaboured his horse.

The level of the sunlit landscape, though flat as a whole, fell away on the farther side of the wood in billows of heavy slope towards the sea, in a way not unlike the lower slope of the Sussex downs. The only difference was that in Sussex the road would have been broken and angular like a little brook, but here the white French road fell sheer in front of them like a waterfall. Down this direct descent the cart clattered at a considerable angle, and in a few minutes, the road growing yet steeper, they saw below them the little harbour of Lancy and a great blue arc of the sea. The travelling cloud of their enemies had wholly disappeared from the horizon.

The horse and cart took a sharp turn round a clump of elms, and the horse's nose nearly struck the face of an old gentleman who was sitting on the benches outside the little café of 'Le Soleil d'Or'.[6] The peasant grunted an apology, and got down from his seat. The others also descended one by one, and spoke to the old gentleman with fragmentary phrases of courtesy, for it was quite evident from his expansive manner that he was the owner of the little tavern.

He was a white-haired, apple-faced old boy, with sleepy eyes and a grey moustache; stout, sedentary, and very innocent, of a type that may often be found in France, but is still commoner in Catholic Germany. Everything about him, his pipe, his pot of beer, his flowers, and his beehive, suggested an ancestral peace; only when his visitors looked up as they entered the inn-parlour, they saw the sword upon the wall.

The Colonel, who greeted the innkeeper as an old friend, passed rapidly into the inn-parlour, and sat down, ordering some ritual refreshment. The military decision of his action interested Syme, who sat next to him, and he took the opportunity when the old innkeeper had gone out of satisfying his curiosity.

'May I ask you, Colonel,' he said in a low voice, 'why we have come here?'

Colonel Ducroix smiled behind his bristly white moustache.

'For two reasons, sir,' he said; 'and I will give first, not the most important, but the most utilitarian. We came here because this is the only place within twenty miles in which we can get horses.'

'Horses!' repeated Syme, looking up quickly.

'Yes,' replied the other; 'if you people are really to distance your enemies it is horses or nothing for you, unless of course you have bicycles and motor-cars in your pocket.'

'And where do you advise us to make for?' asked Syme doubtfully.

'Beyond question,' replied the Colonel, 'you had better make all haste to the police station beyond the town. My friend, whom I seconded under somewhat deceptive circumstances, seems to me to exaggerate very much the possibilities of a general rising; but even he would hardly maintain, I suppose, that you were not safe with the gendarmes.'

Syme nodded gravely; then he said abruptly –

'And your other reason for coming here?'

'My other reason for coming here,' said Ducroix soberly, 'is that it is just as well to see a good man or two when one is possibly near to death.'

Syme looked up at the wall, and saw a crudely painted and pathetic religious picture. Then he said –

'You are right,' and then almost immediately afterwards, 'Has anyone seen about the horses?'

'Yes,' answered Ducroix, 'you may be quite certain that I gave orders the moment I came in. Those enemies of yours gave no impression of hurry, but they were really moving wonderfully fast, like a well-trained army. I had no idea that the anarchists had so much discipline. You have not a moment to waste.'

Almost as he spoke, the old innkeeper with the blue eyes and white hair came ambling into the room, and announced that six horses were saddled outside.

By Ducroix's advice the five others equipped themselves with some portable form of food and wine, and keeping their duelling swords as the only weapons available, they clattered away down the steep, white road. The two servants, who had carried the Marquis's luggage when he was a marquis, were left behind to drink at the café by common consent, and not at all against their own inclination.

By this time the afternoon sun was slanting westward, and by its rays Syme could see the sturdy figure of the old innkeeper growing smaller and smaller, but still standing and looking after them quite silently, the sunshine in his silver hair. Syme had a fixed, superstitious fancy, left in his mind by the chance phrase of the Colonel, that this was indeed, perhaps, the last honest stranger whom he should ever see upon the earth.

He was still looking at this dwindling figure, which stood as a mere grey blot touched with a white flame against the great green wall of the steep down behind him. And as he stared, over the top of the down behind the innkeeper, there appeared an army of black-clad and marching men. They seemed to hang above the good man and his house like a black cloud of locusts. The horses had been saddled none too soon.

12

The Earth in Anarchy

Urging the horses to a gallop, without respect to the rather rugged descent of the road, the horsemen soon regained their advantage over the men on the march, and at last the bulk of the first buildings of Lancy cut off the sight of their pursuers. Nevertheless, the ride had been a long one, and by the time they reached the real town the west was warming with the colour and quality of sunset. The Colonel suggested that, before making finally for the police station, they should make the effort, in passing, to attach to themselves one more individual who might be useful.

'Four out of the five rich men in this town,' he said, 'are common swindlers. I suppose the proportion is pretty equal all over the world. The fifth is a friend of mine, and a very fine fellow; and what is even more important from our point of view, he owns a motor-car.'

'I am afraid,' said the Professor in his mirthful way, looking back along the white road on which the black, crawling patch might appear at any moment, 'I am afraid we have hardly time for afternoon calls.'

'Doctor Renard's house is only three minutes off,' said the Colonel.

'Our danger,' said Dr Bull, 'is not two minutes off.'

'Yes,' said Syme, 'if we ride on fast we must leave them behind, for they are on foot.'

'He has a motor-car,' said the Colonel.

'But we may not get it,' said Bull.

'Yes, he is quite on your side.'

'But he might be out.'

'Hold your tongue,' said Syme suddenly. 'What is that noise?'

For a second they all sat as still as equestrian statues, and for a second – for two or three or four seconds – heaven and earth seemed equally still. Then all their ears, in an agony of attention, heard along the road that indescribable thrill and throb that means only one thing – horses!

The Colonel's face had an instantaneous change, as if lightning had struck it, and yet left it scatheless.

'They have done us,' he said, with brief military irony. 'Prepare to receive cavalry!'

'Where can they have got the horses?' asked Syme, as he mechanically urged his steed to a canter.

The Colonel was silent for a little, then he said in a strained voice –

'I was speaking with strict accuracy when I said that the "Soleil d'Or" was the only place where one can get horses within twenty miles.'

'No!' said Syme violently, 'I don't believe he'd do it. Not with all that white hair.'

'He may have been forced,' said the Colonel gently. 'They must be at least a hundred strong, for which reason we are all going to see my friend Renard, who has a motor-car.'

With these words he swung his horse suddenly round a street corner, and went down the street with such thundering speed that the others, though already well at the gallop, had difficulty in following the flying tail of his horse.

Dr Renard inhabited a high and comfortable house at the top of a steep street, so that when the riders alighted at his door they could once more see the solid green ridge of the hill, with the white road across it, standing up above all the roofs of the town. They breathed again to see that the road was as yet clear, and they rang the bell.

Dr Renard was a beaming, brown-bearded man, a good example of that silent but very busy professional class which France has preserved even more perfectly than England. When the matter was explained to him he pooh-poohed the panic of the ex-Marquis altogether; he said, with the solid French scepticism, that there was no conceivable probability of a general anarchist rising. 'Anarchy,' he said, shrugging his shoulders, 'it is childishness!'

'*Et ça,*' cried out the Colonel suddenly, pointing over the other's shoulder, 'and that is childishness, isn't it?'

They all looked round, and saw a curve of black cavalry come sweeping over the top of the hill with all the energy of Attila.[1] Swiftly as they rode, however, the whole rank still kept well together, and they could see the black vizards of the first line as level as a line of uniforms. But although the main black square was the same, though travelling faster, there was now one sensational difference which they could see clearly upon the slope of the hill, as if upon a slanted map. The bulk of the riders were in one block; but one rider flew far ahead of the column, and with frantic movements of hand and heel urged his horse faster and faster, so that one might have fancied that he was not the pursuer, but the pursued. But even at that great distance they could see something so fantastical, so unquestionable in his figure, that they knew it was the Secretary himself.

'I am sorry to cut short a cultured discussion,' said the Colonel, 'but can you lend me your motor-car, now, in two minutes?'

'I have a suspicion that you are all mad,' said Dr Renard, smiling sociably; 'but God forbid that madness should in any way interrupt friendship. Let us go round to the garage.'

Dr Renard was a mild man with monstrous wealth; his rooms were like the Musée de Cluny,[2] and he had three motor-cars. These, however, he seemed to use very sparingly, having the simple tastes of the French middle class, and when his impatient friends came to examine them, it took them some time to assure themselves that one of them even could be made to work. This with some difficulty they brought round into the street before the Doctor's house. When they came out of the dim garage they were startled to find that twilight had already fallen with the abruptness of night in the tropics. Either they had been longer in the place than they imagined, or some unusual canopy of cloud had gathered over the town. They looked down the steep streets, and seemed to see a slight mist coming up from the sea.

'It is now or never,' said Dr Bull. 'I hear horses.'

'No,' corrected the Professor, 'a horse.'

And as they listened, it was evident that the noise, rapidly coming nearer on the rattling stones, was not the noise of the whole cavalcade, but that of the one horseman, who had left it far behind – the insane Secretary.

Syme's family, like most of those who end in the simple life, had once owned a motor, and he knew all about them. He had leapt at once into the chauffeur's seat, and with flushed face was wrenching and tugging at the disused machinery. He bent his strength upon one handle, and then said quietly –

'I'm afraid it's no go.'

As he spoke, there swept round the corner a man rigid on his rushing horse, with the rush and rigidity of an arrow. He had a smile that thrust out his chin as if it were dislocated. He swept alongside of the stationary car, into which its company had crowded, and laid his hand on the front. It was the Secretary, and his mouth went quite straight in the solemnity of triumph.

Syme was leaning hard upon the steering wheel, and there was no sound but the rumble of the other pursuers riding into the town. Then there came quite suddenly a scream of scraping iron, and the car leapt forward. It plucked the Secretary clean out of his saddle, as a knife is whipped out of its sheath, trailed him kicking terribly for twenty yards, and left him flung flat upon the road far in front of his frightened horse. As the car took the corner of the street with a splendid curve, they could just see the other anarchists filling the street and raising their fallen leader.

'I can't understand why it has grown so dark,' said the Professor at last in a low voice.

'Going to be a storm, I think,' said Dr Bull. 'I say, it's a pity we haven't got a light on this car, if only to see by.'

'We have,' said the Colonel, and from the floor of the car he fished up a heavy, old-fashioned, carved iron lantern with a light inside it. It was obviously an antique, and it would seem as if its original use had been in some way semi-religious, for there was a rude moulding of a cross upon one of its sides.

'Where on earth did you get that?' asked the Professor.

'I got it where I got the car,' answered the Colonel, chuckling, 'from my best friend. While our friend here was fighting with the steering wheel, I ran up to the front steps of the house and spoke to Renard, who was standing in his own porch, you will remember. "I suppose," I said, "there's no time to get a lamp." He looked up, blinking amiably at the beautiful arched ceiling of his own front hall. From this was suspended, by chains of exquisite ironwork, this lantern, one of the hundred treasures of his treasure house. By sheer force he tore the lamp out of his own ceiling, shattering the painted panels, and bringing down two blue vases with his violence. Then he handed me the iron lantern, and I put it in the car. Was I not right when I said that Dr Renard was worth knowing?'

'You were,' said Syme seriously, and hung the heavy lantern over the front. There was a certain allegory of their whole position in the contrast beween the modern automobile and its strange, ecclesiastical lamp.

Hitherto they had passed through the quietest part of the town, meeting at most one or two pedestrians, who could give them no hint of the peace or the hostility of the place. Now, however, the windows in the houses began one by one to be lit up, giving a greater sense of habitation and humanity. Dr Bull turned to the new detective who had led their flight, and permitted himself one of his natural and friendly smiles.

'These lights make one feel more cheerful.'

Inspector Ratcliffe drew his brows together.

'There is only one set of lights that make me more cheerful,' he said, 'and they are those lights of the police station which I can see beyond the town. Please God we may be there in ten minutes.'

Then all Bull's boiling good sense and optimism broke suddenly out of him.

'Oh, this is all raving nonsense!' he cried. 'If you really think that ordinary people in ordinary houses are anarchists, you must be madder than an anarchist yourself. If we turned and fought these fellows, the whole town would fight for us.'

'No,' said the other with an immovable simplicity, 'the whole town would fight for them. We shall see.'

While they were speaking the Professor had leant forward with sudden excitement.

'What is that noise?' he said.

'Oh, the horses behind us, I suppose,' said the Colonel. 'I thought we had got clear of them.'

'The horses behind us! No,' said the Professor, 'it is not horses, and it is not behind us.'

Almost as he spoke, across the end of the street before them two shining and rattling shapes shot past. They were gone almost in a flash, but everyone could see they were motor-cars, and the Professor stood up with a pale face and swore that they were the other two motor-cars from Dr Renard's garage.

'I tell you they were his,' he repeated, with wild eyes, 'and they were full of men in masks!'

'Absurd!' said the Colonel angrily. 'Dr Renard would never give them his cars.'

'He may have been forced,' said Ratcliffe quietly. 'The whole town is on their side.'

'You still believe that?' asked the Colonel incredulously.

'You will all believe it soon,' said the other with a hopeless calm.

There was a puzzled pause for some little time, and then the Colonel began again abruptly –

'No, I can't believe it. The thing is nonsense. The plain people of a peaceable French town—'

He was cut short by a bang and a blaze of light, which seemed close to his eyes. As the car sped on it left a floating patch of white smoke behind it, and Syme had heard a shot shriek past his ear.

'My God!' said the Colonel, 'someone has shot at us.'

'It need not interrupt conversation,' said the gloomy Ratcliffe. 'Pray resume your remarks, Colonel. You were talking, I think, about the plain people of a peaceable French town.'

The staring Colonel was long past minding satire. He rolled his eyes all round the street.

'It is extraordinary,' he said, 'most extraordinary.'

'A fastidious person,' said Syme, 'might even call it unpleasant. However, I suppose those lights out in the field beyond this street are the Gendarmerie. We shall soon get there.'

'No,' said Inspector Ratcliffe, 'we shall never get there.'

He had been standing up and looking keenly ahead of him. Now he sat down and smoothed his sleek hair with a weary gesture.

'What do you mean?' asked Bull sharply.

'I mean that we shall never get there,' said the pessimist placidly. 'They have two rows of armed men across the road already; I can see them from here. The town is in arms as I said it was. I can only wallow in the exquisite comfort of my own exactitude.'

And Ratcliffe sat down comfortably in the car and lit a cigarette, but the others rose excitedly and stared down the road. Syme had slowed down the car as their plans became doubtful, and he brought it finally to a standstill just at the corner of a side street that ran down very steeply to the sea.

The town was mostly in shadow, but the sun had not sunk; wherever its level light could break through it painted everything a burning gold. Up this side street the last sunset light shone as sharp and narrow as the shaft of artificial light at the theatre. It struck the car of the five friends, and lit it like a burning chariot. But the rest of the street, especially the two ends of it, was in the deepest twilight, and for some seconds they could see nothing. Then Syme, whose eyes were the keenest, broke into a little bitter whistle, and he said –

'It is quite true. There is a crowd or an army or some such thing across the end of that street.'

'Well, if there is,' said Bull impatiently, 'it must be something else – a sham fight or the mayor's birthday or something. I cannot and will not believe that plain, jolly people in a place like this walk about with dynamite in their pockets. Get on a bit, Syme, and let us look at them.'

The car crawled about a hundred yards farther, and then they were all startled by Dr Bull breaking into a high crow of laughter.

'Why, you silly mugs!' he cried, 'what did I tell you? That crowd's as law-abiding as a cow, and, if it weren't, it's on our side.'

'How do you know?' asked the Professor, staring.

'You blind bat,' cried Bull, 'don't you see who is leading them?'

They peered again, and then the Colonel, with a catch in his voice, cried out –

'Why, it's Renard!'

There was, indeed, a rank of dim figures running across the road, and they could not be clearly seen; but far enough in front to catch the accident of the evening light was stalking up and down the unmistakable Dr Renard, in a white hat, stroking his long brown beard, and holding a revolver in his left hand.

'What a fool I've been!' exclaimed the Colonel. 'Of course, the dear old boy has turned out to help us.'

Dr Bull was bubbling over with laughter, swinging the sword in his hand as carelessly as a cane. He jumped out of the car and ran across the intervening space, calling out –

'Dr Renard! Dr Renard!'

An instant after Syme thought his own eyes had gone mad in his head. For the philanthropic Dr Renard had deliberately raised his revolver and fired twice at Bull, so that the shots rang down the road.

Almost at the same second as the puff of white cloud went up from this atrocious explosion a long puff of white cloud went up also from the cigarette of the cynical Ratcliffe. Like all the rest he turned a little pale, but he smiled. Dr Bull, at whom the bullets had been fired, just missing his scalp, stood quite still in the middle of the road without a sign of fear, and then turned very slowly and crawled back to the car, and climbed in with two holes through his hat.

'Well,' said the cigarette smoker slowly, 'what do you think now?'

'I think,' said Dr Bull with precision, 'that I am lying in bed at No. 217 Peabody Buildings,[3] and that I shall soon wake up with a jump; or, if that's not it, I think that I am sitting in a small cushioned cell in Hanwell,[4] and that the doctor can't make much of my case. But if you want to know what I don't think, I'll tell you. I don't think what you think. I don't think, and I never shall think, that the mass of ordinary men are a pack of dirty modern thinkers. No, sir, I'm a democrat, and I still don't believe that Sunday could convert one average navvy or counter-jumper.[5] No, I may be mad, but humanity isn't.'

Syme turned his bright blue eyes on Bull with an earnestness which he did not commonly make clear.

'You are a very fine fellow,' he said. 'You can believe in a sanity which is not merely your sanity. And you're right enough about humanity, about peasants and people like that jolly old inn-keeper. But you're not right about Renard. I suspected him from the first. He's rationalistic, and what's worse, he's rich. When duty and religion are really destroyed, it will be by the rich.'

'They are really destroyed now,' said the man with a cigarette, and rose with his hands in his pockets. 'The devils are coming on!'

The men in the motor-car looked anxiously in the direction of his dreamy gaze, and they saw the whole regiment at the end of the road was advancing upon them, Dr Renard marching furiously in front, his beard flying in the breeze.

The Colonel sprang out of the car with an intolerant ex-clamation.

'Gentlemen,' he cried, 'the thing is incredible. It must be a practical joke. If you knew Renard as I do – it's like calling Queen Victoria a dynamiter. If you had got the man's character into your head –'

'Dr Bull,' said Syme sardonically, 'has at least got it into his hat.'

'I tell you it can't be!' cried the Colonel, stamping. 'Renard shall explain it. He shall explain it to me,' and he strode forward.

'Don't be in such a hurry,' drawled the smoker. 'He will very soon explain it to all of us.'

But the impatient Colonel was already out of earshot, advanc-ing towards the advancing enemy. The excited Dr Renard lifted his pistol again, but perceiving his opponent, hesitated, and the Colonel came face to face with him with frantic gestures of remonstrance.

'It is no good,' said Syme. 'He will never get anything out of that old heathen. I vote we drive bang through the thick of them, bang as the bullets went through Bull's hat. We may all be killed, but we must kill a tidy number of them.'

'I won't 'ave it,' said Dr Bull, growing more vulgar in the sincerity of his virtue. 'The poor chaps may be making a mistake. Give the Colonel a chance.'

'Shall we go back, then?' asked the Professor.

'No,' said Ratcliffe in a cold voice, 'the street behind us is held too. In fact, I seem to see there another friend of yours, Syme.'

Syme spun round smartly, and stared backwards at the track which they had travelled. He saw an irregular body of horsemen gathering and galloping towards them in the gloom. He saw above the foremost saddle the silver gleam of a sword, and then as it grew nearer the silver gleam of an old man's hair. The next moment, with shattering violence, he had swung the motor round and sent it dashing down the steep side street to the sea, like a man that desired only to die.

'What the devil is up?' cried the Professor, seizing his arm.

'The morning star has fallen!' said Syme, as his own car went down the darkness like a falling star.

The others did not understand his words, but when they looked back at the street above they saw the hostile cavalry coming round the corner and down the slopes after them; and foremost of all rode the good innkeeper, flushed with the fiery innocence of the evening light.

'The world is insane!' said the Professor, and buried his face in his hands.

'No,' said Dr Bull in adamantine humility, 'it is I.'

'What are we going to do?' asked the Professor.

'At this moment,' said Syme, with a scientific detachment, 'I think we are going to smash into a lamp-post.'

The next instant the automobile had come with a catastrophic jar against an iron object. The instant after that four men had crawled out from under a chaos of metal, and a tall lean lamp-post that had stood up straight on the edge of the marine parade stood out, bent and twisted, like the branch of a broken tree.

'Well, we smashed something,' said the Professor, with a faint smile. 'That's some comfort.'

'You're becoming an anarchist,' said Syme, dusting his clothes with his instinct of daintiness.

'Everyone is,' said Ratcliffe.

As they spoke, the white-haired horseman and his followers came thundering from above, and almost at the same moment a dark string of men ran shouting along the sea-front. Syme snatched a sword, and took it in his teeth; he stuck two others under his arm-pits, took a fourth in his left hand and the lantern in his right, and leapt off the high parade on to the beach below.

The others leapt after him, with a common acceptance of such decisive action, leaving the débris and the gathering mob above them.

'We have one more chance,' said Syme, taking the steel out of his mouth. 'Whatever all this pandemonium means, I suppose the police station will help us. We can't get there, for they hold the way. But there's a pier or breakwater runs out into the sea just here, which we could defend longer than anything else, like Horatius and his bridge.[6] We must defend it till the Gendarmerie turn out. Keep after me.'

They followed him as he went crunching down the beach, and in a second or two their boots broke not on the sea gravel, but on broad, flat stones. They marched down a long, low jetty, running out in one arm into the dim, boiling sea, and when they came to the end of it they felt that they had come to the end of their story. They turned and faced the town.

The town was transfigured with uproar. All along the high parade from which they had just descended was a dark and roaring stream of humanity, with tossing arms and fiery faces, groping and glaring towards them. The long dark line was dotted with torches and lanterns; but even where no flame lit up a furious face, they could see in the farthest figure, in the most shadowy gesture, an organized hate. It was clear that they were the accursed of all men, and they knew not why.

Two or three men, looking little and black like monkeys, leapt over the edge as they had done and dropped on to the beach. These came ploughing down the deep sand, shouting horribly, and strove to wade into the sea at random. The example was followed, and the whole black mass of men began to run and drip over the edge like black treacle.

Foremost among the men on the beach Syme saw the peasant who had driven their cart. He splashed into the surf on a huge cart-horse, and shook his axe at them.

'The peasant!' cried Syme. 'They have not risen since the Middle Ages.'

'Even if the police do come now,' said the Professor mournfully, 'they can do nothing with this mob.'

'Nonsense!' said Bull desperately; 'there must be some people left in the town who are human.'

'No,' said the hopeless Inspector, 'the human being will soon be extinct. We are the last of mankind.'

'It may be,' said the Professor absently. Then he added in his dreamy voice, 'What is all that at the end of the *Dunciad*?[7]

> 'Nor public flame, nor private, dare to shine;
> Nor human light is left, nor glimpse divine!
> Lo! thy dread Empire, Chaos, is restored;
> Light dies before thine uncreating word:
> Thy hand, great Anarch, lets the curtain fall;
> And universal darkness buries all.'

'Stop!' cried Bull suddenly, 'the gendarmes are out,'

The low lights of the police station were indeed blotted and broken with hurrying figures, and they heard through the darkness the clash and jingle of a disciplined cavalry.

'They are charging the mob!' cried Bull in ecstasy of alarm.

'No,' said Syme, 'they are formed along the parade.'

'They have unslung their carbines,' cried Bull, dancing with excitement.

'Yes,' said Ratcliffe, 'and they are going to fire on us.'

As he spoke there came a long crackle of musketry, and bullets seemed to hop like hailstones on the stones in front of them.

'The gendarmes have joined them!' cried the Professor and struck his forehead.

'I am in a padded cell,' said Bull stolidly.

There was a long silence, and then Ratcliffe said, looking out over the swollen sea, all a sort of grey purple –

'What does it matter who is mad or who is sane? We shall all be dead soon.'

Syme turned to him and said –

'You are quite hopeless, then?'

Mr Ratcliffe kept a stony silence; then at last he said quietly –

'No; oddly enough I am not quite hopeless. There is one insane little hope that I cannot get out of my mind. The power of this whole planet is against us, yet I cannot help wondering whether this one silly little hope is hopeless yet.'

'In what or whom is your hope?' asked Syme with curiosity.

'In a man I never saw,' said the other, looking at the leaden sea.

'I know whom you mean,' said Syme in a low voice, 'the man in the dark room. But Sunday must have killed him by now.'

'Perhaps,' said the other steadily; 'but if so, he was the only man whom Sunday found it hard to kill.'

'I heard what you said,' said the Professor, with his back turned. 'I also am holding hard on to the thing I never saw.'

All of a sudden Syme, who was standing as if blind with introspective thought, swung round and cried out, like a man waking from sleep –

'Where is the Colonel? I thought he was with us!'

'The Colonel! Yes,' cried Bull, 'where on earth is the Colonel?'

'He went to speak to Renard,' said the Professor.

'We cannot leave him among all those beasts,' cried Syme. 'Let us die like gentlemen if—'

'Do not pity the Colonel,' said Ratcliffe, with a pale sneer. 'He is extremely comfortable. He is –'

'No! No! No!' cried Syme in a kind of frenzy, 'not the Colonel too! I will never believe it!'

'Will you believe your eyes?' asked the other, and pointed to the beach.

Many of their pursuers had waded into the water shaking their fists, but the sea was rough, and they could not reach the pier. Two or three figures, however, stood on the beginning of the stone footway, and seemed to be cautiously advancing down it. The glare of a chance lantern lit up the faces of the two foremost. One face wore a black half-mask, and under it the mouth was twisting about in such a madness of nerves that the black tuft of beard wriggled round and round like a restless, living thing. The other was the red face and white moustache of Colonel Ducroix. They were in earnest consultation.

'Yes, he is gone too,' said the Professor, and sat down on a stone. 'Everything's gone. I'm gone! I can't trust my own bodily machinery. I feel as if my hand might fly up and strike me.'

'When my hand flies up,' said Syme, 'it will strike somebody else,' and he strode along the pier towards the Colonel, the sword in one hand and the lantern in the other.

As if to destroy the last hope or doubt, the Colonel, who saw him coming, pointed his revolver at him and fired. The shot missed Syme, but struck his sword, breaking it short at the hilt. Syme rushed on, and swung the iron lantern above his head.

'Judas before Herod![8] he said, and struck the Colonel down upon the stones. Then he turned to the Secretary, whose frightful mouth was almost foaming now, and held the lamp high with so rigid and arresting a gesture that the man was, as it were, frozen for a moment, and forced to hear.

'Do you see this lantern?' cried Syme in a terrible voice. 'Do you see the cross carved on it, and the flame inside? You did not make it. You did not light it. Better men than you, men who could believe and obey, twisted the entrails of iron and preserved the legend of fire. There is not a street you walk on, there is not a thread you wear, that was not made as this lantern was, by denying your philosophy of dirt and rats. You can make nothing. You can only destroy. You will destroy mankind; you will destroy the world. Let that suffice you. Yet this one old Christian lantern you shall not destroy. It shall go where your empire of apes will never have the wit to find it.'

He struck the Secretary once with the lantern so that he staggered; and then, whirling it twice round his head, sent it flying far out to sea, where it flared like a roaring rocket and fell.

'Swords!' shouted Syme, turning his flaming face to the three behind him. 'Let us charge these dogs, for our time has come to die.'

His three companions came after him sword in hand. Syme's sword was broken, but he rent a bludgeon from the fist of a fisherman, flinging him down. In a moment they would have flung themselves upon the face of the mob and perished, when an interruption came. The Secretary, ever since Syme's speech, had stood with his hand to his stricken head as if dazed; now he suddenly pulled off his black mask.

The pale face thus peeled in the lamplight revealed not so

much rage as astonishment. He put up his hand with an anxious authority.

'There is some mistake,' he said. 'Mr Syme, I hardly think you understand your position. I arrest you in the name of the law.'

'Of the law?' said Syme, and dropped his stick.

'Certainly!' said the Secretary. 'I am a detective from Scotland Yard,' and he took a small blue card from his pocket.

'And what do you suppose we are?' asked the Professor, and threw up his arms.

'You,' said the Secretary stiffly, 'are, as I know for a fact, members of the Supreme Anarchist Council. Disguised as one of you, I—'

Dr Bull tossed his sword into the sea.

'There never was any Supreme Anarchist Council,' he said. 'We were all a lot of silly policemen looking at each other. And all these nice people who have been peppering us with shot thought we were the dynamiters. I knew I couldn't be wrong about the mob,' he said, beaming over the enormous multitude which stretched away to the distance on both sides. 'Vulgar people are never mad. I'm vulgar myself, and I know. I am now going on shore to stand a drink to everybody here.'

13

The Pursuit of the President

Next morning five bewildered but hilarious people took the boat for Dover. The poor old Colonel might have had some cause to complain, having been first forced to fight for two factions that didn't exist, and then knocked down with an iron lantern. But he was a magnanimous old gentleman, and being much relieved that neither party had anything to do with dynamite, he saw them off on the pier with great geniality.

The five reconciled detectives had a hundred details to explain to each other. The Secretary had to tell Syme how they had come to wear masks originally in order to approach the supposed enemy as fellow-conspirators; Syme had to explain how they had fled with such swiftness through a civilized country. But above all these matters of detail which could be explained rose the central mountain of the matter that they could not explain. What did it all mean? If they were all harmless officers, what was Sunday? If he had not seized the world, what on earth had he been up to? Inspector Ratcliffe was still gloomy about this.

'I can't make head or tail of old Sunday's little game any more than you can,' he said. 'But whatever else Sunday is, he isn't a blameless citizen. Damn it! Do you remember his face?'

'I grant you,' answered Syme, 'that I have never been able to forget it.'

'Well,' said the Secretary, 'I suppose we can find out soon, for tomorrow we have our next general meeting. You will excuse me,' he said, with a rather ghastly smile, 'for being well acquainted with my secretarial duties.'

'I suppose you are right,' said the Professor reflectively. 'I suppose we might find it out from him; but I confess that I should feel a bit afraid of asking Sunday who he really is.'

'Why?' asked the Secretary; 'for fear of bombs?'

'No,' said the Professor, 'for fear he might tell me.'

'Let us have some drinks,' said Dr Bull, after a silence.

Throughout their whole journey by boat and train they were highly convivial, but they instinctively kept together. Dr Bull, who had always been the optimist of the party, endeavoured to persuade the other four that the whole company could take the same hansom-cab from Victoria; but this was overruled, and they went in a four-wheeler, with Dr Bull on the box, singing. They finished their journey at an hotel in Piccadilly Circus, so as to be close to the early breakfast next morning in Leicester Square. Yet even then the adventures of the day were not entirely over. Dr Bull, discontented with the general proposal to go to bed, had strolled out of the hotel at about eleven to see and taste some of the beauties of London. Twenty minutes afterwards, however, he came back and made quite a clamour in the hall. Syme, who tried at first to soothe him, was forced at last to listen to his communication with quite new attention.

'I tell you I've seen him!' said Dr Bull, with thick emphasis.

'Whom?' asked Syme quickly. 'Not the President?'

'Not as bad as that,' said Dr Bull, with unnecessary laughter, 'not as bad as that. I've got him here.'

'Got whom here?' asked Syme impatiently.

'Hairy man,' said the other lucidly, 'man that used to be hairy man – Gogol. Here he is,' and he pulled forward by a reluctant elbow the identical young man who five days before had marched out of the Council with thin red hair and a pale face, the first of all the sham anarchists who had been exposed.

'Why do you worry with me?' he cried. 'You have expelled me as a spy.'

'We are all spies!' whispered Syme.

'We're all spies!' shouted Dr Bull. 'Come and have a drink.'

Next morning the battalion of the reunited six marched stolidly towards the hotel in Leicester Square.

'This is more cheerful,' said Dr Bull; 'We are six men going to ask one man what he means.'

'I think it is a bit queerer than that,' said Syme. 'I think it is six men going to ask one man what they mean.'

They turned in silence into the Square, and, though the hotel was in the opposite corner, they saw at once the little balcony and a figure that looked too big for it. He was sitting alone with bent head, poring over a newspaper. But all his councillors, who had come to vote him down, crossed that Square as if they were watched out of heaven by a hundred eyes.

They had disputed much upon their policy, about whether they should leave the unmasked Gogol without and begin diplomatically, or whether they should bring him in and blow up the gunpowder at once. The influence of Syme and Bull prevailed for the latter course, though the Secretary to the last asked them why they attacked Sunday so rashly.

'My reason is quite simple,' said Syme. 'I attack him rashly because I am afraid of him.'

They followed Syme up the dark stair in silence, and they all came out simultaneously into the broad sunlight of the morning and the broad daylight of Sunday's smile.

'Delightful!' he said. 'So pleased to see you all. What an exquisite day it is. Is the Czar dead?'

The Secretary, who happened to be foremost, drew himself together for a dignified outburst.

'No, sir,' he said sternly, 'there has been no massacre. I bring you news of no such disgusting spectacles.'

'Disgusting spectacles?' repeated the President, with a bright, inquiring smile. 'You mean Dr Bull's spectacles?'

The Secretary choked for a moment, and the President went on with a sort of smooth appeal:

'Of course, we all have our opinions and even our eyes, but really to call them disgusting before the man himself—'

Dr Bull tore off his spectacles and broke them on the table.

'My spectacles are blackguardly,' he said, 'but I'm not. Look at my face.'

'I dare say it's the sort of face that grows on one,' said the President, 'in fact, it grows on you; and who am I to quarrel with the wild fruits upon the Tree of Life?[1] I dare say it will grow on me some day.'

'We have no time for tomfoolery,' said the Secretary, breaking in savagely. 'We have come to know what all this means. Who are you? What are you? Why did you get us all here? Do you know who and what we are? Are you a half-witted man playing the conspirator, or are you a clever man playing the fool? Answer me, I tell you.'

'Candidates,' murmured Sunday, 'are only required to answer eight out of the seventeen questions on the paper. As far as I can make out, you want me to tell you what I am, and what you are, and what this table is, and what this Council is, and what this world is for all I know. Well, I will go so far as to rend the veil of one mystery. If you want to know what you are, you are a set of highly well-intentioned young jackasses.'

'And you,' said Syme, leaning forward, 'what are you?'

'I? What am I?' roared the President, and he rose slowly to an incredible height, like some enormous wave about to arch above them and break. 'You want to know what I am, do you? Bull, you are a man of science. Grub in the roots of those trees and find out the truth about them. Syme, you are a poet. Stare at those morning clouds. But I tell you this, that you will have found out the truth of the last tree and the topmost cloud before the truth about me. You will understand the sea, and I shall be still a riddle; you shall know what the stars are, and not know what I am. Since the beginning of the world all men have hunted me like a wolf – kings and sages, and poets and law-givers, all the churches, and all the philosophers. But I have never been caught yet, and the skies will fall in the time I turn to bay. I have given them a good run for their money, and I will now.'

Before one of them could move, the monstrous man had swung himself like some huge orang-outang[2] over the balustrade of the balcony. Yet before he dropped he pulled himself up again as on a horizontal bar, and thrusting his great chin over the edge of the balcony, said solemnly:

'There's one thing I'll tell you, though, about who I am. I am the man in the dark room, who made you all policemen.'

With that he fell from the balcony, bouncing on the stones below like a great ball of india-rubber,[3] and went bounding towards the corner of the Alhambra, where he hailed a hansom-cab and sprang inside it. The six detectives had been standing thunderstruck and livid in the light of his last assertion: but when he disappeared into the cab, Syme's practical senses returned to him, and leaping over the balcony so recklessly as almost to break his legs, he called another cab.

He and Bull sprang into the cab together, the Professor and the Inspector into another, while the Secretary and the late Gogol scrambled into a third just in time to pursue the flying Syme, who was pursuing the flying President. Sunday led them a wild chase towards the north-west, his cabman, evidently under the influence of more than common inducements, urging the horse at breakneck speed. But Syme was in no mood for delicacies, and he stood up in his own cab shouting, 'Stop thief!' until crowds ran along beside his cab, and policemen began to stop and ask questions. All this had its influence upon the President's cabman, who began to look dubious, and to slow down to a trot. He opened the trap to talk reasonably to his fare, and in so doing let the long whip droop over the front of the cab. Sunday leant forward, seized it, and jerked it violently out of the man's hand. Then, standing up in front of the cab himself, he lashed the horse and roared aloud, so that they went down the streets like a flying storm. Through street after street and square after square went whirling this preposterous vehicle, in which the fare was urging the horse and the driver trying desperately to stop it. The other three cabs came after it (if the phrase be permissible of a cab) like panting hounds. Shops and streets shot by like rattling arrows.

At the highest ecstasy of speed, Sunday turned round on the splashboard where he stood, and sticking his great grinning head out of the cab, with white hair whistling in the wind, he made a horrible face at his pursuers, like some colossal urchin. Then, raising his right hand swiftly, he flung a ball of paper in Syme's face and vanished. Syme caught the thing while instinctively warding it off, and discovered that it consisted of two crumpled papers. One was addressed to himself, and the other to Dr Bull, with a very long, and it is to be feared partly ironical, string of letters after his name. Dr Bull's address was, at any rate, considerably longer than his communication, for the communication consisted entirely of the words:

What about Martin Tupper⁴ *now?*

'What does the old maniac mean?' asked Bull, staring at the words. 'What does yours say, Syme?'

Syme's message was, at any rate, longer, and ran as follows:

No one would regret anything in the nature of an interference by the Archdeacon more than I. I trust it will not come to that. But, for the last time, where are your goloshes.⁵ The thing is too bad, especially after what uncle said.

The President's cabman seemed to be regaining some control over his horse, and the pursuers gained a little as they swept round into the Edgware Road. And here there occurred what seemed to the allies a providential stoppage. Traffic of every kind was swerving to right or left or stopping, for down the long road was coming the unmistakable roar announcing the fire-engine, which in a few seconds went by like a brazen thunderbolt. But quick as it went by, Sunday had bounded out of his cab, sprung at the fire-engine, caught it, slung himself on to it, and was seen as he disappeared in the noisy distance talking to the astonished fireman with explanatory gestures.

'After him!' howled Syme. 'He can't go astray now. There's no mistaking a fire-engine.'

The three cabmen, who had been stunned for a moment, whipped up their horses and slightly decreased the distance between themselves and their disappearing prey. The President acknowledged this proximity by coming to the back of the car, bowing repeatedly, kissing his hand, and finally flinging a neatly folded note into the bosom of Inspector Ratcliffe. When that gentleman opened it, not without impatience, he found it contained the words:

Fly at once. The truth about your trouser-stretchers is known.
– A FRIEND.

The fire-engine had struck still farther to the north, into a region that they did not recognize; and as it ran by a line of high railings shadowed with trees, the six friends were startled, but somewhat relieved, to see the President leap from the fire-engine, though whether through another whim or the increasing protest of his entertainers they could not see. Before the three cabs, however, could reach the spot, he had gone up the high railings like a huge grey cat, tossed himself over, and vanished in a darkness of leaves.

Syme with a furious gesture stopped his cab, jumped out, and sprang also to the escalade. When he had one leg over the fence and his friends were following, he turned a face on them which shone quite pale in the shadow.

'What place can this be?' he asked. 'Can it be the old devil's house? I've heard he has a house in North London.'

'All the better,' said the Secretary grimly, planting a foot in a foothold, 'we shall find him at home.'

'No, but it isn't that,' said Syme, knitting his brows. 'I hear the most horrible noises, like devils laughing and sneezing and blowing their devilish noses!'

'His dogs barking, of course,' said the Secretary.

'Why not say his black-beetles barking!' said Syme furiously, 'snails barking! geraniums barking! Did you ever hear a dog bark like that?'

He held up his hand, and there came out of the thicket a long growling roar that seemed to get under the skin and freeze the flesh – a low thrilling roar that made a throbbing in the air all about them.

'The dogs of Sunday would be no ordinary dogs,' said Gogol, and shuddered.

Syme had jumped down on the other side, but he still stood listening impatiently.

'Well, listen to that,' he said, 'is that a dog – anybody's dog?'

There broke upon their ear a hoarse screaming as of things protesting and clamouring in sudden pain; and then, far off like an echo, what sounded like a long nasal trumpet.

'Well, his house ought to be hell!' said the Secretary; 'and if it is hell, I'm going in!' and he sprang over the tall railings almost with one swing.

The others followed. They broke through a tangle of plants and shrubs, and came out on an open path. Nothing was in sight, but Dr Bull suddenly struck his hands together.

'Why, you asses,' he cried, 'it's the Zoo!'

As they were looking round wildly for any trace of their wild quarry, a keeper in uniform came running along the path with a man in plain clothes.

'Has it come this way?' gasped the keeper.

'Has what?' asked Syme.

'The elephant!'[6] cried the keeper. 'An elephant has gone mad and run away!'

'He has run away with an old gentleman,' said the other stranger breathlessly, 'a poor old gentleman with white hair!'

'What sort of old gentleman?' asked Syme, with great curiosity.

'A very large and fat old gentleman in light grey clothes,' said the keeper eagerly.

'Well,' said Syme, 'if he's that particular kind of old gentleman, if you're quite sure that he's a large and fat old gentleman in grey clothes, you may take my word for it that the elephant has not run away with him. He has run away with the elephant. The elephant is not made by God that could run away with him if he did not consent to the elopement. And, by thunder, there he is!'

There was no doubt about it this time. Clean across the space of grass, about two hundred yards away, with a crowd screaming and scampering vainly at his heels, went a huge grey elephant at an awful stride, with his trunk thrown out as rigid as a ship's bowsprit, and trumpeting like the trumpet of doom. On the back of the bellowing and plunging animal sat President Sunday with all the placidity of a sultan, but goading the animal to a furious speed with some sharp object in his hand.

'Stop him!' screamed the populace. 'He'll be out of the gate!'

'Stop a landslide!' said the keeper. 'He *is* out of the gate!'

And even as he spoke, a final crash and roar of terror announced that the great grey elephant had broken out of the gates of the Zoological Gardens, and was careering down Albany Street like a new swift sort of omnibus.

'Great Lord!' cried Bull, 'I never knew an elephant could go so fast. Well, it must be hansom-cabs again if we are to keep him in sight.'

As they raced along to the gate out of which the elephant had vanished, Syme felt a glaring panorama of the strange animals in the cages which they passed. Afterwards he thought it queer that he should have seen them so clearly. He remembered especially seeing pelicans, with their preposterous, pendent throats. He wondered why the pelican was the symbol of charity, except it was that it wanted a good deal of charity to admire a pelican.[7] He remembered a hornbill, which was simply a huge yellow beak with a small bird tied on behind it. The whole gave him a sensation, the vividness of which he could not explain, that Nature was always making quite mysterious jokes. Sunday had told them that they would understand him when they had understood the stars. He wondered whether even the archangels understood the hornbill.

The six unhappy detectives flung themselves into cabs and followed the elephant, sharing the terror which he spread through the long stretch of the streets. This time Sunday did not turn round, but offered them the solid stretch of his unconscious back, which maddened them, if possible, more than his previous mockeries. Just before they came to Baker Street, however, he was seen to throw something far up into the air, as a boy does a ball, meaning to catch it again. But at their rate of racing it fell far behind, just by the cab containing Gogol; and in faint hope of a clue for some impulse unexplainable, he stopped his cab so as to pick it up. It was addressed to himself, and was quite a bulky parcel. On examination, however, its bulk was found to consist of thirty-three pieces of paper of no value wrapped one round the other. When the last covering was torn away it reduced itself to a small slip of paper on which was written:

The word, I fancy, should be 'pink'.

The man once known as Gogol said nothing, but movements of his hands and feet were like those of a man urging a horse to renewed efforts.

Through street after street, through district after district, went the prodigy of the flying elephant, calling crowds to every window, and driving the traffic left and right. And still through all this insane publicity the three cabs toiled after it, until they came to be regarded as part of a procession, and perhaps the advertisement of a circus. They went at such a rate that distances were shortened beyond belief, and Syme saw the Albert Hall[8] in Kensington when he thought he was still in Paddington. The animal's pace was even more fast and free through the empty, aristocratic streets of South Kensington, and he finally headed towards that part of the sky-line where the enormous Wheel of Earl's Court[9] stood up in the sky. The wheel grew larger and larger, till it filled heaven like the wheel of stars.

The beast outstripped the cabs. They lost him round several corners, and when they came to one of the gates of the Earl's Court Exhibition they found themselves finally blocked. In front of them was an enormous crowd; in the midst of it was an enormous elephant, heaving and shuddering as such shapeless creatures do. But the President had disappeared.

'Where has he gone to?' asked Syme, slipping to the ground.

'Gentleman rushed into the Exhibition, sir!' said an official in a dazed manner. Then he added in an injured voice: 'Funny gentleman, sir. Asked me to hold his horse and gave me this.'

He held out with distaste a piece of folded paper, addressed: 'To the Secretary of the Central Anarchist Council.'

The Secretary, raging, rent it open, and found written inside it:

> When the herring runs a mile,
> Let the Secretary smile;
> When the herring tries to *fly*,
> Let the Secretary die.
>   Rustic Proverb

'Why the eternal crikey,' began the secretary, 'did you let the man in? Do people commonly come to your Exhibition riding on mad elephants? Do—'

'Look!' shouted Syme suddenly. 'Look over there!'

'Look at what?' asked the Secretary savagely.

'Look at the captive balloon!' said Syme, and pointed in a frenzy.

'Why the blazes should I look at a captive balloon?' demanded the Secretary. 'What is there queer about a captive balloon?'

'Nothing,' said Syme, 'except that it isn't captive!'

They all turned their eyes to where the balloon swung and swelled above the Exhibition on a string, like a child's balloon. A second afterwards the string came in two just under the car, and the balloon, broken loose, floated away with the freedom of a soap bubble.

'Ten thousand devils!' shrieked the Secretary. 'He's got into it!' and he shook his fists at the sky.

The balloon, borne by some chance wind, came right above them, and they could see the great white head of the President peering over the side and looking benevolently down on them.

'God bless my soul!' said the Professor with the elderly manner that he could never disconnect from his bleached beard and parchment face. 'God bless my soul! I seemed to fancy that something fell on the top of my hat!'

He put up a trembling hand and took from that shelf a piece of twisted paper, which he opened absently, only to find it inscribed with a true lover's knot, and the words:

Your beauty has not left me indifferent – From LITTLE SNOWDROP.[10]

There was a short silence, and then Syme said, biting his beard:

'I'm not beaten yet. The blasted thing must come down somewhere. Let's follow it!'

The Six Philosophers

Across green fields, and breaking through blooming hedges, toiled six draggled detectives, about five miles out of London. The optimist of the party had at first proposed that they should follow the balloon across South England in hansom-cabs. But he was ultimately convinced of the persistent refusal of the balloon to follow the roads, and the still more persistent refusal of the cabmen to follow the balloon. Consequently the tireless though exasperated travellers broke through black thickets and ploughed through ploughed fields till each was turned into a figure too outrageous to be mistaken for a tramp. Those green hills of Surrey saw the final collapse and tragedy of the admirable light grey suit in which Syme had set out from Saffron Park. His silk hat was broken over his nose by a swinging bough, his coat-tails were torn to the shoulder by arresting thorns, the clay of England was splashed up to his collar; but he still carried his yellow beard forward with a silent and furious determination, and his eyes were still fixed on that floating ball of gas, which in the full flush of sunset seemed coloured like a sunset cloud.

'After all,' he said, 'it is very beautiful!'

'It is singularly and strangely beautiful!' said the Professor. 'I wish the beastly gas-bag would burst!'

'No,' said Dr Bull, 'I hope it won't. It might hurt the old boy.'

'Hurt him!' said the vindictive Professor, 'hurt him! Not as much as I'd hurt him if I could get up with him. Little Snowdrop!'

'I don't want him hurt, somehow,' said Dr Bull.

'What!' cried the Secretary bitterly. 'Do you believe all that tale about our man in the dark room? Sunday would say he was anybody.'

'I don't know whether I believe it or not,' said Dr Bull. 'But it isn't that that I mean. I can't wish old Sunday's balloon to burn because—'

'Well,' said Syme impatiently, 'because?'

'Well, because he's so jolly like a balloon himself,' said Dr Bull desperately. 'I don't understand a word of all that idea of his being the same man who gave us all our blue cards. It seems to make everything nonsense. But I don't care who knows it, I always had sympathy for old Sunday himself, wicked as he was. Just as if he was a great bouncing baby. How can I explain what my queer sympathy was? It didn't prevent my fighting him like hell! Shall I make it clear if I say that I liked him because he was so fat?'

'You will not,' said the Secretary.

'I've got it now,' cried Bull, 'it was because he was so fat and so light. Just like a balloon. We always think of fat people as heavy, but he could have danced against a sylph. I see now what I mean. Moderate strength is shown in violence, supreme strength in levity. It was like the old speculations – what would happen if an elephant could leap up in the sky like a grasshopper?'

'Our elephant,' said Syme, looking upwards, 'has leapt into the sky like a grasshopper.'

'And somehow,' concluded Bull, 'that's why I can't help liking old Sunday. No, it's not an admiration of force, or any silly thing like that. There is a kind of gaiety in the thing, as if he were bursting with some good news. Haven't you sometimes felt it on a spring day? You know Nature plays tricks, but somehow that day proves they are good-natured tricks. I never read the Bible myself, but that part they laugh at is literal truth, "Why leap ye, ye high hills?"[1] The hills do leap – at least, they try to . . . Why do I like Sunday? . . . how can I tell you? . . . because he's such a bounder.'[2]

There was a long silence, and then the Secretary said in a curious, strained voice:

'You do not know Sunday at all. Perhaps it is because you are better than I, and do not know hell. I was a fierce fellow, and a trifle morbid from the first. The man who sits in darkness, and who chose us all, chose me because I had all the crazy look of a conspirator – because my smile went crooked, and my eyes were gloomy, even when I smiled. But there must have been something in me that answered to the nerves in all these anarchic men. For when I first saw Sunday he expressed to me, not your airy vitality, but something both gross and sad in the Nature of Things. I found him smoking in a twilight room, a room with brown blind down, infinitely more depressing than the genial darkness in which our master lives. He sat there on a bench, a huge heap of a man, dark and out of shape. He listened to all my words without speaking or even stirring. I poured out my most passionate appeals, and asked my most eloquent questions. Then, after a long silence, the Thing began to shake, and I thought it was shaken by some secret malady. It shook like a loathsome and living jelly. It reminded me of everything I had ever read about the base bodies that are the origin of life – the deep sea lumps and protoplasm.[3] It seemed like the final form of matter, the most shapeless and the most shameful. I could only tell myself, from its shudderings, that it was something at least that such a monster could be miserable. And then it broke upon me that the bestial mountain was shaking with a lonely laughter, and the laughter was at me. Do you ask me to forgive him that? It is no small thing to be laughed at by something at once lower and stronger than oneself.'

'Surely you fellows are exaggerating wildly,' cut in the clear voice of Inspector Ratcliffe. 'President Sunday is a terrible fellow for one's intellect, but he's not such a Barnum's freak[4] physically as you make out. He received me in an ordinary office, in a grey check coat, in broad daylight. He talked to me in an ordinary way. But I'll tell you what is a trifle creepy about Sunday. His room is neat, his clothes are neat, everything seems in order; but he's absent-minded. Sometimes his great bright eyes go quite blind. For hours he forgets that you are there. Now absent-mindedness is just a bit too awful in a bad man. We think of a wicked man as vigilant. We can't think of a wicked man who is honestly and sincerely dreamy, because we daren't think of a wicked man alone with himself. An absent-minded man means a good-natured man. It means a man who, if he happens to see you, will apologize. But how will you bear an absent-minded man who, if he happens to see you, will kill you? That is what tries the nerves, abstraction combined with cruelty. Men have felt it sometimes when they went through wild forests, and felt that the animals there were at once innocent and pitiless. They might ignore or slay. How would you like to pass ten mortal hours in a parlour with an absent-minded tiger?'

'And what do you think of Sunday, Gogol?' asked Syme.

'I don't think of Sunday on principle,' said Gogol simply, 'any more than I stare at the sun at noonday.'

'Well, that is a point of view,' said Syme thoughtfully. 'What do you say, Professor?'

The Professor was walking with bent head and trailing stick, and he did not answer at all.

'Wake up, Professor!' said Syme genially. 'Tell us what you think of Sunday.'

The Professor spoke at last very slowly.

'I think something,' he said, 'that I cannot say clearly. Or, rather, I think something that I cannot even think clearly. But it is something like this. My early life, as you know, was a bit too large and loose. Well, when I saw Sunday's face I thought it was too large – everybody does, but I also thought it was too loose. The face was so big that one couldn't focus it or make it a face at all. The eye was so far away from the nose that it wasn't an eye. The mouth was so much by itself that one had to think of it by itself. The whole thing is too hard to explain.'

He paused for a little, still trailing his stick, and then went on:

'But put it this way. Walking up a road at night, I have seen a lamp and a lighted window and a cloud make together a most complete and unmistakable face. If anyone in heaven has that face I shall know him again. Yet when I walked a little farther I found that there was no face, that the window was ten yards away, the lamp ten hundred yards, the cloud beyond the world. Well, Sunday's face escaped me; it ran away to right and left, as such chance pictures run away. And so his face has made me, somehow, doubt whether there are any faces. I don't know whether your face, Bull, is a face or a combination in perspective. Perhaps one black disc of your beastly glasses is quite close and another fifty miles away. Oh, the doubts of a materialist are not worth a dump. Sunday has taught me the last and the worst doubts, the doubts of a spiritualist. I am a Buddhist, I suppose; and Buddhism is not a creed, it is a doubt. My poor dear Bull, I do not believe that you really have a face. I have not faith enough to believe in matter.'

Syme's eyes were still fixed upon the errant orb, which, reddened in the evening light, looked like some rosier and more innocent world.

'Have you noticed an odd thing,' he said, 'about all your descriptions? Each man of you finds Sunday quite different, yet each man of you can only find one thing to compare him to – the universe itself. Bull finds him like the earth in spring, Gogol like the sun at noonday. The Secretary is reminded of the shapeless protoplasm, and the Inspector of the carelessness of virgin forests. The Professor says he is like a changing landscape. This is queer, but it is queerer still that I also have had my odd notion about the President, and I also find that I think of Sunday as I think of the whole world.'

'Get on a little faster, Syme,' said Bull; 'never mind the balloon.'

'When I first saw Sunday,' said Syme slowly, 'I only saw his back; and when I saw his back I knew he was the worst man in the world. His neck and shoulders were brutal, like those of some apish god. His head had a stoop that was hardly human, like the stoop of an ox. In fact, I had at once the revolting fancy that this was not a man at all, but a beast dressed up in men's clothes.'

'Get on,' said Dr Bull.

'And then the queer thing happened. I had seen his back from the street, as he sat in the balcony. Then I entered the hotel, and coming round the other side of him, saw his face in the sunlight. His face frightened me, as it did everyone; but not because it was brutal, not because it was evil. On the contrary, it frightened me because it was so beautiful, because it was so good.'

'Syme,' exclaimed the Secretary, 'are you ill?'

'It was like the face of some ancient archangel, judging justly after heroic wars. There was laughter in the eyes, and in the mouth honour and sorrow. There was the same white hair, the same great, grey-clad shoulders that I had seen from behind. But when I saw him from behind I was certain he was an animal, and when I saw him in front I knew he was a god.'

'Pan,'[5] said the Professor dreamily, 'was a god and an animal.'

'Then, and again and always,' went on Syme like a man talking to himself, 'that has been for me the mystery of Sunday, and it is also the mystery of the world. When I see the horrible back, I am sure the noble face is but a mask. When I see the face but for an instant, I know the back is only a jest. Bad is so bad that we cannot but think good an accident; good is so good that we feel certain that evil could be explained. But the whole came to a kind of crest yesterday when I raced Sunday for the cab, and was just behind him all the way.'

'Had you time for thinking then?' asked Ratcliffe.

'Time,' replied Syme, 'for one outrageous thought. I was suddenly possessed with the idea that the blind, blank back of his head really was his face – an awful, eyeless face staring at me: And I fancied that the figure running in front of me was really a figure running backwards, and dancing as he ran.'

'Horrible!' said Dr Bull, and shuddered.

'Horrible is not the word,' said Syme. 'It was exactly the worst instant of my life. And yet ten minutes afterwards, when he put his head out of the cab and made a grimace like a gargoyle, I knew that he was only like a father playing hide-and-seek with his children.'

'It is a long game,' said the Secretary, and frowned at his broken boots.

'Listen to me,' cried Syme with extraordinary emphasis. 'Shall I tell you the secret of the whole world? It is that we have only known the back of the world. We see everything from behind, and it looks brutal. That is not a tree, but the back of a tree. That is not a cloud, but the back of a cloud. Cannot you see that everything is stooping and hiding a face? If we could only get round in front—'

'Look!' cried out Bull clamorously, 'the balloon is coming down!'

There was no need to cry out to Syme, who had never taken his eyes off it. He saw the great luminous globe suddenly stagger in the sky, right itself, and then sink slowly behind the trees like a setting sun.

The man called Gogol, who had hardly spoken through all their weary travels, suddenly threw up his hands like a lost spirit.

'He is dead!' he cried. 'And now I know he was my friend – my friend in the dark!'

'Dead!' snorted the Secretary. 'You will not find him dead easily. If he has been tipped out of the car, we shall find him rolling as a colt rolls in a field, kicking his legs for fun.'

'Clashing his hoofs,' said the Professor. 'The colts do, and so did Pan.'

'Pan again!' said Dr Bull irritably. 'You seem to think Pan is everything.'

'So he is,' said the Professor, 'in Greek. He means everything.'

'Don't forget,' said the Secretary, looking down, 'that he also means Panic.'

Syme had stood without hearing any of the exclamations.

'It fell over there,' he said shortly. 'Let us follow it!'

Then he added with an indescribable gesture –

'Oh, if he has cheated us all by getting killed! It would be like one of his larks.'

He strode off towards the distant trees with a new energy, his rags and ribbons fluttering in the wind. The others followed him in a more footsore and dubious manner. And almost at the same moment all six men realized that they were not alone in the little field.

Across the square of turf a tall man was advancing towards them, leaning on a strange long staff like a sceptre. He was clad in a fine but old-fashioned suit with knee-breeches; its colour was that shade between blue, violet and grey which can be seen in certain shadows of the woodland. His hair was whitish grey, and at first glance, taken along with his knee-breeches, looked as if it was powdered. His glance was very quiet; but for the silver frost upon his head, he might have been one of the shadows of the wood.

'Gentlemen,' he said, 'my master has a carriage waiting for you in the road just by.'

'Who is your master?' asked Syme, standing quite still.

'I was told you knew his name,' said the man respectfully.

There was a silence, and then the Secretary said:

'Where is this carriage?'

'It has been waiting only a few moments,' said the stranger. 'My master has only just come home.'

Syme looked left and right upon the patch of green field in which he found himself. The hedges were ordinary hedges, the trees seemed ordinary trees; yet he felt like a man entrapped in fairyland.

He looked the mysterious ambassador up and down, but he could discover nothing except that the man's coat was the exact colour of the purple shadows, and that the man's face was the exact colour of the red and brown and golden sky.

'Show us the place,' Syme said briefly, and without a word the man in the violet coat turned his back and walked towards a gap in the hedge, which let in suddenly the light of a white road.

As the six wanderers broke out upon this thoroughfare, they saw the white road blocked by what looked like a long row of carriages, such a row of carriages as might close the approach to some house in Park Lane. Along the side of these carriages stood a rank of splendid servants, all dressed in the grey-blue uniform, and all having a certain quality of stateliness and freedom which would not commonly belong to the servants of a gentleman, but rather to the officials and ambassadors of a great king. There were no less than six carriages waiting, one for each of the tattered and miserable band. All the attendants (as if in court-dress) wore swords, and as each man crawled into his carriage they drew them, and saluted with a sudden blaze of steel.

'What can it all mean?' asked Bull of Syme as they separated. 'Is this another joke of Sunday's?'

'I don't know,' said Syme as he sank wearily back in the cushions of his carriage; 'but if it is, it's one of the jokes you talk about. It's a good-natured one.'

The six adventurers had passed through many adventures, but not one had carried them so utterly off their feet as this last adventure of comfort. They had all become inured to things going roughly; but things suddenly going smoothly swamped them. They could not even feebly imagine what the carriages were; it was enough for them to know that they were carriages, and carriages with cushions. They could not conceive who the old man was who had led them; but it was quite enough that he had certainly led them to the carriages.

Syme drove through a drifting darkness of trees in utter abandonment. It was typical of him that while he had carried his bearded chin forward fiercely as long as anything could be done, when the whole business was taken out of his hands he fell back on the cushions in a frank collapse.

Very gradually and very vaguely he realized into what rich roads the carriage was carrying him. He saw that they passed the stone gates of what might have been a park, that they began gradually to climb a hill which, while wooded on both sides, was somewhat more orderly than a forest. Then there began to grow upon him, as upon a man slowly waking from a healthy sleep, a pleasure in everything. He felt that the hedges were what hedges should be, living walls; that a hedge is like a human army, disciplined, but all the more alive. He saw high elms behind the hedges, and vaguely thought how happy boys would be climbing there. Then his carriage took a turn of the path, and he saw suddenly and quietly, like a long low sunset cloud, a long, low house, mellow in the mild light of sunset. All the six friends compared notes afterwards and quarrelled; but they all agreed that in some unaccountable way the place reminded them of their boyhood. It was either this elm-top or that crooked path, it was either this scrap of orchard or that shape of a window; but each man of them declared that he could remember this place before he could remember his mother.

When the carriages eventually rolled up to a large, low, cavernous gateway, another man in the same uniform, but wearing a silver star on the grey breast of his coat, came out to meet them. This impressive person said to the bewildered Syme:

'Refreshments are provided for you in your room.'

Syme, under the influence of the same mesmeric sleep of amazement, went up the large oaken stairs after the respectful attendant. He entered a splendid suite of apartments that seemed to be designed specially for him. He walked up to a long mirror with the ordinary instinct of his class, to pull his tie straight or to smooth his hair; and there he saw the frightful figure that he was – blood running down his face from where the bough had struck him, his hair standing out like yellow rags of rank grass, his clothes torn into long wavering tatters. At once the whole enigma sprang up, simply as the question of how he had got there, and how he was to get out again. Exactly at the same moment a man in blue, who had been appointed as his valet, said very solemnly:

'I have put out your clothes, sir.'

'Clothes!' said Syme sardonically. 'I have no clothes except these,' and he lifted two long strips of his frock-coat in fascinating festoon, and made a movement as if to twirl like a ballet girl.

'My master asks me to say,' said the attendant, 'that there is a fancy dress ball tonight, and that he desires you to put on the costume that I have laid out. Meanwhile, sir, there is a bottle of Burgundy and some cold pheasant, which he hopes you will not refuse, as it is some hours before supper.'

'Cold pheasant is a good thing,' said Syme reflectively, 'and Burgundy is a spanking good thing. But really I do not want either of them so much as I want to know what the devil all this means, and what sort of costume you have got laid out for me. Where is it?'

The servant lifted off a kind of ottoman[6] a long peacock-blue drapery, rather of the nature of a domino,[7] on the front of which was emblazoned a large golden sun, and which was splashed here and there with flaming stars and crescents.

'You're to be dressed as Thursday, sir,' said the valet somewhat affably.

'Dressed as Thursday,' said Syme in meditation. 'It doesn't sound a warm costume.'

'Oh yes, sir,' said the other eagerly, 'the Thursday costume is quite warm, sir. It fastens up to the chin.'

'Well, I don't understand anything,' said Syme, sighing. 'I have been used so long to uncomfortable adventures that comfortable adventures knock me out. Still, I may be allowed to ask why I should be particularly like Thursday in a green frock spotted all over with the sun and moon. Those orbs, I think, shine on other days. I once saw the moon on Tuesday, I remember.'

'Beg pardon, sir,' said the valet, 'Bible also provided for you,' and with a respectful and rigid finger he pointed out a passage in the first chapter of Genesis.[8] Syme read it wondering. It was that in which the fourth day of the week is associated with the creation of the sun and moon. Here, however, they reckoned from a Christian Sunday.

'This is getting wilder and wilder,' said Syme, as he sat down in a chair. 'Who are these people who provide cold pheasant and Burgundy, and green clothes and Bibles? Do they provide everything?'

'Yes, sir, everything,' said the attendant gravely. 'Shall I help you on with your costume?'

'Oh, hitch the bally thing on!' said Syme impatiently.

But though he affected to despise the mummery, he felt a curious freedom and naturalness in his movements as the blue and gold garment fell about him; and when he found that he had to wear a sword, it stirred a boyish dream. As he passed out of the room he flung the folds across his shoulder with a gesture, his sword stood out at an angle, and he had all the swagger of a troubadour. For these disguises did not disguise, but reveal.

15

The Accuser

As Syme strode along the corridor he saw the Secretary standing at the top of a great flight of stairs. The man had never looked so noble. He was draped in a long robe of starless black, down the centre of which fell a band or broad stripe of pure white, like a single shaft of light. The whole looked like some very severe ecclesiastical vestment. There was no need for Syme to search his memory or the Bible in order to remember that the first day of creation marked the mere creation of light out of darkness. The vestment itself would alone have suggested the symbol; and Syme felt also how perfectly this pattern of pure white and black expressed the soul of the pale and austere Secretary, with his inhuman veracity and his cold frenzy, which made him so easily make war on the anarchists, and yet so easily pass for one of them. Syme was scarcely surprised to notice that, amid all the ease and hospitality of their new surroundings, this man's eyes were still stern. No smell of ale or orchards could make the Secretary cease to ask a reasonable question.

If Syme had been able to see himself, he would have realized that he, too, seemed to be for the first time himself and no one else. For if the Secretary stood for that philosopher who loves the original and formless light, Syme was a type of the poet who seeks always to make the light in special shapes, to split it up into sun and star. The philosopher may sometimes love the infinite; the poet always loves the finite. For him the great moment is not the creation of light, but the creation of the sun and moon.

As they descended the broad stairs together they overtook Ratcliffe, who was clad in spring green like a huntsman, and the pattern upon whose garment was a green tangle of trees. For he stood for that third day on which the earth and green things were made, and his square, sensible face, with its not unfriendly cynicism, seemed appropriate enough to it.

They were led out of another broad and low gateway into a very large old English garden, full of torches and bonfires, by the broken light of which a vast carnival of people were dancing in motley dress. Syme seemed to see every shape in Nature imitated in some crazy costume. There was a man dressed as a windmill with enormous sails, a man dressed as an elephant, a man dressed as a balloon; the two last, together, seemed to keep the thread of their farcical adventures. Syme even saw, with a queer thrill, one dancer dressed like an enormous hornbill, with a beak twice as big as himself – the queer bird which had fixed itself on his fancy like a living question while he was rushing down the long road at the Zoological Gardens. There were a thousand other such objects, however. There was a dancing lamp-post, a dancing apple-tree, a dancing ship. One would have thought that the untamable tune of some mad musician had set all the common objects of field and street dancing an eternal jig. And long afterwards, when Syme was middle-aged and at rest, he could never see one of those particular objects – a lamp-post, or an apple-tree, or a windmill – without thinking that it was a strayed reveller from that revel of masquerade.

On one side of this lawn, alive with dancers, was a sort of green bank, like the terrace in such old-fashioned gardens.

Along this, in a kind of crescent, stood seven great chairs, the thrones of the seven days. Gogol and Dr Bull were already in their seats; the Professor was just mounting to his. Gogol, or Tuesday, had his simplicity well symbolized by a dress designed upon the division of the waters, a dress that separated upon his forehead and fell to his feet, grey and silver, like a sheet of rain. The Professor, whose day was that on which the birds and fishes – the ruder forms of life – were created, had a dress of dim purple, over which sprawled goggle-eyed fishes and outrageous tropical birds, the union in him of unfathomable fancy and of doubt. Dr Bull, the last day of Creation, wore a coat covered with heraldic animals in red and gold, and on his crest a man rampant.[1] He lay back in his chair with a broad smile, the picture of an optimist in his element.

One by one the wanderers ascended the bank and sat in their strange seats. As each of them sat down a roar of enthusiasm rose from the carnival, such as that with which crowds receive kings. Cups were clashed and torches shaken, and feathered hats flung in the air. The men for whom these thrones were reserved were men crowned with some extraordinary laurels. But the central chair was empty.

Syme was on the left hand of it and the Secretary on the right. The Secretary looked across the empty throne at Syme, and said, compressing his lips:

'We do not know that he is not dead in a field.'

Almost as Syme heard the words, he saw on the sea of human faces in front of him a frightful and beautiful alteration, as if heaven had opened behind his head. But Sunday had only passed silently along the front like a shadow, and had sat in the central seat. He was draped plainly, in a pure and terrible white, and his hair was like a silver flame on his forehead.

For a long time – it seemed for hours – that huge masquerade of mankind swayed and stamped in front of them to marching and exultant music. Every couple dancing seemed a separate romance; it might be a fairy dancing with a pillar-box, or a peasant girl dancing with the moon; but in each case it was, somehow, as absurd as Alice in Wonderland,[2] yet as grave and kind as a love story. At last, however, the thick crowd began to thin itself. Couples strolled away into the garden-walks, or began to drift towards that end of the building where stood smoking, in huge pots like fish-kettles, some hot and scented mixtures of old ale or wine. Above all these, upon a sort of black framework on the roof of the house, roared in its iron basket a gigantic bonfire, which lit up the land for miles. It flung the homely effect of firelight over the face of vast forests of grey or brown, and it seemed to fill with warmth even the emptiness of upper night. Yet this also, after a time, was allowed to grow fainter; the dim groups gathered more and more round the great cauldrons, or passed, laughing and clattering, into the inner passages of that ancient house. Soon there were only some ten loiterers in the

garden; soon only four. Finally the last stray merry-maker ran
into the house whooping to his companions. The fire faded, and
the slow, strong stars came out. And the seven strange men were
left alone, like seven stone statues on their chairs of stone. Not
one of them had spoken a word.

They seemed in no haste to do so, but heard in silence the
hum of insects and the distant song of one bird. Then Sunday
spoke, but so dreamily that he might have been continuing a
conversation rather than beginning one.

'We will eat and drink later,' he said. 'Let us remain together
a little, we who have loved each other so sadly, and have fought
so long. I seem to remember only centuries of heroic war, in
which you were always heroes – epic on epic, iliad on iliad,[3] and
you always brothers in arms. Whether it was but recently (for
time is nothing), or at the beginning of the world, I sent you out
to war. I sat in the darkness, where there is not any created thing,
and to you I was only a voice commanding valour and an
unnatural virtue. You heard the voice in the dark, and you never
heard it again. The sun in heaven denied it, the earth and sky
denied it, all human wisdom denied it. And when I met you in
the daylight I denied it myself.'

Syme stirred sharply in his seat, but otherwise there was
silence, and the incomprehensible went on.

'But you were men. You did not forget your secret honour,
though the whole cosmos turned an engine of torture to tear it
out of you. I knew how near you were to hell. I know how
you, Thursday, crossed swords with King Satan, and how you,
Wednesday, named me in the hour without hope.'

There was complete silence in the starlit garden, and then the
black-browed Secretary, implacable, turned in his chair towards
Sunday, and said in a harsh voice:

'Who and what are you?'

'I am the Sabbath,' said the other without moving. 'I am the
peace of God.'

The Secretary started up, and stood crushing his costly robe
in his hand.

'I know what you mean,' he cried, 'and it is exactly that that
I cannot forgive you. I know you are contentment, optimism,

what do they call the thing, an ultimate reconciliation. Well, I am not reconciled. If you were the man in the dark room, why were you also Sunday, an offence to the sunlight? If you were from the first our father and our friend, why were you also our greatest enemy? We wept, we fled in terror; the iron entered into our souls – and you are the peace of God! Oh, I can forgive God His anger, though it destroyed nations; but I cannot forgive Him His peace.'

Sunday answered not a word, but very slowly he turned his face of stone upon Syme as if asking a question.

'No,' said Syme, 'I do not feel fierce like that. I am grateful to you, not only for wine and hospitality here, but for many a fine scamper and free fight. But I should like to know. My soul and heart are as happy and quiet here as this old garden, but my reason is still crying out. I should like to know.'

Sunday looked at Ratcliffe, whose clear voice said:

'It seems so *silly* that you should have been on both sides and fought yourself.'

Bull said:

'I understand nothing, but I am happy. In fact, I am going to sleep.'

'I am not happy,' said the Professor with his head in his hands, 'because I do not understand. You let me stray a little too near to hell.'

And then Gogol said, with the absolute simplicity of a child:

'I wish I knew why I was hurt so much.'

Still Sunday said nothing, but only sat with his mighty chin upon his hand, and gazed at the distance. Then at last he said:

'I have heard your complaints in order. And here, I think, comes another to complain, and we will hear him also.'

The falling fire in the great cresset[4] threw a last long gleam, like a bar of burning gold, across the dim grass. Against this fiery band was outlined in utter black the advancing legs of a black-clad figure. He seemed to have a fine close suit with knee-breeches such as that which was worn by the servants of the house, only that it was not blue, but of this absolute sable. He had, like the servants, a kind of sword by his side. It was only when he had come quite close to the crescent of the seven and flung up his face to look at them, that Syme saw, with thunder-struck clearness, that the face was the broad, almost ape-like face of his old friend Gregory, with its rank red hair and its insulting smile.

'Gregory!' gasped Syme, half rising from his seat. 'Why, this is the real anarchist!'

'Yes,' said Gregory, with a great and dangerous restraint, 'I am the real anarchist.'

' "Now there was a day," '[5] murmured Bull, who seemed really to have fallen asleep, ' "when the sons of God came to present themselves before the Lord, and Satan came also among them." '

'You are right,' said Gregory, and gazed all round. 'I am a destroyer. I would destroy the world if I could.'

A sense of a pathos far under the earth stirred up in Syme, and he spoke brokenly and without sequence.

'Oh, most unhappy man,' he cried, 'try to be happy! You have red hair like your sister.'

'My red hair, like red flames, shall burn up the world,' said Gregory. 'I thought I hated everything more than common men hate anything; but I find that I do not hate everything as much as I hate you!'

'I never hated you,' said Syme very sadly.

Then out of this unintelligible creature the last thunders broke.

'You!' he cried. 'You never hated because you never lived. I know what you are, all of you, from first to last – you are the people in power! You are the police – the great fat, smiling men in blue and buttons! You are the Law, and you have never been broken. But is there a free soul alive that does not long to break you, only because you have never been broken? We in revolt talk all kind of nonsense doubtless about this crime or that crime of the Government. It is all folly! The only crime of the Government is that it governs. The unpardonable sin of the supreme power is that it is supreme. I do not curse you for being cruel. I do not curse you (though I might) for being kind. I curse you for being safe! You sit in your chairs of stone, and have never come down from them. You are the seven angels of heaven, and you have had no troubles. Oh, I could forgive you everything, you that rule mankind, if I could feel for once that you had suffered for one hour a real agony such as I—'

Syme sprang to his feet, shaking from head to foot. 'I see everything,' he cried, 'everything that there is. Why does each thing on the earth war against each other thing? Why does each small thing in the world have to fight against the world itself? Why does a fly have to fight the whole universe? Why does a dandelion have to fight the whole universe? For the same reason that I had to be alone in the dreadful Council of the Days. So that each thing that obeys law may have the glory and isolation of the anarchist. So that each man fighting for order may be as brave and good a man as the dynamiter. So that the real lie of Satan may be flung back in the face of this blasphemer, so that by tears and torture we may earn the right to say to this man, "You lie!" No agonies can be too great to buy the right to say to this accuser, "We also have suffered."

'It is not true that we have never been broken. We have been broken upon the wheel. It is not true that we have never descended from these thrones. We have descended into hell. We were complaining of unforgettable miseries even at the very moment when this man entered insolently to accuse us of happiness. I repel the slander; we have not been happy. I can answer for every one of the great guards of Law whom he has accused. At least—'

He had turned his eyes so as to see suddenly the great face of Sunday, which wore a strange smile.

'Have you,' he cried in a dreadful voice, 'have you ever suffered?'

As he gazed, the great face grew to an awful size, grew larger than the colossal mask of Memnon, which had made him scream as a child. It grew larger and larger, filling the whole sky; then everything went black. Only in the blackness before it entirely destroyed his brain he seemed to hear a distant voice saying a commonplace text that he had heard somewhere, 'Can ye drink of the cup that I drink of?'[6]

When men in books awake from a vision, they commonly find themselves in some place in which they might have fallen asleep;

they yawn in a chair, or lift themselves with bruised limbs from a field. Syme's experience was something much more psychologically strange if there was indeed anything unreal, in the earthly sense, about the things he had gone through. For while he could always remember afterwards that he had swooned before the face of Sunday, he could not remember having ever come to at all. He could only remember that gradually and naturally he knew that he was and had been walking along a country lane with an easy and conversational companion. That companion had been a part of his recent drama; it was the red-haired poet Gregory. They were walking like old friends, and were in the middle of a conversation about some triviality. But Syme could only feel an unnatural buoyancy in his body and a crystal simplicity in his mind that seemed to be superior to everything that he said or did. He felt he was in possession of some impossible good news, which made every other thing a triviality, but an adorable triviality.

Dawn was breaking over everything in colours at once clear and timid; as if Nature made a first attempt at yellow and a first attempt at rose. A breeze blew so clean and sweet that one could not think that it blew from the sky; it blew rather through some hole in the sky. Syme felt a simple surprise when he saw rising all round him on both sides of the road the red, irregular buildings of Saffron Park. He had no idea that he had walked so near London. He walked by instinct along one white road, on which early birds hopped and sang, and found himself outside a fenced garden. There he saw the sister of Gregory, the girl with the gold-red hair, cutting lilac before breakfast, with the great unconscious gravity of a girl.

Appendix

Extract from an article by G. K. Chesterton concerning
The Man Who Was Thursday *published in the*
Illustrated London News, *13 June 1936*

. . . I recur here to my personal point about the tendency to miss what the title means; or even what the title says . . . In a rambling column, whether because it is personal or impersonal, it is permissible to introduce personal trifles about oneself, as well as about other people, so long as it is made sufficiently obvious that they are trifling. And I may remark in this connexion, or disconnexion, that I happen to have a very strong objection to that trick of missing the point of a story, or sometimes even the obvious sense of the very name of a story. I have sometimes had occasion to murmur meekly that those who endure the heavy labour of reading a book might possibly endure that of reading the title-page of a book. For there are more examples than may be imagined, in which earnest critics might solve many of their problems about what a book is, merely by discovering what it professes to be.

. . . It is odd that one example occurred in my own case . . . in a book called *The Man Who Was Thursday*. It was a very melodramatic sort of moonshine, but it had a kind of notion in it; and the point is that it described, first a band of the last champions of order fighting against what appeared to be a world of anarchy, and then the discovery that the mysterious master both of the anarchy and the order was the same sort of elemental elf who had appeared to be rather too like a pantomime ogre. This line of logic, or lunacy, led many to infer that this equivocal being was meant for a serious description of the Deity; and my work even enjoyed a temporary respect among those who like the Deity to be so described. But this error was entirely due to the fact that they had read the book but had not read the title-page. In my case, it is true, it was a question of a subtitle rather than a title. The book was called *The Man Who Was Thursday: A Nightmare*. It was not intended to describe the real world as it was, or as I thought it was, even when my thoughts were considerably less settled than they are now. It was intended to describe the world of wild doubt and despair which the

pessimists were generally describing at that date; with just a gleam of
hope in some double meaning of the doubt, which even the pessimists
felt in some fitful fashion.

Notes

DEDICATION

1. *Edmund Clerihew Bentley*: E. C. Bentley (1875–1956), a lifelong friend of Chesterton, who first met him at St Paul's School, was a journalist, poet and novelist. As a poet, he is chiefly remembered for devising the 'clerihew', an epigrammatic verse form comprising two rhymed couplets, in his *Biography for Beginners* (1905). His fiction included *Trent's Last Case* (1913), an influential novel that Chesterton described as 'the best detective story of modern times'. In his *Autobiography* (1936), Chesterton celebrated Bentley's talent for constructing 'strategic maps of nonsense' and 'preposterous plots'.

2. *Whistler*: James Abbott McNeill Whister (1834–1903), an American painter who moved to London in 1859 and then became the most celebrated exponent of aestheticism in the visual arts, was for many of his contemporaries the embodiment of dandiacal decadence (he was a close friend of Oscar Wilde, who admired his mordant wit). In 1877, the influential critic John Ruskin, appalled by Whistler's 'Nocturne in Black and Gold', accused him of 'flinging a pot of paint in the public's face'; Whistler successfully sued Ruskin, but in the process ruined himself financially.

3. *showed their own white feather*: white feathers, which are characteristic of fighting cocks that are cross-bred rather than pure-bred, were, in the nineteenth-century British army, emblems of cowardice. Chesterton might have two recent novels in mind: A. E. W. Mason's *The Four Feathers* (1902); and P. G. Wodehouse's *The White Feather* (1907).

4. *Baal*: in the north-west Semitic language, this was a generic term applied to gods associated with particular cities, such as Carthage and Tyre, though it could also be used to refer to Hadad, the lord

of heaven. In Christian demonology, the name became associated with Satan, especially in the shape of Beelzebub.

5. *Paumanok*: the Algonquian name for Long Island, New York, meaning 'fish-shaped'. Long Island was the home of the American poet Walt Whitman (1819–92), an important influence on Chesterton, who refers to 'fish-shape [sic] Paumanok, where I was born' in the 1860 edition of *Leaves of Grass* (see Dedication, n. 7).

6. *Green Carnation*: *The Green Carnation* (1894), an anonymous novel by Robert Smythe Hichens (1864–1950), which featured characters manifestly based on Oscar Wilde and Lord Alfred Douglas, caused a scandal when it was first published, and was subsequently cited as evidence in Wilde's trial of 1895. Chesterton uses it in this context to emblematize Wildean aestheticism.

7. *leaves of grass*: the American poet Walt Whitman's *Leaves of Grass*, written in a form of free verse, was published in a series of ever-expanding editions from 1855 to 1891. According to his brother Cecil, Chesterton first read *Leaves of Grass* at about the time he was leaving school, and its spirit of democratic optimism had 'a profound and decisive influence on the growth of his mind' (this formative impact is evident in *The Wild Knight*, a collection of poems published in 1900). In *The Thing: Why I am a Catholic* (1929), Chesterton reflected that his entire youth had been 'filled, as with sunrise, with the sanguine glow of Walt Whitman'.

8. *Tusitala*: a Samoan name, meaning 'Teller of Tales', adopted by the Scottish novelist Robert Louis Stevenson (1850–94), who died of tuberculosis on the island of Upolu, where he had bought an estate in 1890. Stevenson, who had himself praised Whitman's optimism in *Essays in the Art of Writing* (1905), also exercised a decisive influence on Chesterton's intellectual development. In the final chapter of *Robert Louis Stevenson* (1927), Chesterton predicts that the novelist's importance will ultimately be understood when the contemporary modernist novel reaches its limits: 'The story, the first of childish and the oldest of human pleasures, will nowhere reveal its structure and its end so swiftly and simply as in the tales of Tusitala.'

9. *Dunedin to Samoa spoke*: 'Dunedin' is the Gaelic name for Edinburgh, where Stevenson was born, so this phrase alludes to his passage from Scotland to Samoa.

10. *the City of Mansoul*: the site of a battle between Satan and Emmanuel in John Bunyan's *The Holy War* (1682). William Oddie has commented in *Chesterton and the Romance of Orthodoxy* (2008) that Chesterton's interest in this spiritual allegory was

probably prompted by the fact that 'it is about the struggle for the salvation of a whole culture as much as for the salvation of individual souls'. In his edition of *The Man Who Was Thursday*, Denis Conlon observes that 'the image of Mansoul (Man's Soul) being relieved from siege was suggested to Chesterton by the sieges of Ladysmith and of Mafeking during the Boer War of 1899–1902'.

I

The Two Poets of Saffron Park

1. *Saffron Park*: a barely disguised portrait of Bedford Park, close to Turnham Green in west London, an almost self-contained community consisting of affordable red-brick houses built by Richard Norman Shaw (1831–1912) and other architects in the 1870s. This attractive tree-lined suburb, with its atmosphere of respectable bohemianism, became closely associated with aestheticism in the 1880s, when a number of artists, authors and intellectuals, notably the Irish poet W. B. Yeats (1865–1939) and the Russian anarchist Sergius Stepniak (1851–95), lived there. In the autumn of 1896, Chesterton became a member of a debating club that met in Bedford Park at the family home of Frances Blogg, whom he married in 1901. In the sixth chapter of his *Autobiography*, entitled 'The Fantastic Suburb', Chesterton describes seeing it for the first time after an aimless walk across London: 'it was evening, and I think it was then I saw in the distance of that grey landscape, like a ragged red cloud of sunset, the queer artificial village of Bedford Park.' He goes on to discuss 'the manufactured quaintness' of the place: 'Bedford Park did look like what it partially professed to be; a colony for artists who were almost aliens; a refuge for persecuted poets and painters hiding in their red-brick catacombs or dying behind their red-brick barricades.' The 'speculative builder, faintly tinged with art' to whom Chesterton refers in the succeeding sentence is Jonathan Thomas Carr (1845–1915), the cloth merchant who masterminded the construction of Bedford Park (he was assisted in this by his brother, J. W. Comyns Carr (1849–1916), the art critic and co-director of the Grosvenor Gallery).

2. *new women*: this refers to late nineteenth-century feminists, who were caricatured in the conservative press, from the second half of the 1880s, as aggressively masculine women who wore rational

dress, rode bicycles and smoked cigarettes. The term was finally coined in an article on 'The Social Standing of the New Woman', published in the *Woman's Herald* in August 1893: 'Without warning, woman suddenly appears on the scene of man's activities, as a sort of new creation, and demands a share in the struggles, the responsibilities and the honours of the world, in which, until now, she has been a cipher.'

3. *pre-Raphalite picture*: the Pre-Raphaelite Brotherhood (PRB), an attempt to develop a pictorial aesthetic shaped both by naturalism and symbolism, was formed in 1848 by the painters William Holman Hunt (1827–1910), John Everett Millais (1829–96) and Dante Gabriel Rossetti (1828–82), among others. For a concrete sense of Chesterton's allusion, see for instance Rossetti's 'The Girlhood of Mary Virgin' (1849), the first picture to be exhibited with the initials of the PRB. Incidentally, compare the description of 'dark red hair' in this sentence to Chesterton's sketch of 'the Diabolist', 'a man with a long ironical face, and close and red hair', in his article of that name, printed in the *Daily News* on 9 November 1907.

4. *the end of the world*: this recalls the apocalyptic conclusion to *The Time Machine* (1895), by H. G. Wells (1866–1946), when the Time-Traveller is transported into an entropic, far-distant future: 'At last, some time before I stopped, the sun, red and very large halted motionless upon the horizon, a vast dome glowing with a dull heat, and now and then suffering a momentary extinction.'

5. *local patriotism*: from the time of the Boer War (1899–1902), when jingoism was rife in England, Chesterton argued energetically for a form of patriotism that was committedly anti-imperialist. In 'A Defence of Patriotism', published in *The Speaker* in 1901, he referred with characteristic passion to 'this strange and perverted fact that, while a unifying vision of patriotism can ennoble bands of brutal savages or dingy burghers, and be the best thing in their lives, we, who are – the world being judge – humane, honest, and serious individually, have a patriotism that is the worst thing in ours'. Chesterton's first novel, *The Napoleon of Notting Hill* (1904), is an elaborate celebration of 'local patriotism', or, as Chesterton came to call it, 'distributism'.

6. *the name of Gabriel Syme*: as a number of critics have pointed out, this name confers an archangelic identity on Syme, just as the name Lucian implicitly confers a Luciferan one on Gregory.

7. *the Underground Railway*: the Metropolitan Railway, which

inaugurated the London Underground, opened in 1863. Turnham Green station, on the line from Richmond to the City, was built by the London and South Western Railway Company in 1869. The Metropolitan District Railway, known as the District, which ran its trains on this line from 1877, constructed an additional line from Turnham Green to Ealing in 1879.

8. *Bradshaw*: the compendious train timetable published by the printer George Bradshaw (1801–53). It has served as an important plot device in English detective and adventure fiction. In *The Riddle of the Sands* (1903), by Erskine Childers (1870–1922), the narrator provides this parenthetical description: 'an extraordinary book, Bradshaw, turned to from habit, even when least wanted, as men fondle guns and rods in the close season.'

9. *no man born of woman*: see the Second Apparition's speech in *Macbeth* 4.1: 'Be bloody, bold, and resolute: laugh to scorn / The power of man, for none of woman born / Shall harm Macbeth.' (It transpires of course that Macduff, who finally kills Macbeth, 'was from his mother's womb / Untimely ripp'd.')

10. *flâneur*: from the French verb *flâner*, meaning to stroll, this refers to someone who transforms strolling in the metropolis into an almost full-time occupation. Although the *flâneur* was a fairly common Parisian archetype in the first half of the nineteenth century, his most celebrated appearance is probably in 'The Painter of Modern Life' (1863), by Charles Baudelaire (1821–67): 'For the perfect *flâneur*, for the passionate spectator, it is an immense joy to set up house in the heart of the multitude, amid the ebb and flow of movement, in the midst of the fugitive and the infinite.'

11. *Colney Hatch*: the Colney Hatch Pauper Lunatic Asylum, close to London, which opened in 1851.

2

The Secret of Gabriel Syme

1. *crème de menthe*: a syrupy mint liqueur, either green or colourless.
2. *a kind of screw*: if in the previous sentence Gregory had used this term in the ordinary sense of a cylindrical mechanical appliance, Syme sardonically repeats it in order to signify a means of coercion ('the screws' or 'the screw', derived from 'thumbscrew', indicated an instrument of torture).
3. *Mr Joseph Chamberlain*: Joseph Chamberlain (1836–1914) was the Liberal MP who led the Unionists in the later 1880s and so

played a decisive part in opposing Home Rule. As Secretary for
the Colonies under the Conservatives between 1895 and 1903,
he was largely responsible for prosecuting the Boer War. He
resigned from this government in order to campaign for tariff
reform, an issue that split the Conservatives and led, in 1906, to
a Liberal landslide.

4. *New Anarchists*: the late nineteenth century, when this novel is
set, is the period in which the anarchist movement was most
dramatically defined by 'propaganda of the deed', a form of direct
action that, in spite of the impression created in the popular press,
did not necessarily entail individual acts of violence. In 'The Spirit
of Revolt' (1880), for example, the celebrated Russian anarchist
Peter Kropotkin (1842–1921), who was to spend much of his
exile in England, argued as follows: 'When a revolutionary situation arises in a country, before the spirit of revolt is sufficiently
awakened in the masses to express itself in violent demonstrations
in the streets, or by rebellions and uprisings, it is through *actions*
that minorities succeed in awakening that feeling of independence
and that spirit of audacity without which no revolution can come
to a head.' Kropotkin's opposition to spectacular acts of violence
did not however prevent others from using his insistence that
'one such act may, in a few days, make more propaganda than
thousands of pamphlets' to justify terroristic attacks. For anarchists performed a number of such acts of violence in the 1890s and
1900s: in 1893, the Chamber of Deputies in Paris was bombed;
in 1894, there was an unsuccessful bomb attack on the Royal
Observatory at Greenwich in London, an episode that famously
formed the basis for *The Secret Agent* (1907) by Joseph Conrad
(1857–1924); also in 1894, the French president was assassinated;
in 1897, the Spanish prime minister was assassinated; in 1900,
the King of Italy was assassinated; in 1906, there was a failed
attempt to bomb the King of Spain, Alfonso XIII (in 'The Folly
of Anarchists', printed in the *Illustrated London News*, Chesterton
opined that 'the attempt at Madrid is too atrocious to be taken
seriously'); and, finally, in February 1908, the month in which
The Man Who Was Thursday was published, the King of Portugal
and his son were assassinated.

5. *Nietzsche*: in an attack on so-called 'levellers' in *Beyond Good
and Evil* (1886), the German philosopher Friedrich Nietzsche
(1844–1900) argued: 'We believe that severity, violence, slavery,
danger in the street and in the heart, secrecy, stoicism, tempter's
art and devilry of every kind – that everything wicked, terrible,

tyrannical, predatory and serpentine in man, serves as well for the elevation of the human species as its opposite.'

6.   *the Central Anarchist Council*: the acronym CAC irresistibly evokes the Greek word *kakos*, meaning 'bad' or 'evil'. The word 'cacotopia', originally coined in 1818 by Jeremy Bentham (1748–1832), had been used in 1868 by John Stuart Mill (1806–73) during a parliamentary debate about Ireland: the Conservatives, he insisted, were not 'Utopians' in their policy-making, but 'dystopians, or cacotopians'.

7.   *Bloody Sunday*: this alludes to a demonstration in Trafalgar Square on Sunday 13 November 1887, organised by anarchists, radicals, socialists and Irish nationalists in response to a ban against open-air meetings there. The demonstration, consisting of about ten thousand people, was brutally suppressed by policemen and soldiers, who severely injured several hundred working-class demonstrators. In consequence, this event played an important part in the mythology of class conflict in late nineteenth-century England. William Morris (1834–96), who attended the demonstration, used the events of Bloody Sunday as the basis for his portrait of socialist revolution in *News from Nowhere* (1891).

3
The Man Who Was Thursday

1.   *Mr Tim Healy*: Tim Healy (1855–1931), the Irish barrister and anti-Parnellite politician, a small, bespectacled, bearded man with a reputation for scurrilous debate, was MP for North Louth from 1892 to 1910. In *Heretics* (1905), Chesterton describes him as 'the most serious intellect in the present House of Commons'.

2.   *Sabbatarian*: either, generally, a Christian 'whose opinion and practice with regard to Sunday observance are unusually strict'; or, specifically, 'a member of a Christian sect founded towards the close of the sixteenth century, the members of which maintained that the Sabbath should be observed on the seventh and not on the first day of the week' (*OED*).

3.   *Ally Sloper's Half-Holiday and the Sporting Times*: *Ally Sloper's Half-Holiday*, a weekly comic paper, priced at a penny and published from 1884 to 1923, was popular both among the working classes and some bohemian sections of the middle classes (William Morris was, for example, a keen reader); the *Sporting Times*,

published weekly between 1865 and 1932, purveyed social gossip as well as news about horse racing.

4. *Catacombs*: in Chesterton's short story 'The Nightmare', probably written in 1907, though published posthumously in *The Coloured Lands* (1938), the narrator wakes up to discover that London is ruled by Nietzschean pessimists and that, in consequence, Christians have secreted themselves in the Underground, like those who sought refuge from the persecution of the Romans in the catacombs.

5. *the shopwalker*: either someone who supervises customers in a particular department of a shop; or 'an attendant who directs customers to that part of the premises where the goods they wish to inspect or purchase are to be found' (*OED*).

4
The Tale of a Detective

1. *a Chinese Invasion*: this recalls anxieties in Europe at the time of the so-called Boxer Rebellion, an anti-imperialist struggle that took place in China from 1898 to 1901. *The Yellow Danger* (1898), by M. P. Shiel (1865–1947), a fantastical novel depicting Chinese domination of the globe, was especially popular in England during the uprising.

2. *a stream of literal fire*: compare the 'boiling red water' of the rivers in the seventh circle of Hell in Canto XIV of Dante's *Inferno*.

3. *Bulwer Lytton*: Edward George Earle Lytton Bulwer Lytton (1803–73), one of the most prolific and popular novelists of the nineteenth century, was the author of *Night and Morning* (1841) and *Zanoni* (1842), among many other more or less sensational fictions.

4. *the Board Schools*: these secular elementary schools, controlled by local elected boards, were instituted in areas of 'educational destitution' in England and Wales as a result of the Education Act of 1870.

5. *Harrow*: founded in 1572, Harrow is a public school (that is, an independent, fee-paying school) located at the north-west edge of London.

6. *pot-houses*: taverns or public houses, in which ale was served in pots.

7. *triolet*: from the French meaning 'little three', this refers to a verse form consisting of eight lines and two rhymes, in which the first line is repeated as the fourth and seventh, and the second as the

eighth line. In the late nineteenth century it was associated with Austin Dobson (1840–1921), W. E. Henley (1849–1903) and Robert Bridges (1844–1930) in particular.

8. *that disastrous twilight which Milton spoke of as shed by the sun in eclipse*: see John Milton (1608–74), *Paradise Lost* Book I, lines 594–9: '. . . as when the sun new risen / Looks through the horizontal misty air / Shorn of his beams, or from behind the moon / In dim eclipse disastrous twilight sheds / On half the nations, and with fear of change / Perplexes monarchs.' In the early 1890s, Chesterton was a leading member of a school debating society, the Junior Debating Club ('JDC'), and published a discussion of *Paradise Lost* in its undated magazine, *The Debater*: 'Milton's intellect could get as high as the Devil's, but no higher', was his judgement.

9. *stirrup-cup*: 'a cup of wine or other drink handed to a man when already on horseback setting out for a journey; a parting glass' (OED).

10. *some Egyptian Palace*: in 1878, the ancient Egyptian obelisk popularly called Cleopatra's Needle, which had been transplanted from Alexandria, was erected on the Victoria Embankment beside the Thames.

5
The Feast of Fear

1. *Leicester Square: More New Arabian Nights: The Dynamiter* (1885), by Robert Louis Stevenson and his wife Fanny van de Grift Stevenson (1840–1914), begins with an encounter 'on the broad northern pavement of Leicester Square'. In 'Zero's Tale of the Explosive Bomb', a chapter in the same volume, the arch-anarchist villain Zero describes one of his diabolical attempts to cause destruction in London: 'Our objective was the effigy of Shakespeare in Leicester Square: a spot, I think, admirably chosen; not only for the sake of the dramatist, still very foolishly claimed as a glory by the English race, in spite of his disgusting political opinions; but from the fact that the seats in the immediate neighbourhood are often thronged by children, errand-boys, unfortunate young ladies of the poorer class and infirm old men – all classes making a direct appeal to public pity, and therefore suitable with our designs.'

2. *the Alhambra*: a theatre and music-hall with a number of Moorish architectural features first built in 1854 on the east side of

Leicester Square. The decadent poet Arthur Symons (1865–1945) had celebrated its charms in 'At the Alhambra: Impressions and Sensations' (1896).

3. *the mask of Memnon in the British Museum*: this probably refers to the colossal bust of Rameses II, the remaining fragment of a vast granite sculpture built in about 1250 BCE, which was excavated from the mortuary temple of Rameses at Thebes by Giovanni Belzoni (1778–1824) in 1816. This monumental head, which had arrived in London in 1818, was bought by the British Museum in 1821, when it came to be called the 'Younger Memnon'. The prospect of its imminent appearance is thought to have inspired Percy Bysshe Shelley (1792–1822) to compose 'Ozymandias' (1818).

4. *diablerie*: 'business belonging to or connected with the devil, or in which the devil is employed or has a hand; dealings with the devil; sorcery or conjuring in which the devil is supposed to assist; wild recklessness, devilry' (*OED*). In his *Autobiography*, Chesterton described the decadent culture of the *fin de siècle* as 'that world of diabolism'. Note incidentally that he regarded the 'grotesque' as a significant aesthetic and even 'philosophical' category; so in *Robert Browning* (1903), for instance, he argues positively that 'to present a matter in a grotesque manner does certainly tend to touch the nerve of surprise and thus to draw attention to the intrinsically miraculous character of the object itself'.

5. *cicerone*: 'a guide who shows and explains the antiquities or curiosities of a place to strangers' (*OED*). Cicero was Dante's guide in *Inferno*.

6. *the darker poems of Byron and Poe*: see, for example, 'Lara' (1814) by George Gordon, Lord Byron (1788–1824): ''Twas midnight – all was slumber; the lone light / Dimm'd in the lamp, as loth to break the night'; and 'The Raven' (1845) by Edgar Allan Poe (1809–49): 'And his eyes have all the seeming of a demon's that is dreaming / And the lamp-light o'er him streaming throws his shadows on the floor; / And my soul from out that shadow that lies floating on the floor / Shall be lifted – nevermore!'

6

The Exposure

1. *the super-man*: in *George Bernard Shaw* (1909), Chesterton complained that Nietzsche had 'succeeded in putting into [Shaw's]

head a new superstition, which bids fair to be the chief superstition of the dark ages which are possibly in front of us – I mean the superstition of what is called the Superman'.

2. *Strasbourg pie*: Strasbourg or Strasburg pie is a pâté made with fatty goose livers. In *Vanity Fair* (1848), by W. M. Thackeray (1811–63), for example, it is reported that, as a young man in the diplomatic service at Pumpernickel, Pitt Crawley used to bring home 'dispatches, consisting of Strasburg pie, to the Foreign Minister of the day'.

3. '*Païens ont tort et Chrétiens ont droit*': literally, 'the Pagans are wrong and the Christians are right' (it should read: '*Paien unt tort e Chestïens unt dreit*'). In Chesterton's introduction to a translation of 'The Song of Roland' by Charles Scott Moncrieff (1889–1930), published in 1919, he asserts that 'the value of the tale was that it hinted that there is a heart in history, even remote history'. This essay concludes: 'The poem ends, as it were, with a vision and vista of wars against the barbarians; and the vision is true. For that war is never ended, which defends the sanity of the world against all the stark anarchies and rending negations which rage against it for ever. That war is never finished in this world; and the grass has hardly grown on the graves of our own friends who fell in it.'

7

The Unaccountable Conduct of Professor De Worms

1. *de trop*: too much, superfluous.

2. *Timbuctoo*: the name of an ancient city on the edge of the Sahara in West Africa which, since the mid-nineteenth century, has been proverbial for an almost unimaginably distant place.

3. *splash-board*: 'a board fixed over or beside a wheel to intercept splashings' (*OED*). Here it refers to the open platform at the back of the bus.

4. *the great orb and the cross*: these symbols ornament the top of St Paul's Cathedral in London. They are of considerable symbolic importance to *The Ball and the Cross*, first published in serial form from 1905 to 1906, though it remained uncompleted until it appeared in book form in 1910. In his *Autobiography*, Chesterton summarized it as a novel 'about two men perpetually prevented by the police from fighting a duel about the collision of blasphemy and worship'. In its opening scene, Professor Lucifer

and the monk called Michael hurtle past the dome of St Paul's in the former's 'flying ship': 'A plain of sad-coloured cloud lay along the level of the top of the Cathedral dome, so that the ball and the cross looked like a buoy riding on a leaden sea.' 'What could possibly express your philosophy and my philosophy better than the shape of that cross and the shape of this ball?' Lucifer goes on to ask; 'This globe is reasonable; that cross is unreasonable. It is a four-legged animal, with one leg longer than the others. The globe is inevitable. The cross is arbitrary. Above all the globe is at unity with itself; the cross is primarily and above all things at enmity with itself.' Compare too 'The Nightmare' (see Chapter 3, note 4), in which the narrator, rushing up from the safety of the Underground, finds himself standing before St Paul's Cathedral, which is 'like the lost temple of some empty planet'.

8

The Professor Explains

1. *If heaven were his throne and the earth his footstool*: see Isaiah 66: 1: 'Thus saith the Lord, the heaven *is* my throne, and the earth *is* my footstool: where *is* the house that ye build unto me? And where *is* the place of my rest?'; and Acts 7: 49: 'Heaven *is* my throne, and earth *is* my footstool: what house will ye build me? saith the Lord: or what *is* the place of my rest?'

2. *Tower of Babel*: in Genesis 11: 1-9, the people of the earth, who are 'of one language, and of one speech', build a tower 'whose top *may reach* unto heaven', though they do so in the name of humanity rather than God. On seeing the tower, God announces that, as a result, 'nothing will be restrained from them, which they have imagined to do', and he therefore 'confound[s] their language, that they may not understand one another's speech', and scatters them abroad: 'Therefore is the name of it called Babel; because the Lord did there confound the language of all the earth: and from thence did the Lord scatter them abroad upon the face of all the earth.'

3. *Argus*: in Greek mythology, Argus Panoptes, often depicted as possessing up to one hundred eyes, was a giant employed by Hera to guard Io.

4. *Mâcon*: a red or white wine produced in the Mâconnais region of Burgundy in France.

5. *the false pig in Aesop*: probably a nonsense formulation, though

in his edition, Stephen Medcalf identifies the phrase with 'the fable of the Buffoon and the Countryman, actually by Phaedrus but ascribed by him to Aesop': 'A Buffoon at a theatre imitated a pig's squeak so perfectly that the audience insisted he must have a pig hidden about his person, but applauded him deafeningly when he convinced them he had not. A countryman claimed he could do better, and made a pig which he had beneath his smock squeak. The audience unanimously declared that the buffoon's imitation was much more true to life. The countryman, producing the pig, said "that shows what sort of judges you are".' In 1912, Chesterton provided the Introduction to V. S. Vernon Jones's translation of *Aesop's Fables*, illustrated by Arthur Rackham. There he insists that, in contrast to fairy tales, fables like those for which Aesop was famous are premised on the idea 'that everything is itself, and will in any case speak for itself. The wolf will be always wolfish; the fox will be always foxy.' According to this theory, the idea of a 'false pig' is completely incompatible with Aesop.

6.   *the hedgehog in Montaigne*: another nonsense formulation, as Chesterton indicates in the succeeding sentence, though Medcalf observes that 'there is actually a hedgehog in Montaigne, which forecasts changes of the wind'. Michel Eyquem de Montaigne (1533–92) was a French humanist philosopher famed for his essays.

9

The Man in Spectacles

1.   *a tyrant once advised us to eat grass*: in his edition, Medcalf notes that 'Joseph François Foulon (1717–89) was alleged to have said this when minister of the king's household in France, probably untruly: but grass was thrust into his mouth when he was hanged on 22 July 1789, a story which fascinated Chesterton'.

2.   *Acheron*: in the *Aeneid*, Charon ferries the dead across the Acheron to reach the Underworld.

3.   *Marat or a more slipshod Robespierre*: along with Georges Danton (1759–94), Jean-Paul Marat (1743–93) and Maximilien Robespierre (1758–94) were the most important leaders of the French Revolution. Robespierre's appearance was notoriously neat, even at the height of the Terror in 1793 and 1794.

4.   *Jacobins*: radicals belonging to the Jacobin Club, led by Robespierre, Marat and Danton, the most influential of the

political clubs to appear during the French Revolution.

5. *golliwog*: a black-faced minstrel doll made famous by Florence Kate Upton (1873–1922) in the children's stories she published from the mid-1890s.

6. *Bogy*: a term either for 'the evil one, the devil' or for 'a goblin; a person much dreaded', apparently in use in children's nurseries since the 1820s (see *OED*). Interestingly, the *OED* claims that, at least from the 1920s, it was also criminals' slang for a detective.

7. *the Savoy*: a grand hotel on the Strand in London, designed by Thomas Edward Collcutt (1840–1924) and opened in 1889.

8. *blue devils in blue hell*: the phrase 'blue devils' is proverbial for a state of depression; in 'Half Hours in Hades: An Elementary Handbook of Demonology', composed in 1891 when he was seventeen, and published in *The Coloured Lands* (1938), Chesterton taxonomizes the 'Blue Devil (Caeruleus Lugubrius)' thus: 'These creatures are gregarious, being usually seen and spoken of in the plural. Though formed by super-Nature in their habits and exterior apparently for the filling of waste moors, mountains, churchyards and other obsolete places, these animals, like the Red Devil, have frequently been domesticated in rich and distinguished houses, and many of the wealthiest aristocrats and most successful men of commerce may be seen with a string of these blue creatures led by a leash in the street or seated round him in a ring on his own fireside.'

9. *the British Constitution*: in *The English Constitution* (1867), Walter Bagheot (1826–77) began by observing that 'the British Constitution has continued in connected outward sameness, but hidden inner change, for many ages', comparing it to 'an old man who still wears with attached fondness clothes in the fashion of his youth: what you see of him is the same; what you do not see is wholly altered'.

10. *josser*: slang for 'a simpleton; a soft or silly fellow' (*OED*).

11. *the Grey Nose*: the Cap Gris-Nez, a cape on the coast of northern France to the south-west of Calais, is the closest point of France to England.

12. *the Romans who held the bridge*: this refers to the legend, narrated by Livy and others, of the Roman soldier Horatius Cocles and his comrades, who heroically defended the Pons Sublicius, the oldest recorded bridge across the Tiber in Rome, against the Etruscans. In 'Horatius', from his *Lays of Ancient Rome* (1842), Thomas Babington Macaulay (1800–59) described this incident: 'Haul down the bridge, Sir Consul, / With all the speed ye may; / I, with

two more to help me, / Will hold the foe in play. / In yon strait path a thousand / May well be stopped by three. / Now who will stand on either hand, / And keep the bridge with me?' See also Chapter 12, note 6.

13.   *Bruce at Bannockburn*: on 24 June 1314, Robert the Bruce (1274–1329), King of Scotland, defeated Edward II (1284–1327), in spite of the fact that the former's army was far smaller than the latter's.

14.   '*argent a chevron gules charged with three cross crosslets of the field*': a silver coat of arms consisting of a red chevron bearing three silver crosses each limb of which terminates in a smaller cross.

10

The Duel

1.   *Saumur*: a sparkling wine from the Saumur region of the Loire in France.

2.   *café chantant*: a café in which music is performed, associated especially with the *belle époque*.

3.   *Legion of Honour*: the Ordre national de la Légion d'honneur, a decoration founded by Napoleon Bonaparte (1769–1821) in 1802.

4.   *décoré*: decorated.

5.   *Peste*: an expletive, meaning 'Plague!'

6.   *Going to Jericho to throw a Jabberwock*: in his edition, Conlon notes that this is equivalent to 'going to Hell', and adds (a little dogmatically) that 'Jericho in this case is not the city to the north of the Dead Sea in Palestine but a country estate of that name where Henry VIII had assignations with young ladies'. The 'jabberwock' is the fantastic beast described in 'Jabberwocky', a nonsense poem by Lewis Carroll (1832–98), which appeared in *Through the Looking-Glass and What Alice Found There* (1871): 'Beware the Jabberwock, my son! / The jaws that bite, the claws that catch!' See also Chapter 13, note 10; and Chapter 15, note 2.

7.   *paper-chase*: 'a cross-country race in which the runners follow a trail marked by torn-up paper' (*OED*).

8.   *blind man's buff*: a game in which a player in a blindfold attempts to capture other players who deliberately poke at him and provoke him.

II
The Criminals Chase the Police

1. *cinematograph*: the *cinématographe* was the means of producing
    motion pictures first patented, used and exhibited by Auguste
    (1862–1954) and Louis (1864–1948) Lumière in 1895. In 1896,
    the *Daily News* reported on the first exhibition of the cine-
    matograph in London: 'The "Cinématographe" is an invention of
    MM. Lumiere, and it is a contrivance by which a real scene of life
    and movement may be reproduced before an audience in a life
    size picture.'

2. *Impressionism*: Chesterton's most significant encounter with
    Impressionism came in 1893, when he enrolled at the Slade School
    of Art, where Whistler was especially fashionable. He identified
    its aesthetic with the extreme philosophical relativism that, in
    opposition to his deepest spiritual convictions, seemed character-
    istic of the *fin de siècle*. In his *Autobiography*, he attacked
    Impressionist painting in passionate tones, adducing it as an
    example of 'scepticism in the sense of subjectivism': 'Its principle
    was that if all that could be seen of a cow was a white line and a
    purple shadow, we should only render the line and the shadow;
    in a sense we should only believe in the line and shadow, rather
    than in the cow. [. . .] Whatever may be the merits of this as a
    method of art, there is obviously something highly subjective and
    sceptical about it as a method of thought. It naturally lends itself
    to the metaphysical suggestion that things only exist as we perceive
    them, or that things do not exist at all.' See also the Introduction
    to this edition.

3. *Lancy*: probably Bourbon-Lancy, an ancient town close to the
    Loire in Bourgogne, eastern France.

4. *barons' wars*: the civil war, from 1264 to 1268, between Henry
    III (1207–72) and the rebellious barons led by Simon de Montfort
    (1208–65), who were determined to enforce the limitations on
    royal power set out in the Provisions of Oxford (1258) and the
    Provisions of Westminster (1259).

5. *dévot*: devout.

6. *Le Soleil d'Or*: The Golden Sun.

12

The Earth in Anarchy

1. *Attila*: Attila (406–53) was emperor of the Huns, a people whose impressive incursions into the Roman Empire from the East were achieved by armies on horseback.

2. *Musée de Cluny*: the Musée de Cluny, the Musée National du Moyen Age in Paris, which was originally built by the abbots of Cluny in the fourteenth century, contains a rich collection of mediaeval manuscripts, sculptures and tapestries.

3. *Peabody Buildings*: the capitalist and philanthropist George Peabody (1795–1869) had founded the Peabody Donation Fund to build housing for the poor in the east end of London in the 1860s.

4. *Hanwell*: the Hanwell Insane Asylum, to the west of London, was opened in 1829. Note that in Chapter 2 of *Orthodoxy* (1908), 'The Maniac', Chesterton illustrates his opening argument, that so-called worldly people do not understand the world but rely instead 'on a few cynical maxims which are not true', by relating an anecdote about a publisher who pompously announces of a common acquaintance, 'That man will get on; he believes in himself.' Chesterton continues: 'And I remember that as I lifted my head to listen, my eye caught an omnibus on which was written "Hanwell". I said to him, "Shall I tell you where the men are who believe most in themselves? For I can tell you. I know of men who believe in themselves more colossally than Napoleon or Caesar. I know where flames the fixed star of certainty and success. I can guide you to the thrones of the Super-men. The men who really believe in themselves are all in lunatic asylums."'

5. *navvy or counter-jumper*: manual labourer or shop assistant.

6. *Horatius and his bridge*: see Chapter 9, note 12.

7. *the Dunciad*: these are the final lines of *The Dunciad* (1743) by Alexander Pope (1688–1744), and should read: 'Nor *public* Flame, nor *private*, dares to shine; / Nor *human* Spark is left, nor Glimpse *divine*! / Lo! thy dread Empire, CHAOS! Is restor'd; / Light dies before thy uncreating word: / Thy hand, great Anarch! lets the curtain fall; / And Universal Darkness buries All' (Book IV, lines 651–6).

8. *Judas before Herod*: Judas is led before Herod and humiliated by him in the Gospel of Barnabas, an account of the life of Jesus recorded in sixteenth-century manuscripts composed in Italian and Spanish.

13
The Pursuit of the President

1. *Tree of Life*: the 'tree of life' appears in numerous different ancient religious and folkloric traditions, but presumably Chesterton is above all thinking of its importance in Genesis, and especially in the account of the Fall. See Genesis 3: 22–4: 'And the Lord God said, Behold, the man is become as one of us, to know good and evil: and now, lest he put forth his hand, and take also of the tree of life, and eat, and live for ever: / Therefore the Lord God sent him forth from the garden of Eden, to till the ground from whence he was taken. / So he drove out the man; and he placed at the east of the garden of Eden Cherubims, and a flaming sword which turned every way, to keep the way of the tree of life.'

2. *like some huge orang-outang*: perhaps an allusion to Poe's 'The Murders in the Rue Morgue' (1841), often regarded as the first detective story, in which an escaped orang-utan violently kills one Madame L'Espanaye and her daughter and flees through a casement.

3. *a great ball of india-rubber*: in Chapter 9 of *Charles Dickens* (1906), Chesterton writes that Dickens's life was full of the 'unexpected energies' of a pantomime clown: 'He liked high houses, and sloping roofs, and deep areas. But he would have been really happy if some good fairy of the eternal pantomime had given him the power of flying off the roofs and pitching harmlessly down the height of the houses and bounding out of the areas like an india-rubber ball. The divine lunatic in *Nicholas Nickleby* comes nearest to his dream.'

4. *Martin Tupper*: Martin Tupper (1810–89) was the author of *Proverbial Philosophy: A Book of Thoughts and Arguments* (1838), a collection of commonplace poetic aphorisms which proved an immense popular success in the mid-nineteenth century. In the later nineteenth century, under the impact of scientific advance in particular, Tupper's Christian platitudes became to some the embodiment of an empty and outdated ideology of progress.

5. *goloshes*: an over-shoe, made of leather or (from the late nineteenth century) india-rubber, designed to protect the shoe itself from damp and dirt.

6. *The elephant*: in *Chesterton: Man and Mask* (1961), Gary Wills noted that 'the final chase through monstrous scenes, thronged

with trumpeting and incredible beasts, is a glimpse of [the] animal world which Jehovah called up for Job. Syme is answered by the elephant, as Job was by Behemoth.'

7. *pelican*: the pelican, a common heraldic device, is the Christian symbol both of charity and of Christ crucified because, according to legend, it savaged its own breast in order to feed life-giving blood to its hungry young.

8. *the Albert Hall*: the Royal Albert Hall, a vast amphitheatrical concert hall dedicated to Queen Victoria's late husband Prince Albert (1819–61), who had helped organize the Great Exhibition of 1851 in nearby Hyde Park, was opened in 1871. It is approximately two kilometres, across the park, from Paddington.

9. *Wheel of Earl's Court*: the Great Wheel, a ferris wheel modelled on the Chicago Wheel, was opened in 1895 at the Empire of India Exhibition in Earl's Court, an event devised by the impresario Imre Kiralfy (1845–1919). It was demolished in 1907. In his *Descriptive Album of London* (c.1896), the architect George Birch (1842–1904) wrote that 'the big wheel always has its crowd of patrons who like to experience the exhilarating effects of an ascent into the air, minus the dangers attending a balloon and the probability of making an ascent rather higher than they originally intended, and the improbability of landing on the earth again in a perfect condition'.

10. *Snowdrop*: in his edition, Gardner points out that 'it may not be a coincidence that Snowdrop was the name of Alice's kitten, as we learn from the last chapter of Lewis Carroll's *Through the Looking Glass*'. See also Chapter 10, note 6; and Chapter 15, note 2.

14
The Six Philosophers

1. *Why leap ye, ye high hills*: see Psalm 68: 16: 'Why leap ye, ye high hills? *this is* the hill *which* God desireth to dwell in; yea, the Lord will dwell *in it* for ever.'

2. *bounder*: Chesterton probably has three associations in mind: someone who leaps about; someone characterized by objectionable or anti-social manners; and, to cite the *OED*, someone 'who sets or marks out bounds or limits' ('All my life I have loved edges,' Chesterton writes in his *Autobiography*; 'and the boundary-line that brings one thing sharply against another').

3. *the deep sea-lumps and protoplasm*: this recalls 'the Thing' sent from Mars in H. G. Wells's *The War of the Worlds* (1898), and the Martians that emerge from it: the first of these is described as 'a big, greyish rounded bulk, the size, perhaps, of a bear', which 'glistened like wet leather' and 'heaved and pulsated convulsively'. It also evokes the end of the penultimate chapter of *The Time Machine*, where the Time Traveller, briefly marooned in the far-distant future, glimpses life on earth beginning again (see Chapter 1, note 4).

4. *Barnum's freak*: Phineas Taylor Barnum (1810–91) was an American impresario and circus-owner, famous in England for his 'Barnum and London Circus', the central attraction of which was an elephant called Jumbo, which he bought from London Zoo in 1882. The roster of 'freaks' who performed for Barnum included, most famously, General Tom Thumb.

5. *Pan*: Pan, who has the hooves, legs, hindquarters and horns of a goat, is in Greek mythology the god of shepherds and of all things pastoral. In the Greek language, *pan* means 'all'.

6. *ottoman*: 'a low upholstered seat without a back or arms, typically serving also as a box, with the seat hinged to form a lid' (*OED*).

7. *domino*: 'a kind of loose cloak, apparently of Venetian origin, chiefly worn at masquerades, with a small mask covering the upper part of the face, by persons [im]personating a character' (*OED*).

8. *a passage in the first chapter of Genesis*: see Genesis 1: 14–18: 'And God said, Let there be lights in the firmament of the heaven to divide the day from the night; and let them be for signs, and for seasons, and for days, and years: / And let them be for lights in the firmament of the heaven to give light upon the earth: and it was so. / And God made two great lights; the greater light to rule the day, and the lesser light to rule the night: *he made* the stars also. / And God set them in the firmament of the heaven to give light upon the earth, / And to rule over the day and over the night, and to divide the light from the darkness: and God saw that *it was* good.'

15

The Accuser

1. *a man rampant*: in heraldry, this generally refers to a four-legged animal standing on its hind feet with its forepaws in the air;

applied to humans, as in this rather mischievous image, it signifies a fierce disposition.

2.   *Alice in Wonderland*: a reference to *Alice's Adventures in Wonderland* (1865) by Lewis Carroll. In Chapter 3, 'A Caucus-Race and a Long Tale', the Dodo presents Alice with a thimble she has found in her own pocket as a prize: 'Alice thought the whole thing very absurd, but they all looked so grave that she did not dare to laugh.' See also Chapter 10, note 6; and Chapter 13, note 7.

3.   *iliad*: an epic poem like the *Iliad*, the celebrated account, traditionally attributed to Homer, of the Greeks' siege of Troy.

4.   *cresset*: 'an iron basket to hold pitched rope, wood, or coal, to be burnt for light; usually mounted on the top of a pole or building, or suspended from a roof' (*OED*). This is, of course, a reference to the description in a previous paragraph of the 'gigantic bonfire' that from its 'iron basket' on the roof of the house 'lit up the land for miles'.

5.   *Now there was a day*: see Job 1: 6–7: 'Now there was a day when the sons of God came to present themselves before the Lord, and Satan came also among them. / And the Lord said unto Satan, whence comest thou? Then Satan answered the Lord, and said, From going to and fro in the earth, and from walking up and down in it.'

6.   *Can ye drink of the cup that I drink of*: see Mark 10: 37-40: 'They [James and John] said unto him [Jesus], Grant unto us that we may sit, one on thy right hand, and the other on thy left hand, in thy glory. / But Jesus said unto them, Ye know not what ye ask: can ye drink of the cup that I drink of? And be baptized with the baptism that I am baptized with? / And they said unto him, We can. And Jesus said unto them, Ye shall indeed drink of the cup that I drink of; and with the baptism that I am baptized with shall ye be baptized. / But to sit on my right hand and on my left hand is not mine to give; but *it shall be given to them* for whom it is prepared.' Compare too Matthew 26: 26–56.